Jo Thomas worked for many years as a reporter and producer, including time at Radio 4's *Woman's Hour* and Radio 2's Steve Wright show.

Jo's debut novel, *The Oyster Catcher*, was a runaway bestseller and won both the RNA Joan Hessayon Award and the Festival of Romance Best EBook Award. Her book *Escape to the French Farmhouse* was a No. 1 bestselling ebook. In every one of her novels Jo loves to explore new countries and discover the food produced there, both of which she thoroughly enjoys researching. Jo lives in Pembrokeshire with her husband and three children, where cooking and gathering around the kitchen table are a hugely important and fun part of their family life.

Visit Jo's website: jothomasauthor.com
or follow her on:
𝕏 Jo_Thomas01
◼ JoThomasAuthor
◎ JoThomasAuthor

Sign up for Jo's newsletter at:
www.penguin.co.uk/jo-thomas-newsletter

Also by Jo Thomas

THE OYSTER CATCHER
THE OLIVE BRANCH
LATE SUMMER IN THE VINEYARD
THE HONEY FARM ON THE HILL
SUNSET OVER THE CHERRY ORCHARD
A WINTER BENEATH THE STARS
MY LEMON GROVE SUMMER
COMING HOME TO WINTER ISLAND
ESCAPE TO THE FRENCH FARMHOUSE
FINDING LOVE AT THE CHRISTMAS MARKET
CHASING THE ITALIAN DREAM
CELEBRATIONS AT THE CHÂTEAU
RETREAT TO THE SPANISH SUN
KEEPING A CHRISTMAS PROMISE
SUMMER AT THE ICE CREAM CAFE
COUNTDOWN TO CHRISTMAS
LOVE IN PROVENCE
A RECIPE FOR CHRISTMAS

Ebook short stories:
THE CHESTNUT TREE
THE RED SKY AT NIGHT
NOTES FROM THE NORTHERN LIGHTS

A PLACE IN THE SUN

Jo Thomas

PENGUIN BOOKS

TRANSWORLD PUBLISHERS

UK | USA | Canada | Ireland | Australia
India | New Zealand | South Africa

Transworld is part of the Penguin Random House group of companies whose
addresses can be found at global.penguinrandomhouse.com.

Penguin Random House UK, One Embassy Gardens,
8 Viaduct Gardens, London SW11 7BW

penguin.co.uk

Penguin
Random House
UK

First published in Great Britain in 2025 by Penguin Books
an imprint of Transworld Publishers

001

Typeset in 11/14pt ITC Giovanni Std by Jouve (UK), Milton Keynes.
Printed and bound in Great Britain by Clays Ltd, Elcograf S.p.A.

The authorized representative in the EEA is Penguin Random House Ireland,
Morrison Chambers, 32 Nassau Street, Dublin D02 YH68.

A CIP catalogue record for this book is available from the British Library

ISBN: 9781804993866

Penguin Random House is committed to a sustainable future
for our business, our readers and our planet. This book is made
from Forest Stewardship Council® certified paper.

MIX
Paper | Supporting
responsible forestry
FSC® C018179
www.fsc.org

Dedicated to Belinda Jones, a wonderful, inspiring, supportive author, taken too soon.

'Recipes don't make food taste great, people do!'
Samin Nosrat

1

'You have arrived at your destination. Make a U-turn. Turn left. Make a U-turn. Turn right. You have arrived at your destination.'

It feels like *Groundhog Day*, but it's not wet or snowy, like the film. It's hot. We have all the windows open. The aircon packed up when we were leaving France, and it's getting hotter.

'Make a U-turn! Turn left. Make a U-turn!'

'All right, all right!' I say, tired, flustered, and trying to switch off the satnav, punching the button. I stop the car and put my head into my hands. The heat sweeps in, wrapping itself around us, like a goose-down duvet. I fan myself with an empty paper bag from one of the many roadside meals we've had on our journey from the UK. At first I tried to make the road trip to Italy an adventure. And the B-and-Bs we've stayed in for the last couple of nights have been small, friendly and lovely. But now I want it to be over. I just want to have reached our destination.

'Mum,' Luca says, from the passenger seat beside me, my iPad on his lap, 'this could be it. It's like one of the pictures Dad took. Look at the village up there.' He points towards a hilltop we must have driven past at least three times, maybe four.

'Are we nearly there yet?' asks Aimee, from the back seat.

'Nearly, love.'

'You said that ages ago,' she says.

In the rear-view mirror I can see her flushed cheeks. 'I know, love. But I promise we're nearly there now.' Just wishing we could find the place.

'Make a U-turn!' interrupts the satnav, bossily.

'You and I are going to fall out, lady!'

Aimee giggles, cheering me up. 'She's not real, Mummy!'

'Isn't she?' I tease. 'I thought she was. I thought *she*'d eaten all the wine gums.'

Aimee giggles some more. 'No, that was you.'

'Me? It wasn't! It was the satnav lady – I heard her burp.'

And even Luca smiles.

It'll be fine, I tell myself firmly.

'She didn't. She's a machine!' Aimee laughs now.

In the rear-view mirror, she's clasping Mr Fluffy to

her chest as I turn the car and set off up a narrow lane towards the hilltop village. It's overgrown and banked by tumbledown stone walls at either side, so tight that I'm not sure I should be driving along it . . . I've spent three days in the car with these two and they've been brilliant. I couldn't be prouder. Luca has read the map all the way, regardless of the satnav. Belt and braces! Aimee has watched films, played with her toys and slept.

Now I can smell the sun on the fields around us and herbs: rosemary, a hint of mint and wild fennel as the car and wing mirrors brush against the hedge. Aimee is still laughing, and I can't help smiling.

'Mum, watch out!' Luca shouts, jolting my attention to the road.

I slam on the brakes and a man with three goats crosses from a field on one side of the road to another. I nod when he and the animals are safely over and he nods slowly back.

The children are no longer smiling and I need to find the house. My tetchiness returns.

'Well, she's clearly gone to sleep,' I say, tapping at the satnav but getting no response.

I take the next left, then left again.

It has to be around here somewhere. I attempt to drive straight on but the road is even narrower. I reverse, passing the man and his goats again, this time raising a hand, trying to look as if we're not totally lost and to convince the children that everything's fine.

3

'Mr Fluffy really needs a wee. He can't hold it!' Aimee brandishes the well-worn stuffed rabbit, its head lolling to one side.

I know she isn't joking. Mr Fluffy needing a wee tells me I must find her a toilet very quickly.

'You have arrived at your destination.' The satnav bursts into life again and I slam on the brakes.

'Up there, Mum. I think we have to go up there,' says Luca, peering at the photos on the iPad and pointing towards the narrow lane.

'I can't get the car up there,' I say, straining to see what's ahead over the steering wheel.

'Well, maybe we have to walk,' says my ever-sensible son.

He's right. We've exhausted the options by car. I pull into a passing point, a clearing in the hedge, and try, without luck, to push open the car door.

'I'll have to get out your side,' I say to Luca, who is on the road, stretching, the iPad in his hand. I lift my leg over the handbrake and, with his help, haul myself out, as a stray sweet wrapper and a McDonald's bag fly past me. We chase after them, pick them up, throw them back into the footwell and shut the door. I'll deal with them later. I look around. It seems as good a place as any to park the car. But it has all our worldly belongings in it – I don't want to leave it for long.

We grab a few things from the boot and I lock up.

I hold my face to the Tuscan sun, which makes my cheeks tingle. It feels good to be out of the car.

But in no time at all I'm keen to be out of the bright sunlight and in the shade.

'Come on, let's see if we can find it up here,' I say to Aimee.

'I can't. Mr Fluffy still needs a wee,' she says. 'And he's too tired to walk.'

'Come on, Aimee, it'll be fun,' says Luca, and again my heart swells with pride as he helps jolly his sister along. 'Come on, let's sing. And we'll find Mr Fluffy a loo soon.'

The three of us hold hands, like Dorothy on the yellow brick road, and begin to sing the Italian lessons we've listened to all the way down.

'*Piacere.*'

'*Piacere.*'

'It's nice to meet you.'

'*Piacere mio.*'

'It's nice to meet you too!' we sing, and swing our arms with Aimee, walking in the shade up a steep hill, the midday heat bouncing off the walls along narrow cobbled streets and neglected buildings.

'Hey!' I hear someone shout, as we pass a row of rundown but typically Tuscan terraced houses, with a dining chair outside the front door and washing hanging from the upstairs balcony. 'No! No, no, no!'

'*Signora!* Madam! *Cosa fai?* What are you doing?'

My Italian is rusty but I understand what's been said. For a moment I wonder if the voice is speaking to us. I glance around, then up.

A large-chested woman is leaning out of her balcony with a stick, flicking it at some sheets hanging on the line there.

There's another shout from a second woman. 'Hey! Stop! That is my clean washing!'

'And it is on my side of the boundary. Keep your washing to yourself!'

There is another shout: 'Please keep the noise down. I can hardly hear my television,' says a third woman.

'Madam, do not touch my washing with your stick!'

'Don't let it flap in my window. I don't want to be disturbed by your sheets while I'm trying to rest.'

'And shut your window when you're cooking. The smell puts me off my dinner.'

'Yours makes my washing smell bad so I have to do it again.'

'Perhaps this time it'll turn out clean.'

I hurry the children along. They're fascinated by the altercation, their heads turned back the way we came to watch the women, who are still berating each other from the balconies of their stone houses.

Eventually I spot it. I recognize it straight away from the pictures. The house with peeling paintwork on the door is Casa Luna. I take the iPad from Luca and hold it up, secretly hoping the photo will show something a little less tired and neglected further up the street, but this is definitely the right one. It's barely changed since the snap was taken. Maybe the shutters are a little more weatherworn, and even more weeds are growing around the front door between the cracks in the paving stones. I take a big loin-girding breath.

'We're here,' I say, a touch of disappointment mixed with a sigh of relief. 'We've made it. Finally, we've found you, Casa Luna.'

For a moment, I stand and stare. The house I've heard so much about, in which I've invested so many dreams. It's real. If only the dreams were. There's a tug at my hand.

'Mum . . . Mr Fluffy still really needs the toilet.'

'Oh, yes. I just need to unlock the door.' I reach into my bag and pull out the big metal key with the cardboard tag on it. I push it into the lock but I can't get it to turn.

'Mum, Mr Fluffy really doesn't like this.'

'Me neither,' says Luca, quietly. 'It's too hot here.'

'It'll be fine.' I try to sound calm. 'Really. Once we're in and sorted it'll be lovely, you'll see.' My heart is pounding with the heat and I'm wondering what I'll find once I open the door. I feel queasy.

'I really need to wee, Mum! And so does Mr Fluffy!'

My nerves are jangling. This was the best plan. It was the only plan, a voice says in my head.

I give the key another firm twist and the lock clunks. Finally. We're in the right place.

'There!' I say, wiping my brow and pushing at the door. It won't open.

'Mr Fluffy can't hold it, Mum!' Aimee does a little dance.

And now she's said it, I really want to go too. It's been a long journey from our last overnight stop at the border.

'Help me,' I say to the kids, who step forward and shove at the door. It opens with a creak.

I'm out of breath. 'Well done, both of you. I'm really proud of you. Let's just get inside and find the light switch.' I feel for it. It's pitch black in there with the shutters closed and, despite the warmth of the day, the house is cool.

I can feel rough stone crumbling under my hand as I try to locate the switch, running my fingers over the uneven surface. I touch something soft and sticky and pull them back. 'Argh!' I shake my hand.

'What was it?'

'Did something bite you?'

'Mr Fluffy is scared!'

'It's fine,' I repeat.

I think even the kids know it's not. We're some-where in the middle of Tuscany in a hilltop village called Città dei Castagni, town of the chestnut trees. It's supposedly full of Tuscan charm, according to Marco. He'd come home and told me what he'd done with our life savings, which didn't amount to much.

'Hey, both.' I turn back to them standing on the door-step. 'There's nothing to be scared of. Dad wouldn't have bought this place if he didn't think we'd love it and want to spend time here, would he?' I put my hands on their shoulders to reassure them and myself. I remind myself of Marco's good intentions and how impulsive he was. I loved that about him.

They nod.

'He chose this place for us to have holidays here. One day it'll be our for-ever home . . . once you guys have flown the nest.' I smile, unable to imagine that right now.

Then Aimee says, her voice wavering, 'I don't want to live in a nest and neither does Mr Fluffy.' She starts to sob.

I crouch down to her. 'Not a real nest, honey.' My chest tightens: I've got it all wrong again, a fairly con-stant state right now. I wish I knew it would be fine. But I don't.

'Come on.' I straighten and take her hand. 'We just need to find the light . . . It'll be like camping. Like the time Dad put the tent up in the garden.'

'And a mole tried to burrow under it and scared you to death!' Luca laughs, then Aimee joins in and so do I. It's how we've got through, with laughter and our memories of the fun times. We're a tight little unit, helping each other. I'd tried to hide the worst of it from them but they've seen me struggle these last couple of years. When I thought they were in bed and sat crying my eyes out over reruns of *Virgin River*, I'd discover them sitting at the top of the stairs and have to blame the tears on my favourite TV characters. Then I'd chivvy them back to bed, knowing they hadn't believed a word I'd said. I'd often fall asleep with them, all of us tucked up in my bed. With Marco dying, the restaurant going, losing the house and now moving to another country, these children have had more than most to deal with. But the holiday home is all I've got left. Even thinking about losing the house makes my blood boil, and tears sting my eyes. It was our home. I tried, I really tried, to keep it all going.

'Mum?'

'I'm fine.' There's that word again. Fine.

'I wish Papa was here,' says Aimee.

I pull her to my side. 'Me too, honey.'

'Me three,' says my son, coming in to hug us.

'Maybe he is,' I say quietly.

Then, with a squeeze, I let them go and reach back through the door for the light switch.

'Found it!' I say, with my hand over it. 'Ready?'

I push down the switch and suddenly there's light. I push the door further open. It feels as if we're walking into a museum, dark with falling wallpaper and a sagging ceiling. It's packed to the gunwales with stuff. Piles of chairs and tables, clothes and books. I do what I've learnt to do over the two years since Marco died: I pull up my big-girl pants. Then I step inside.

It's not too bad, cleaner than I was expecting, just crammed with belongings that someone has clearly been hoarding. The kitchen looks usable.

'See? I told you it would be fine. A bit of a sort-out will work wonders!'

A loud crackling sound, like the fuse of a firework being lit, and a bang, makes us jump. All the lights go out and there's a whiff of burning.

For a moment, none of us speaks. Then Luca asks, 'Mum, how long do we have to stay for?'

'When can we go home?' Aimee clings to me.

'Soon, lovelies, very soon. We just have to get this place looking like it's wearing its Sunday best, then sell it to someone who wants to love it and live in it. After that, we can go back to England and find a lovely little house for the three of us near your school and your friends. Just think of it as a lovely long summer holiday.'

I hug them even closer. What on earth have I done, bringing them here?

2

I scan the walls with the torch on my phone, then open the first set of windows and push aside the shutters to let in the light. It's still dark, but not half as bad as it might have been.

'Let's open all the windows and shutters for some air,' I say, navigating the big kitchen table as I head to the back door to open that too.

'Mr Fluffy needs a wee!'

'Oh, yes.' I push open another door. 'In here,' I say, checking the loo first. Again, it's relatively clean.

'Leave the door open,' says Aimee, as she sidles in.

'We'll get settled and Mr Fluffy sorted, and then I'll try to find an electrician,' I say, as brightly as I can.

'Will the electrician make the place less scary?' Aimee says, as I flush the loo and turn on the taps for her to wash her hands. It's cold but it's water. I hold out my T-shirt for her to dry them and she walks out, hugging Mr Fluffy, her head down, her nose on the top of his head.

I feel like crying, but if I started I probably wouldn't be able to stop. I swallow the lump in my throat. 'There's nothing to be scared of. Remember, Dad chose this place for us,' I repeat. 'This is an adventure.'

'Mr Fluffy's hungry,' says Aimee.

'I'm starving,' says Luca, and his stomach growls. His hands fly to it and he looks surprised, making us all smile.

We're standing in what looks like someone's front room after they've just walked out, leaving everything they've ever owned in it. There are photographs on the walls, vying for space, and it smells musty. It's as if time has stood still, since the door was closed on the place, however many years ago that was.

'It's not scary. It was someone's home,' I say. 'We just need to make it our home. Make it how we'd like it.'

I stare at the photographs, the lace doilies on the dark-wood sideboard, loaded with china ornaments and crockery, and wonder where to start.

'Let's go and find something to eat,' I suggest, 'and ask around for an electrician. Then we'll come back and make our beds. Everything will look better in the morning. And we'll go shopping now, get what we need for breakfast,' I say cheerily, looking at their wary, yet trusting faces. Inside I feel tired, scratchy, and my spirits are dipping. Oh, Marco! Why did you have to leave me? A bloody heart attack of all things, I think angrily. And why didn't we get round to tackling proper grown-up issues like life insurance? Because we were always too busy trying to make the restaurant the best it could be, dreaming of the day when life would be easier and we'd come to stay in our little piece of Italy. My eyes prickle.

I usher the children out of the door – it takes the three of us to pull it shut. I lock it, although, looking around the quiet street, I'm not sure why. I turn in the direction of the terraced houses where the three older women were arguing. It's quiet now.

'Come on, Dad wouldn't have wanted us to feel like this.' I put on a smile. 'He'd have wanted us to enjoy ourselves. We'll go and find a restaurant or café. Papa wouldn't have bought a holiday home without somewhere good to eat nearby!'

I stop and take in the view. Now I know why Marco bought this place. He said he could see us sitting out here in our old age. There is a heat-haze over the golden hills in front of me and the higgledy-piggledy village houses seem to be tumbling down the hillside towards huge open fields, punctuated by cypresses and what may be chestnut trees too. The sun is sinking a little lower in the sky, and tears spring to my eyes. It really is beautiful, and I wish Marco was here to see it.

Maybe he is, I muse, imagining him beside me admiring at the view.

'You okay, Mum?' asks Luca, touching my hand.

'Fine, my lovely. Fine.' I smile at him, take hold of their hands and squeeze. The three of us walk out onto the road and, following my instinct, which is about all I have to rely on, these days, we head up the hill towards the remote village Marco described to me after he'd put in an offer on the house. 'How could I not, Thea?' he'd said. 'It was a steal!' I remember him grinning, which made me smile, because however madcap his ideas were, I'd loved them – and him.

I breathe in the warm air. Maybe if Marco and I had taken time off, closed the restaurant for a few days, planned a proper holiday together, he wouldn't have been trying to make plans for our future on his own. And I wouldn't be trying to sell this house alone.

3

It's still really hot. The sort of hot that means you have to take your time, whatever you're doing. July in Tuscany is always going to be like this. We're dragging our feet as we stumble up the cobbled street, which is leading us, I hope, to the heart of the village.

A cat wanders across our path and stops to lie down in the shade of a building. Aimee bends to stroke it, smiling as the cat purrs. That little smile means everything to me right now.

'I'm starving,' says Luca again. And I know he must be. He's not usually one to complain, and since Marco died he's hardly complained at all. I worry that he's trying to be strong for Aimee and me and keep his feelings to himself. Aimee lets me know how she's feeling via Mr Fluffy. God forbid anything ever happens to that rabbit. She's had him since she was a baby but

16

has held on to him even tighter over the last couple of years, when other children of her age had long left their childhood toys behind. Mr Fluffy still goes everywhere with us. I worry she'll be picked on for having a soft toy in school in September, but haven't the heart to encourage her to leave him at home. That's a conversation I'll have with the teachers when we're back in England. Right now, we'll take one day at a time, one foot in front of the other.

'There must be somewhere around here to eat,' I say, passing the quiet, dark houses.

The old man and his three goats are wandering up the middle of the road behind us. The children huddle against me, more used to electric scooters and e-bikes taking up pavement space rather than four-legged animals.

'*Scusi?*' I try to call over the goats, which are bleating, and the bells around their necks clang as they walk. '*Scusi?*' How do I ask if there's somewhere to eat around here? I hold my fingers to my lips. '*Mangia?*' It's as much as I can remember from Marco and the Italian conversation course we played on the journey here. I'd always meant to learn more Italian, but there was never any time for any of the things we promised ourselves once the hard months of Covid and the squeeze on the hospitality industry were over.

The man directs me up the hill with a gnarled finger. '*Mangiare!*' He encourages me, with a toothless smile, to follow the road.

'*Grazie*,' I call, and turn the children back in the direction he's pointing, uphill, and we hurry ahead of the goats, grazing now at the side of the road.

Just when I think none of us can go any further, I spot it. 'There,' I say, relieved. There's a doorway in a wall, with a wooden gate, and a small handmade sign, La Tavola. The table. At least I recognize that word. I step through the gate into a small courtyard, with a large chestnut tree in the middle creating welcome shade. There's a table with chairs, just outside a stone archway with a door in it, and oil cans with plants in them. There's even a white loo in which red geraniums are blooming, making the children giggle. 'There.' I smile. 'I said we'd find somewhere.'

The children rush towards the table and I hurry after them, practically collapsing into an old plastic chair. I breathe a sigh of relief. The quiet courtyard is full of buckets and pots brimming with flowers and herbs. It smells amazing, and it's cool under the branches of the tree.

Aimee has turned pale.

'Aimee, are you okay?'

At first she says nothing.

'Aimee?'

'Mr Fluffy feels a bit *wooo* . . .' She rolls her head around.

'I'll get some water for us,' I say. 'Hello? *Buongiorno?*' I call, but no one comes. It's just silent. '*Ciao?*' I call again but louder. Still there is no sign of anyone. I stand, getting impatient, worrying about Aimee. I understand the problems that result from keeping staff to a minimum – I've been trying to do that for the last couple of years – but there really should be someone to greet us.

I walk to the worn wooden door and push it open. 'Hello? *Ciao?*'

A man appears from the kitchen, wearing a pair of workman's trousers with padded knees. His appearance takes me by surprise. He's tall, wide-shouldered and clearly very fit. He has dark, curly hair and no shirt, which I find a little alarming.

'*Buongiorno*. Um, I'm . . .we're sitting outside. Could we have some water, please?' I make a drinking action with my hand. '*Acqua?*'

'Yes, of course.' He replies in perfect English with a strong Italian accent. He wipes his hands. 'I'll just clean up.' He holds up his hands and smiles. 'Doing a bit of maintenance.'

I can't help thinking that maintenance should be kept outside opening hours. But it's not my business. As long as the food is good, that's all that matters. 'And could we have the menus, too, please?' I turn and hurry back to Aimee. 'There's some water coming,' I say, sitting down again on the plastic chair, which is weather-worn and aged. I hope it doesn't give way. 'Mr Fluffy probably just needs a drink.'

'Me too,' says Luca.

'And me. A large glass of wine!' I add. And the children laugh, making me smile.

After a little wait, the door to the stone building opens and the maintenance man, who has put on a clean white T-shirt, I'm pleased to see, comes with a jug of water and three short glasses, stacked together. 'It's a hot one,' he says, in his very good English. 'Are you okay?' he asks Aimee kindly.

'She's hot,' I say. 'And tired. It's been a long few days.'

He pours the water and hands it to Aimee first. She drinks it, and he passes one to Luca, then finally to me.

'*Grazie.* Thank you,' I say.

He pulls over an umbrella and adjusts it to make sure we're all in shade.

'*Grazie,*' I say again. He gives me a warm, attractive smile. I'm not usually halted by someone's looks, but he's handsome, with that dark hair and those shoulders. Marco was my type. Well, I didn't realize he was until I met him. Before him I was seeing someone quite the opposite. But once I met Marco, I realized I had a type and he was it. Just like this man is. I shake my head. I have no idea why I'm thinking about my type, and how good-looking this waiter is. I put it down to the heat, and the relief of being here. He's very like Marco, I muse, as he stands with the three of us. Perhaps he's waiting to start a conversation. But I don't want to explain who we are and what we're doing here right now.

'Menus?' I remind him gently.

He has his hands on his hips. 'I can do you some pasta,' he tells me. '*Cacio e pepe?*'

I stare at him in amazement. I know it's late in the afternoon, but surely there must be something else on the menu, other than plain pasta with Parmesan and pepper. I know how hungry and tired the children are, though, so I say, 'That'll be great. Yes, please,' too tired and hot to suggest looking for somewhere else where we might be offered a choice. 'Don't worry, Aimee. Food is on its way. Pasta, like we had at home.'

She holds her rabbit to her nose. 'Mr Fluffy wants to go home,' she says into his worn, tear-stained head.

'You'll feel better after something to eat. Papa always said so, didn't he?'

Luca gazes up at the man. 'And could my mum have a large glass of wine, please?' he says, sounding so grown-up that he makes me smile . . . but I want to cry too.

The man smiles. 'I'll see what I can do,' he says, and goes back inside.

Maybe he's just being jokey with the customers. When we had the restaurant I bent over backwards to get customers what they wanted. But that didn't help me hang on to the place. Maybe I should have been a bit more *laissez-faire*. My mind flits back to the CCTV, the straw that finally broke the restaurant's and my back. The family of seven who came in and

21

ordered royally from the menu, making me think I could just about pay the staff that weekend ... that I could hang on to the place for another month and everything would be fine. Their bill was huge and I thought I'd be able to make ends meet that week, until their card didn't work. They went to get another from the car, leaving their son in the restaurant. He took his cue to scarper when they were outside with the engine running. It was evidently a practised routine. I should have realized I was being mugged when the card was declined. They had eaten and drunk my most expensive food and wine, then left without paying. All I could do was to let other restaurateurs in the area know about them. My takings were down, my kitchen stock cleared out and my credit at full capacity. I had to close. With my years of experience I should have seen the red flags that were flying in my face when they came in, drinking champagne and ordering the most expensive dishes. One of the party was so drunk she threw up all over the cloakroom floor and left it for my young waitress to clear up.

But I'm not here as a restaurateur. I don't need to contemplate what you could do with this place to make it a really good business. I'm just here to eat. I'm never going back to the world of hospitality. My eyes sting with exhaustion and, to honest, I'm with Mr Fluffy: I want to go home. But there's no home to go back to. The restaurant has gone, the house too. I remortgaged it to help the restaurant and in the end I lost the lot. All I have left in the world is the house in this village, which I've never been to before, in a country I hardly know.

We're grateful for the shade over the table and chairs. Aimee gets up to greet another cat, lounging in the heat, and introduces him or her to Mr Fluffy.

Finally the door opens and the waiter comes out, this time with a small, white dog at his feet. Not sure what breed it is. A mix, I expect. Like a small, white retriever, with dark eyes and nose. 'Gently, gently, Bello,' he tells the dog as it joyously bounds up to Luca, and then lies on its back waiting for its stomach to be stroked. I'm not sure it's great restaurant etiquette. Right now, though, anything goes. I'm just keen to get us all fed, then find out about an electrician.

The man is carrying the pasta and three plates. He puts the steaming bowl down, and serves it, piling long strands onto the plates, then handing them to the children and me. I have to say it smells fantastic. Buttery, cheesy and peppery. The children dive in, twisting the spaghetti with their forks and eating enthusiastically, reminding me again of Marco and his insistence that the children should learn to eat pasta correctly. He'd also said never, ever to put pineapple on pizza. One of our many differences of opinion, I think, a smile pulling at the corners of my mouth. Since we arrived here I've thought of Marco. Every day since he died I've thought of him, but being here, in the village, in the house, his dream for us, he hasn't left my thoughts.

The man goes back inside and returns with an opened bottle of wine, the cork halfway into the neck, and a glass, then puts them on the table. 'Help yourself,' he says.

'Oh, just a glass would be fine,' I say.

He picks up the bottle, pulls the cork and pours the dark red wine for me. Then he puts the bottle back on the table.

'Let me know if there's anything else you'd like. I'll just be inside.'

We eat hungrily, mopping up the buttery sauce with bread from a basket. It's probably one of the best meals I've ever eaten and I feel guilty, thinking of Marco and the passion he poured into his dishes. But we were so hungry today and it hit the spot. The children have cleared their plates, the colour returning to their cheeks.

'How was the food?' says the man, reappearing through the big door, his dog at his heels.

'*Buono!*' says Luca, and kisses the tips of his fingers, like Marco used to, making us all laugh.

'I'm afraid I have only *gelato* for dessert,' he says, putting down three bowls of thick, creamy pistachio ice cream. The children fall on it with enthusiasm, as do I.

He pours me another glass of wine. 'Take your time,' he tells me. Then, to my surprise, he pulls up a chair, putting two cups of coffee on the table. 'So, how do you come to be in our village? Are you on holiday?' He stirs a sugar cube from his saucer into his coffee and leans back in the chair.

'Erm . . .' I'm alarmed by him sitting at our table and my guard comes up. I try to stop the children telling our story to a complete stranger. Too late . . .

'We're here on a long holiday,' says Luca. 'We're putting the house into its Sunday best so someone can love it, like my papa did.'

'Actually,' I cut in, 'I'm wondering if you know of an electrician? I have a problem with the electrics.'

He frowns. 'Where are you staying exactly?'

'Just down there.' Luca points. 'In the falling-down house. Casa Luna.'

'It's dark. The lights don't work. Mr Fluffy doesn't like it. He wants to go home.'

'Ah,' he nods, 'Casa Luna. It sold a couple of years ago.'

'Yes!' say the children. 'Our papa bought it, but—'

'It's time we were going.' I stand up. 'Could we have the bill, please?'

The man stands up too, as does the dog, which has been lying between him and Luca.

'He died,' Luca finishes.

I pull out my purse to pay.

The man holds up his hand.

'Just let me have the bill, please,' I say.

'There's no charge.'

'I – I'm not looking for charity! Or sympathy.' I'm suddenly hot and cross.

'I'm not giving it. It's just there's no charge. We're not a restaurant. We don't charge.'

I put my purse away. 'I'm so sorry,' I say, and hurry the children to their feet. 'Quick, time to go!', I say, trying to entice Luca away from the dog.

'Oh, but you wanted to know of someone to help with the electrics. I can.'

'No, no, it's fine. It'll be fine.' My cheeks are burning as I hurry the children out of the courtyard and down the hill to the house. Have I just sat down and ordered food in someone's home? I want the hot, dusty cobbles to open and swallow me. I don't need help. I can do this myself. I pull out my phone and google 'blown electrics'. The sooner I get things sorted, the sooner we can leave.

4

'But, Mum,' Luca sounds as frustrated as I feel, 'the man back there said he could help.' He throws his arms into the air, just like Marco did. 'Why don't we ask him?'

I'm holding my torch in one hand and staring at the fuse-box, my eyes starting to blur with tiredness. I've tried every different combination I can think of to get the electricity back on. Outside, the sun is setting and I know that evening will soon be here and it'll get darker. From what I can see, there are no streetlights to ease the situation.

'Mum, we need help,' he says. Aimee is clutching Mr Fluffy and telling him not to be scared because Mum'll sort it.

'I've phoned someone I found online. Left a message. I'm sure they'll be here soon. Hopefully they'll understand my garbled message in English with the odd

Italian word thrown in,' I say, trying to reassure him and still hoping I can fix it myself: there's no way I'm going back to ask the man whose home I'd sat outside to help sort my electrics. He'd done more than enough already. I couldn't have been more embarrassed.

That night, the electricity still isn't on. As night falls, we close the windows downstairs and climb up to where we're going to share the one double bed in the largest bedroom – Mr Fluffy insisted on it. I make the bed, pulling a sheet over the heavy mattress as dusk starts to fall.

The room is full of cases of clothes, but the bed is lovely and the windows are open to amazing views of fields stretching from the house down the hillside. I can smell the warm air as it creeps in through the open window, earthy scents from the ground below, and hear the whirring of cicadas.

'But Dad always left a light on at night.'

'I know.' I wonder how to do this. 'Tell you what, we'll leave the torch on my phone on. It'll be like camping! Like when we set up the tent in the garden.'

'Yes, and never went anywhere, like other kids in school, because summers were too busy in the restaurant, and winter was office Christmas parties, and January and February were too cold and we were back in school,' says Luca.

I flinch, the mistakes of the past coming back to haunt me again. If only we had made the time, for all our sakes. But, then, we didn't know how hard it would be to keep the restaurant going, or that I'd be doing it on my own after Marco had gone, like a fish trying to swim upstream. It had been a losing battle, with everything becoming so expensive and the chance of making any profit practically non-existent. It was like drowning in quicksand, every day, with more and more bills that I just couldn't pay.

'But we're here now. Like Dad planned. A place for holidays and for us to enjoy being together. This'll be fun. We're in Italy. The sun is shining and we're here for a whole six weeks! Just like a summer of camping.'

I can tell they're not convinced, as we climb up onto the high dark-wood bed and the children fall asleep after the three-day journey in the car. It's hot, sticky and still. I toss the covers aside and lie there listening to their regular breathing and watching the bats flit to and fro outside the window, eventually dropping off myself. I've left the window and shutters open, and between bouts of light sleep, I wait for dawn to come, my only accompaniment the sound of cicadas and mosquitoes.

The following morning my legs itch. They're red and soon raw from my scratching where the mosquitoes feasted on me last night. They didn't bother with the children, which is a good thing.

I stare at my phone. I can't ring the electrician to find out if he's coming, because the battery's died after we used it as a torch last night. I don't say anything. It's no one's fault. We made it through our first night and that's what matters.

'There's no Wi-Fi here anyway,' Luca says, with obvious disappointment. 'I can't get the iPad to work. What are we going to do all summer?'

'Mr Fluffy is hungry,' says Aimee.

'Let's find a shop and get some bits for breakfast,' I say, shoving my dead phone into my bag and pulling it up onto my shoulder. 'We could all do with something to eat.'

'Perhaps we could stop at that man's house again,' Luca says, making me cringe and laugh at the same time. My stomach gives a treacherous rumble at the memory of yesterday's glorious *cacio e pepe* while my cheeks burn all over again.

I pull the door closed behind us as we step out into the already scalding hot day and lock it with the giant key that is the only one I have for the house. I must think about getting the locks changed and new keys.

Another cat wanders up the slope at the side of the house. I look down to the view over the fields with the sun already baking the soil.

'Me and Aimee could go and find the shop on our own,' says Luca. 'You could wait for the electrician.'

'Not yet you can't,' I say, terrified that something will happen to them. Maybe it's irrational or maybe I'm being sensible. I'm scared of them not coming back, like Marco didn't that day he left for work. I know I'll have to start to let go, but not yet.

I write a quick note saying 'Back soon' in case the electrician turns up while we're out, using a pen from my bag and the back of a fuel receipt. I hope his English is better than my Italian. I add *presto* because it's all I can remember. I leave it under a stone on the doorstep, and as I step back, I can hear voices from down the cobbled street. The same voices from yesterday, I think. My ear seems to be getting attuned to the language and I can just about make out what they're saying.

'Madam, please move your washing. I have no desire to look at your undergarments all day.'

'Close your windows, then!'

'Keep the noise down, you two. You're hurting my ears.'

I raise my eyebrows and turn down my mouth at Luca and Aimee and we walk up the hill. I hurry them past the wooden door with 'La Tavola' written on it, the gate ajar, just as it was yesterday. I get a sneak peek at the table and chairs under the tree and embarrassment overcomes me again. I chivvy us on up the street to where the road opens out into a small square.

We stand and look around. There seems to be little here. Houses that were once shops now look as if they've been closed for a long time. I notice a small corner shop with crates of vegetables outside. 'This way,' I tell the children and point. We cross the small square in the hot, bright sunlight.

Jo Thomas

We step into the shop, which is small, dark and quiet, but has everything we need. The owner greets me with a nod and watches me, clearly intrigued to see an outsider shopping there.

As I let my eyes become accustomed to the gloom and study the shelves, I realize that although the range of products might be minimal, it's wonderful. Home-made salami, bottles to buy and fill from a barrel of wine. In a corner, I spot fresh lemons and oranges, piles of dark aubergines, fragrant tomatoes and misshapen peppers. My spirits lift at just the smell of the place. I fill a basket with ingredients: onions, big fat bulbs of garlic, a bottle of olive oil and salt and pepper, dried pasta, and lots of tomatoes, big, red and smelling like tomatoes should. I wish Marco was here to enjoy them.

I hear a little bell from another room and the shop-keeper excuses himself. We wait. He returns, smiles and apologizes. I tell him there's no need, curious as to where he went, but it's none of my business.

He adds up my bill on a pad, glancing between me and the pad, and shows me the figure. When I pay, clearly a good customer for the day, he hands the children a lollipop each. They smile widely. Then he gives another to Aimee for Mr Fluffy and tears prick my eyes at his kindness. We thank him in Italian and say good-bye. The children are much chirpier for the lollipops and I'm humbled to see the difference that such a small gesture can make.

We head down the hill with our bags, the children with their school rucksacks, which contain bread and cheese. I'm carrying two baskets, which I'd found on the back of the kitchen door, old but serviceable, with a bottle of wine, the tomatoes, pancetta, pasta, milk and the rest of the ingredients we bought.

We pass the man with the goats who smiles at us and asks if we enjoyed the food . . .

'*Noi mangiamo bene.*' I'm not sure if he's heard about my mistake at La Tavola or is telling us to have a good meal. But I smile anyway. '*Buongiorno.*'

The goats walk slowly but surefootedly up the hill, snatching at grass and leaves on the verges. One looks up at Aimee and Mr Fluffy, and she clutches him protectively to her chest.

I nod and smile and we move on.

'Do you think the electrician has been?' asks Luca. I realize I need to go down to the car to check on it and charge my phone.

At the house, the note is in the same place as I left it, under the stone on the doorstep. 'No,' I say, deflated.

Luca drops his smile and his head.

'I'm sure he'll be here soon,' I say.

I turn the key in the door and push it open. It squeaks – I must oil it, I think. The sun is making its way up the sky with fiery determination, but it's lovely and cool inside and we fall into the dark room. I navigate the big table and lots of stacked chairs and head for the kitchen. I put a big bottle of water on the table, find glasses in the old dresser, pour the water and pass them round.

'Help yourselves to a snack – you can tear off some bread from the loaf we bought. I'm going to charge my phone,' I say. 'And then I'll be back to organize some proper lunch for us. Don't answer the door to strangers.'

I walk down the hill, past the terraced houses with the washing on the lines that's causing so many arguments.

The car is where I left it, as good a place as any. I plug my phone in, turn on the ignition and gather a few more of our belongings to carry to the house. By the time I've staggered up the hill, I'm hot and hungry. 'Right, lunch,' I say, clapping my hands together, suddenly quite excited at the prospect of the cheeses and bread in our bags. Luca and Aimee help me wipe down the table and open the packages.

'Mum, a man came to the door,' says Luca.

'But we told him we weren't allowed to open it,' Aimee jumps in quickly.

'A man? Who?' My heart starts to race. 'Was it the electrician?'

Luca shakes his head. 'I opened the window and asked him. He said he wasn't an electrician. He was the mayor. I said you were out and he said he would come back later to see you and welcome you to the village.'

'Okay, okay, good,' I say. 'That was nice of him.'

I walk to the back door and open it. When I look

above the overgrown grass and bushes, the view is amazing. I breathe it in, then have a thought. I go back into the house, pick up a chair and bring it outside. I stamp down some grass and place the chair under a fig tree, with what looks like a swing hanging from a big branch. Luca appears at the back door, then does the same thing. Aimee joins in with the stamping and we create a pathway to the house. Then Luca helps me move one of the many small tables from the living room under the tree. I fling a single duvet cover over it from the bedding bag I've brought from the car.

Then we look in all the cupboards in the packed dresser, pull out piles of plates, bowls and cutlery, and take them to the sink. I turn on the tap, which gurgles and splutters. For a moment I think it's about to give up trying, but it gives a big cough and splurges out water, showering us. We jump back, laughing. We rinse the plates and dry them with a hand towel from the bag. Then we wash the big fat tomatoes with water and carefully lay the table under the fig tree. I even pick some daisies and find a small jug to put them in. From its place in the shade we can sit at the table and see over the fields.

'We'll hear the door when the electrician comes,' I say, reassuring Luca.

I pour a small glass of wine and take it to the table under the tree, the branches wrapping themselves around and over us, protecting us from the sun. At first the children say nothing as they stare at the food.

'Look, I know it's not . . .' I'm waiting for complaints and demands for chicken nuggets, which are what they were living on while I ran the restaurant on my own. Anything that was quick and easy and could be pulled from the freezer. Sometimes I'd bring back food from the restaurant but they'd turn up their noses and I didn't have the energy to argue. As long as they were fed.

To my amazement, the children dive in, filling their plates with the bread, cheese and salami. They eat hungrily, without saying they don't like tomatoes or asking for cheese triangles. I watch in amazement. This is a far cry from the life we've just left.

Aimee devours the bread with butter and slices of cucumber. Luca eats salami as if it's a quarter-pounder with cheese. Neither complains about having water to drink, not squash or something fizzy. Just for a moment, time seems to stand still. I wish it could stay like this, I think, with us all content in the moment. Even if we are in a rundown house with a neglected, overgrown garden.

As we finish, Aimee slides from her chair and strokes a cat that has strolled in and lain down beside us on the flattened grass. She is grey and white, and is lazily stretching out her paw to pat at passing butterflies. Aimee leaves Mr Fluffy on the chair as she strokes the cat, then reaches for her rabbit and introduces him.

The cat is neither interested in nor bothered by Mr Fluffy's presence.

I sit and sip the robust red wine, which is rough yet fortifying. I gaze at the fields and, just for a moment, I don't worry about what I have to do next. The long list of things I need to achieve so that I can sell the house, then find a property I can afford back home and a job that will have nothing to do with hospitality. I wonder if, once we're home and sorted, I'll feel this kind of peace again. I hope so.

I look at Aimee playing happily, watch the butterflies and finish my wine. Then I shut my eyes and fall into a deep, welcoming sleep. I dream that Marco is here, laughing and playing with Aimee, until the cat has grown huge and is chasing us—I jolt awake.

For a moment, I have no idea where I am. My heart is racing as I remind myself I'm in Italy with the children. We're in a remote hilltop village in Tuscany that seems to have been ignored by holidaymakers and abandoned by its residents but, just for a moment, I thought it was the most peaceful place I'd ever been. A large fly buzzes, insistent on settling on our leftovers from lunch. The peace has gone. I look around for Luca but can't see him. And the list of things I must do is piling up in my head.

'Luca!' I call, with the familiar anxiety of not knowing exactly where either child is.

'Luca's not here,' says Aimee, casually, as the cat wanders off.

I swing round. 'What?' Alarm bells are ringing in my head.

'He said he was going for a walk. He wouldn't let me or Mr Fluffy go. 'Spect he's 'sploring.'

My heart is thundering now. He's only eleven! He can't just go exploring on his own, in a foreign country, when we don't know the place or anyone in it. I jump to my feet and check my phone, I have no idea why. He has my old one, but it's not charged, because we have no electricity. What made me think I was in some kind of rural idyll, sitting there drinking wine and dozing in the sunshine? There's a reason we give youngsters phones these days: to keep in contact and ensure they're safe.

Oh, Luca! I wish he didn't feel older than eleven. I should be happy he's gone exploring but he hasn't even got his phone.

I can't leave Aimee, who's only seven, on her own. I go to the front door and open it, then look up and down the street. He's not there. I chew my lip. He can't have gone far. I step back into the house and leave the door open, wondering how long I should wait before alerting the police. How would I get in touch with them? I'm reminded me all over again of the night Marco kissed me goodbye as he left for work, saying that he'd be back as soon as he could. An hour passed, two hours. He didn't answer his phone. I couldn't leave the children. In the end, I bundled them into the car in their pyjamas and we went to find him.

But, I tell myself firmly, today Luca has only gone for a walk. I was asleep. It's fine if he wants to explore. I'm just glad he didn't take Aimee with him. I mustn't let myself fall asleep again in the middle of the day. I shouldn't have let down my guard like that.

I turn to Aimee. 'Let's get tidied away and start emptying the cupboards so we see what's there.' I'm keen to keep busy, with one ear on the door.

As we put the crockery into the dresser and on the shelves under the work surface, I hear a voice.

'*Ciao?*'

I jump up, 'Hello? *Ciao?*' and run to the door.

'Are you the electrician? *Elettricista?* I'm pleased you're here.'

Distracted, I glance up and down the road again for Luca. 'Sorry, I'm waiting for my son.'

'I met him earlier,' he says.

My heart sets up the familiar panicky pace that has been ever-present for the last couple of years. 'You saw him? Is he okay?'

He smiles. 'Yes. He said he wasn't allowed to open the door, but spoke to me through the window.'

'Ah.' The penny drops. This isn't someone who has seen Luca out exploring, or the electrician. 'You're the mayor.'

'*Sì.*' He holds out a hand to shake. I give mine a quick wipe on my shorts and take his. 'Welcome to our village,' he smiles, 'and this is our local police officer.' I notice a second man standing behind him. 'Here in Italy we check people are who they say they are when they move in.' He introduces the other man.

'*Grazie*,' I say distractedly.

'And Marco, he is your husband?'

'Erm, yes. He was . . .'

He frowns.

'My husband passed away.' I wish I didn't have to say that every time I meet someone.

'I'm sorry to hear that.' He looks around me into the house. 'And you have some work to do here,' he says.

'Yes – *sì*.'

He nods. 'And, of course, not much time to do it.'

'Well, yes, it's true. I want to get back to the UK as soon as possible.'

'Without having to pay the penalty.'

I look out and around him for Luca. 'The . . . the what?'

'The penalty.' He seems to hesitate, then continues: 'You know about the penalty?'

'What penalty?' I say slowly.

He takes a deep breath. 'Your husband, he bought this place for a very good price.'

'Yes, I know.'

'And he was going to do it up and bring it back to life.'

'Yes.'

'The contract he signed, it gave him two years exactly to get it to a cared-for state.'

'Well, as you say, there's a lot to do, and that's what I plan to do.'

'If it's not done, by two years, then the owner, that is you, has to pay the full amount for the property. It's all there in the contract, with the agreed amount. The house has to be fit for the market, so it can be sold or lived in or rented. We have an estate agent in the neighbouring town who will evaluate the property.'

I feel as if another sack of weights has been added to my shoulders. 'You're telling me that if this house isn't "fit for the market" by a certain time I have to find a sum of money to pay?'

He nods. 'It is a local project. Some towns and villages are selling houses for one euro with all sorts of restrictions and clauses. Others are paying people to move there. We are selling houses where the owner has died and has no family to pass it on to. We sell for a nominal fee and, if nothing is done to the house to renovate it within two years, the owner must pay the market value. Bit like the one-euro houses, but,' he shrugs, 'this house is habitable . . . just.'

I take in the enormity of what needs to be done to get the house 'fit for the market'. 'How long have I got?'

'It's in the paperwork,' he says, handing it to me. I look at the page and try to focus my eyes. Just six weeks, the end of August. The day before Marco died. And then I look at the amount I'll have to pay if it's not done. I don't have that sort of money. I have only enough for us to live on until this house can be sold. I look back at the mayor, who gives a slightly apologetic shrug.

'It's for the good of the community,' he says. 'We are in need of all the help we can get right now. Many people would like to come here, I'm sure. I just need to find them.'

I don't trust myself to say anything.

Then I hear voices. I recognize Luca's. He is strolling down the cobbled street, arms swinging, with another figure I recognize. I stand and stare as they walk up to the front door.

'Giovanni, *ciao*,' says the mayor.

He and Giovanni shake hands and Giovanni smiles at the police officer. '*Buongiorno*,' he says to the mayor, and then to me.

'Well, I'll leave you to it,' says the mayor, and walks away.

I'm still staring at his back when Giovanni, the man from the not-restaurant, says, '*Ciao.*'

This is like some hideous nightmare. He raises his hand in the hot afternoon sun. 'Luca tells me you've been let down by your electrician.'

I look at Luca, not knowing whether to hug him or be cross with him for disappearing without telling me.

But I'm desperately relieved he's back, even if he's with the one person I was trying to avoid.

'We're fine,' I hear myself say, and I'm even irritating myself now. Things are clearly not fine. 'I'm sure he'll be here at some point.' I raise my eyebrows. Then, without thinking, 'Luca, I've been so worried!' I say, and hate myself for telling him off.

'Sorry, Mum.'

'Don't be.' I'm getting this all wrong. 'I drifted off in the peace of the back garden.'

'I'm sure it's lovely,' says Giovanni. 'The views from this house are great.'

'Yes,' I say stiffly, hoping it will be a good selling point when I've got the house ready – in just six weeks! I need to get it renovated and sold. My panic returns.

'I'm Giovanni,' says the man, cutting in and diverting the conversation. I think I should be grateful to him. 'You are Thea, yes? Your son told me.' He smiles politely. 'I'm a handyman, you could say. A bit of this, a bit of that. I can take a look at your electrics, no problem. I'm used to the electrics around here. I've been in this house a few times.'

I put up my hands. 'No, it—'

'No, Mum,' Luca shouts. 'It's not fine. We're living here in the dark. Mr Fluffy hates the dark!' Even my son is using that rabbit to make a point. I can't be cross with him. He's just trying to help.

I step forward and try to hug him, but he's upset and

moves away from me. I don't want to embarrass him further, so I slide back, giving him the space he wants. I feel completely useless, as I often do these days, and wish I wasn't trying to navigate parenthood on my own, that I was doing this with Marco.

I still don't really know why he bought a house here and not where he came from in Le Marche. But, knowing Marco, it was just too good a bargain. He saw it online, flew out and bought it. That was Marco all over. He lived life to the full. He laughed and loved with passion. He argued with me and we made up just as passionately. It still seems unreal that he isn't here now, to help sort this place out.

The house will be beautiful when it's done up. If only he'd told me about that clause. I suppose he thought he wouldn't have to. He'd probably have told me once we hit the two-year mark and the house was finished. I can see him now – telling me life was for taking risks! Well, this one hasn't paid off. Because either I get it done up and on the market or, instead of making money from it, I'll be in debt.

'I can help here,' says Giovanni, gently, breaking into my thoughts.

'See?' says Luca, straightening.

Giovanni smiles at him. 'Luca explained you only arrived yesterday, just before I met you, and that the electrics have gone and the electrician you called hasn't turned up.'

'I've had a go myself, but I can't fix it.'

'I would suggest it could be some time before the man appears. Work doesn't always happen to a schedule around here.'

Luca tugs crossly at the hem of my T-shirt. 'Mum!' he hisses.

'Okay, okay.' I look back at Giovanni. 'Sorry. Thank you for coming. *Grazie.*' I stand aside to let him in, feeling a little uneasy about allowing this stranger into our house. A stranger whose home I invaded yesterday. I've found it's just easier not to let people help, having to explain why I'm on my own, what happened to Marco and our home. But I need the electricity so that I can start work on this place. 'As I say, I've done everything I can think of already.' I hate feeling I might have missed something simple, that I have to lean on other people. I could do this, if I had some time, but clearly that is something I lack.

He dips his head and steps into the cool, dark house. I can smell him as he passes me, freshly showered, with a hint of lemon, making me think of lemon meringue pie, a restaurant favourite, with caramelized peaks. It was one of Marco's specialities and regular customers always requested it. It was never the same after he died and I had to take it off the menu, replacing it with lemon cheesecake.

Giovanni puts his tool-bag on the kitchen table. Suddenly I can imagine Marco standing in this house, just as he dreamed. It was what he talked about after a tough day at work while he waited for all the paper-work for the sale to go through. I see him watching with interest, arms folded across his chest, smiling, reminding me why he'd brought me here. I've heard his voice before, but not imagined him like this. It's as if I could reach out and touch him. But I know I can't. It's just my mind playing tricks.

'He's good-looking!' I imagine him saying about Giovanni. 'He'd better not try anything funny!' I give a sudden laugh, to Luca and Giovanni's surprise.

'She does that sometimes,' says Luca to Giovanni.

'When she remembers one of Papa's jokes,' Aimee says, startling me.

'Or something he used to do,' Luca adds. 'Then she usually cries, when she thinks we can't hear.'

Giovanni says nothing, puts on a head torch and switches it on.

I cough and take a breath, trying to block out the sound of Marco's voice in my head. 'Is this the guy whose house you sat outside and ordered food from?' I hear him laughing.

I bite my lip, trying to stop the nervous laughter bubbling up. I'm embarrassed, but in comparison with what we've been through in the last couple of years, it's not the worst.

'Look, erm, about yesterday.' I decide to address this head on. Giovanni turns to me, practically blinding me with his head torch. I put my hand up against the light, making Aimee laugh.

'Sorry, sorry,' he says, switching it off. 'What were you saying?'

I clear my throat. 'About yesterday . . .'

Giovanni grabs a chair, climbs onto it, then switches on the head torch again. With his back to me, I notice his wide shoulders and muscular behind . . .

'I want to apologize. I didn't realize you weren't a restaurant.' I try to focus and hurry on with my apology. 'We were tired, hot . . . a little confused. I saw an old man.'

'Giuseppe, I expect,' he says, reaching up to take off the cover to the fuse-box. 'Did he have goats?'

'Yes! Hairy ones!' says Aimee, surprising me again by talking. She only speaks to strangers when absolutely necessary these days, and usually from Mr Fluffy's perspective.

'Yes, hairy ones!' I agree.

'Bit smelly too!' Luca waves a hand and we all manage a laugh, to my relief, including Giovanni. I'm feeling bad that I wanted to send him away when he's trying to help. I must let people help me more. Since Marco died I seem to feel I have to do it all on my own, and usually I believe I can. But clearly I can't or we wouldn't have been without life insurance, lost the restaurant and our home. If Marco was here, he'd be feeling bad too. And I know I'll never replace him.

47

He'll always be here, part of the children's lives and mine, by my side.

'The man with the goats, Giuseppe, pointed me in the direction of your house. I just assumed. I should have kept walking up the road,' I explain quickly. 'I would have found the shop. Sorry.'

'Luca, pass me a screwdriver, will you?' Giovanni points to it on the table and, again, I see Marco standing there, arms folded, a slight frown on his forehead.

Luca steps forward and does as he's asked. I stand and stare but I'm not hopeful. I've been over and over the fuse-box with Google and YouTube before my phone battery died.

Giovanni turns off the torch and jumps down from the chair to stand in front of us.

'Don't worry,' I say. 'I'm sure the electrician will arrive at some point.'

'Luca, give the lights a try,' he says. Luca goes to the switch by the front door and presses it down with a clunk.

There's a fraction of a second and then – the lights are on!

'You did it!'

'Fiddly things, these old fuse-boxes. Be good to get it replaced. But that should keep you going until you do.' He tosses the screwdriver into his tool-bag. We have light, and the fridge comes on with a loud hum.

'I don't know what to say. Thank you!'

He's smiling, pulling his torch off. 'It's no problem.'

I spin quickly round to see if Marco is still where he was with the lights out. He is.

'Just glad I could help,' says Giovanni. He closes his tool-bag and heads for the door, glancing around the shabby little house, the walls covered with black-and-white photographs, and cobwebs showing up even more now there's light.

Suddenly Aimee tugs at Giovanni's hand. 'Would you like something to drink?' she asks. 'Mr Fluffy wants to know.'

My heart swells with pride at my daughter's good manners, and I'm cross with myself for forgetting mine.

He looks down at her, pushes his dark curls off his face and smiles. 'Some water would be lovely, please.'

'Probably the saftest option,' Luca jokes, his eyes roaming around the stacks of boxes and someone else's belongings. He moves to the kitchen area, and pours a glass from the bottle we brought back from the shop and gives it to Giovanni.

He takes a big gulp of the water and nearly finishes it. Then he looks around. 'You have a lot to do here.'

I try not to sigh or think of the mayor and his deadline. I lift my chin. 'Yes. But it'll be fine.'

He smiles, and I can't help but smile back. I hold up both hands and look at Luca, 'I know, I know.'

'And, really, no problem about yesterday. It was my pleasure.' He finishes the water, puts the glass on the table and turns to leave. 'Well, I'll be off. *Ciao.*' He opens the front door, and the bright light from the sun streams in.

'Just one thing, Giovanni,' I call.

He holds up a hand up against the sun and turns back.

'Why did you serve us yesterday?'

Luca frowns at me as if I'm embarrassing him.

'If you'd waited long enough and not rushed off,' Giovanni replies, 'I could have told you.'

It's my turn to frown. 'Told me what?'

'La Tavola, where I live. The house I rent. It's not a restaurant, but it is a community kitchen.'

'What's that?' asks Luca.

Giovanni explains patiently, 'It's somewhere people come for company, to help their community, and where we provide meals for some of the people who need it in the village.'

I jump in quickly. 'I wasn't looking for charity, honestly. I can pay.'

'Really, no need to be so prickly. I was happy to help. You looked ready to drop!'

Luca frowns at me again, clearly to remind me of my manners.

'Well, thank you, and it looks like you're doing a good thing. Let me know if I can repay the favour some time, while we're here, which won't be for too long,' I gabble.

'Well, we could always do with a helping hand at La Tavola. As I said, we provide meals for those who need them, delivering on a Friday night, and on a Sunday we make dinner for anyone who wants to come, those without family, on their own. Or who need company.'

'That sounds great!' says Luca. 'My dad was a chef! And Mum . . .'

'Maybe you could help me some time,' he says to Luca. 'If your mum lets you.'

'I'd love that! Mum?'

All my fears rush up to meet me, a tsunami of worries about us, a tiny family, the children, their future. I suddenly feel hot. Really hot. 'Well, we're not sure how long we'll be here. I need to tidy this place and get it on the market.' I'm floundering, reaching for the back of a chair to lean on, hoping he can't see my flushing cheeks, or the worry that's etched on my face that Luca will start to love cooking, like his dad. What if he wanted to go into that industry? It destroyed us. The long hours, the stress, the pressure of rising costs, fewer people going out to eat . . . Unexpected tears rush into my eyes. We lost everything.

And with the lights on and the shabbiness of the house laid bare, I brush away any traces of tears.

'It's good this place is going to get some attention,' says Giovanni, looking around.

'It's rammed with stuff but surprisingly well kept, considering no one's been living here for so long. Did you know the person who owned it?'

'A little. She was well respected and much liked but she was the last of the line for a big family. Their Sunday lunches were legendary apparently, hence all the furniture. She had no siblings or cousins, so no one to leave it to when she was gone.'

I'm suddenly seeing not the mess or the dreams Marco had for this place, but someone's home, their place of safety. And now it's mine too, safety for me and my family. The door is open: Aimee spots the cat and skips off to stroke her on the step. It makes me smile and I want to remind them that it's okay to be happy. We don't have to be sad all the time.

'Are you from here?' I ask Giovanni, even though I'm determined not to get involved in local life. We're not staying. I don't want the children to become too attached, then have to uproot them again.

He shakes his head. He looks through the arch, into the kitchen and out of the back door towards the gently rolling hills. 'This village was just here when I needed it most,' he says. 'I was travelling through and . . . I got stuck here, I suppose.' He gives a little laugh.

'And La Tavola?'

'I like to think I'm giving something back. And, as I said, I'm always looking for more volunteers,' he says, with his lovely smile.

For a moment I see a face peering through the open front door. I squint, but it may be the bright sunlight playing tricks with my eyes, creating patterns and images, a bit like seeing Marco standing in this kitchen. I shake my head, focusing on the here and now and what I know to be certain.

'Sorry, kitchens and I aren't a good match. Besides, I'll have my hands full here!' I look around the room, taking in imperfections that were barely noticeable in the half-light but are now illuminated, showing the work that needs to be done. I wonder where I'm going to start.

'Okay . . .' Giovanni says. 'If you need anything, you know where I am.'

I raise a grateful smile. I'm back in the here and now, not in some far-off place where Marco had made plans for our future, telling me about the house and the village as we cleared away in the restaurant kitchen after a busy dinner service. 'You will love it, *cara*,' he would often say as we waited for the sale to be finalized. I loved hearing about his plans, about a time when life would be easier and everything would work out perfectly.

'I won't be calling on you again,' I tell him. 'But thank you so much. I think I've used up all my helpful-neighbour tokens.'

He smiles at me, a small dimple in his left cheek. Even his eyes smile. 'This village is keen to help each other, well, mostly . . . whether you want it or not,' he says thoughtfully, then adds, 'If only they would do it together.'

I have no idea what he's talking about but follow

him through the front door into the sunshine and thank him again.

'Mum,' Aimee says, 'a lady came by and gave me this.' Aimee is holding a dish wrapped in a tea-towel. It looks heavy and I take it from her. 'She said to give it to my *mamma*. A welcome gift.'

'What lady?' I spin round, but no one's there. I lift the dish to my nose and breathe in the warm, seasoned herby, tomatoey smell. 'Did she say who she was?'

Giovanni is beside us, one hand across his body, the other to his chin.

'She asked my name and how long I was staying.'

'And what did you say?' I'm concerned. Stranger danger, and all that.

'That this was the house my dad bought. But I said I wasn't allowed to tell strangers my name.'

Giovanni looks down at the tea-towel-covered dish.

'What is this?' I ask him.

'As she says, a gift,' he says, taking the corner of the tea-towel. 'May I?' He looks up at me with dancing, playful eyes.

'But why? Who's it from?'

He lifts the tea-towel, bends his head and breathes in. 'Aaah, I would say that's Teresa's . . . definitely Teresa's sauce.'

'Teresa? But why?'

He straightens up, his T-shirt tight across his broad chest.

'She'll have brought it for you for dinner, lasagne, a welcome gift. We look out for our own here.' He turns to leave.

'Well, that's very kind but . . .' I'm not sure what to do with such a generous gift from a stranger.

'I know – you're fine.' He raises a hand in the air, still smiling, his tool-bag in the other.

'Yes.' I bite my lip and wishing I was better at accepting help. 'But it's very kind of her.'

'Kind, but also a way of finding out who you are and what you're doing here.' He winks. The dog I saw at La Tavola yesterday has been lying patiently outside and now gets to his feet to join Giovanni. 'The ladies round here don't cook unless they have to, these days, which is why the community kitchen helps those who need it.' He looks at the dish. 'This may be the first of many, I would assume . . . Like I say, you know where I am if you need me. Just call up to La Tavola.' He sets off, walking up the cobbled street, the dog at his side, and I'm left standing, with the warm dish of lasagne, which smells amazing.

'At least that's dinner sorted,' I say, as I head back inside and put it on the kitchen table. I imagine Marco leaning over it, breathing in deeply, just like Giovanni did, and nodding approvingly.

Suddenly, I have memories of the lasagnes we'd make for birthdays and on Sundays before we had the restaurant. The early days when Marco was a chef on tour with different bands, not just in this country but abroad, catering for the musicians, world-class acts, and crew. I was working in the city, a professional headhunter . . . We met one night after he'd done a gig at the O2 in south-east London and I was having a late drink with friends after work. We clicked straight away, and after we'd messaged for a while I broke off my engagement. We met up as often as his work allowed it. It was the most impetuous thing I had ever done and I felt awful about hurting my lovely fiancé. Otherwise everything about it felt right. When Marco came up with the idea of us putting down roots and opening a restaurant of our own, I jumped at it, first because I wanted to be with him and, second, it sounded like a wonderful adventure. I loved hosting events, which was part of my job. We headed west, to my home town of Cardiff, where things were cheaper than they were in London, and found a restaurant to call our own. Marco knew I could make our customers feel looked after and also manage the staff. He wanted to be liked, not to be the boss, and always referred the staff to me for anything official.

'See my wife! She's the boss!' he would tell them, knowing we were equal partners. We were happy with the way we'd fallen into our roles in the business. He was creative, friendly and encouraging to the staff. I generated the warm, welcoming atmosphere in the restaurant and kept a firm hand on the books. But the business wasn't a business without the two of us. The harder it became to make ends meet, the harder it was to keep up the appearance of a smooth-running ship.

'Mum?' Luca says, interrupting my thoughts of the past. 'What did Giovanni mean, "the first of many"?'

'I'm not sure, Luca.'

Something tells me, though, that all is not as it seems in the sleepy little village.

5

That night, after making up the beds in the two other rooms upstairs, next to the small, basic bathroom, we sit outside at the table under the big fig tree. I've found a candle, pushed it into a dusty old wine bottle from under the sink and light it to try to keep the mosquitoes away as we eat the delicious lasagne. Layers of pasta and béchamel sauce, with a rich, tomatoey *ragù*. But there's far too much for the three of us.

'Any more?' I ask the children.

Luca accepts a second helping, but Aimee is full.

'We have plenty left,' I say.

'We could eat it for breakfast,' giggles Aimee, and makes Mr Fluffy's head bounce up and down as if he's agreeing.

'Or save it for tomorrow evening,' Luca says sensibly.

We put the remainder into a dish from the dresser

and into the noisy fridge, which sounds like a small aircraft revving up to take off. I wash the dish it came in and wonder what to do with it.

'We'll dry up!' says Aimee, making me smile. 'We all have to help because Papa isn't here. Mr Fluffy says so.'

I look at where I can imagine Marco, smiling at the children from a chair he's pulled up to the table, sipping a glass of red wine.

Maybe being here for the summer wouldn't be so bad after all. Marco's here with me, or so it feels, and that's all I need.

I head back into the garden where our friendly neighbour cat is lounging in the cooler evening air. I sit at the table in the overgrown garden with the view over the fields and hedges below.

'Mum?' Luca comes into the garden.

'Yes, lovely?'

He's carrying something. Something that looks a lot like a dish with a tea-towel over it. I frown in the dusky light. 'What's that?'

'A woman just came to the door. I answered. She asked if Papa was here and gave me this.'

I peer at the dish he's holding, then stand up and join him. 'Who was it?'

'Said her name was Lucia. She asked to speak to Papa.'

'What did you say?'

He swallows. 'That he wasn't here.' He lowers his

head. 'I thanked her for the dish, in Italian. Dad would have liked that.'

'He would,' I say softly. I take the dish from him and carry it inside to the kitchen table where I pull back the tea-towel to reveal golden-brown pasta with béchamel sauce. 'It's another,' I say to the children, whose eyes widen. 'Another lasagne!'

'We can't eat all this!' squeaks Aimee.

'We could try,' says Luca, eyeing the lasagne warily.

'Mr Fluffy has a full tummy too, but he'll try.'

'Let's have a bit, just to be polite. The fridge is already fairly full and I don't want them seeing it in our bin and thinking we're ungrateful.'

We sit at the kitchen table, each grab a spoon and take a mouthful, chewing slowly.

'Interesting. Different from the last,' I say.

'Meatier,' says Luca.

'Different kind of meat in the sauce, I think.'

'Mr Fluffy's full!' Aimee sits back on her chair, holding her stomach.

'That's fine, lovely. We'll put it in the fridge for tomorrow.'

'With the rest of the other one,' Luca says seriously, and grins.

'Yes,' I join in. 'If only we had a freezer.'

'Mr Fluffy is tired,' says Aimee.

'Well, in that case, he should go to bed. Why don't you take him upstairs and show him the beds we made today in the other bedrooms, so you and Mr Fluffy can have your own room?'

'Mr Fluffy would rather share with Luca. There's two single beds in there.'

'That's fine too,' I say. I don't want to rush her. 'Now off you go.'

I stand up and squeeze the dish into the now quite full fridge.

'I'll check on Aimee and Mr Fluffy,' says Luca. 'Read them a story.'

'Thank you.' I'm reminded that he's taken on a more responsible role than other eleven-year-old boys.

I pour a glass of wine and stroll out to the garden. I sit down, with a pen and my refillable notebook that Marco gave me when we had the restaurant idea, and begin to write a list. What to do? Where to start? Just like I've always done when I'm at a crossroads, I make a priority list. I run my hand over the notebook that never left my side when I was running the restaurant, making orders for suppliers, lists of jobs to do, and in the pocket on the inside cover, the postcards Marco sent me from places he was visiting as a chef for touring bands and we hatched the plan for our own place, the dream.

In my mind, Marco has followed me into the garden and sat on the other side of the table I put there, gazing at the view. Just as he told me it would be: the two of us, either side of the table, in the candlelight. The evening is sultry and I can feel him, hear him.

'Okay, let's get this list sorted,' I say to myself.

1. Clear out the rubbish.
2. Find the dump.
3. Clean.
4. Paint.
5. Get an estate agent to value it.
6. Sell and move home before school starts again.
7. Find a job.

I put down my pen, pick up my glass, take a sip of wine and stare at the sky, the slowly setting sun a huge ball of fire, streaking the horizon with orange and gold. I breathe in deeply.

'Well, I think I know why you chose this place, Marco. This view . . . and the price, of course. It's beautiful. I just wish you were really here to see it and enjoy it.'

A knock at the front door startles me, catapulting me out of my daydream. I stand up quickly, hoping Aimee hasn't woken if she was asleep. I hurry in through the back door and run through the kitchen, past the clean lasagne dish on the table.

'Let's hope it's not another!' I say aloud, and laugh. Then, cautiously, I open the heavy front door.

6

A large-bosomed woman in a black dress, a cardigan draped over her shoulders, is holding a dish, covered with a tea-towel. I've got a good idea of what it might be, and my heart sinks.

'*Buona sera*. I brought you lasagne,' she says, unsmiling, and holding out the dish to me. 'Proper Tuscan lasagne.' She emphasizes each word.

'Oh . . .' I hesitate, unsure of the etiquette, but I feel I should politely refuse it. 'Really, we have so much . . .' Her stare burns into me, like the intense heat of the midday summer sun. She is holding out the lasagne dish firmly and steadily to me. Of course I can't decline it. 'That's so kind of you,' I say. I put out my hand and take one side of the dish. I realize it would be rude not to lift the cloth and look at it. The sight of another lasagne makes me sigh and not in a good way. 'It smells delicious,' I say, barely able to look at it.

'It is proper Tuscan lasagne. Made as it should be,' she says fiercely. 'Others may copy, but they don't know the real secret to the sauce, even if they think they do. This is how it should be done.'

'Okay,' I say, still holding one side of the dish. I give it a gentle tug, only to find she keeps holds of the other side, assessing me.

'And what is your name?' she asks directly, with a jut of the chin.

'Thea,' I answer.

She narrows her eyes. 'Who are you here with?'

I'm contemplating letting go of the dish, but if I do it will crash to the ground, causing all sorts of extra problems. My arm aches and I have no idea how much longer the interrogation will last. It's a clever move on her part. She has me trapped and won't let go until she has the information she wants.

'Er . . .' I'm taken a little aback by her conversation skills, or lack of them '. . . just me and my children.'

She gives a sharp nod and attempts to peer into the house past me, while still holding her end of the lasagne dish. 'It's been empty for a long time,' she tells me.

'Yes,' I say. I wonder if I have to tell this stranger that my husband died suddenly, that I lost our business and our house, before she'll let go of the dish and release me from the interview. Or maybe I can hold back some information and get away from the situation unscathed. 'It certainly needs updating.'

'It is sad. No one to take it on or care for it after she was gone. And there is no one else here?' She looks past me again.

I give the lasagne dish another little tug. She's still not letting go of it.

I glance over my shoulder at the tired room, then back at her. Day is turning to night, as dusk sets in, and the bats flit about outside the front door.

'Anyway, *grazie mille*!' I nod to the lasagne, wondering what on earth I'm going to do with it. The food bin isn't big enough for all these lasagnes. I look at the cat and wonder if it would like some, maybe tell its mates. No, not a good idea. I'll be inundated.

She finally lets go. 'And where is your husband? The man who came here?'

She's pulled the rug from under my feet. She met him. She saw Marco, here, in what was supposed to become our happy place.

There's no way out of it. I'm cornered. 'He died,' I say. 'Very suddenly. A heart attack at work. Just after we signed for this place . . .' I peter out.

She says nothing, and then I'm bursting with questions for her, what she remembers of Marco being there, what his face looked like when he turned it to the sun. Does she remember him laughing? That laugh! But I don't. Instead, she nods to me.

'I'm very sorry,' she says, then adds, 'I hope the lasagne helps.' She turns and starts to walk down the hill, her large hips rolling from side to side under her black dress. I wonder why the women hadn't come together, perhaps brought one lasagne between them. And then I remember I heard neighbours arguing over the washing. They all know we're here. They've brought lasagnes. We must be the talk of the village, wondering who we are.

From upstairs I can hear Luca reading aloud. Tears prick my eyes.

I turn back into the house and close the door with my hip. I look back to the kitchen. I can see Marco at the table again, laughing.

'They are just trying to make you feel welcome, *cara*. They want to find out more.'

'You can laugh. You haven't got to eat it all! The children will have lasagne coming out of their ears! And I'll have to remember which was which, make sure I can tell the difference. This one,' I sniff, 'smells much the same at the last one. Maybe there's something different in it. If you were really here you could tell me.'

'Mum?' Luca is on the stairs. 'Who are you talking to? Who was at the door?'

'No one, lovely. Well, yes, someone.' I don't want to tell him I'm talking to a vision of his dead father. 'It was . . .' I hold up the dish and tilt my head to one side.

'Oh, no! Not another!'

'Luca . . .' I try to scold him but end up laughing. 'They're being friendly,' I say, although the woman I just met was anything but. And I'm going to have to get the empty dishes back to them tomorrow, tell them it was delicious and thank them. How on earth am I going to remember which was which and find out where they live?

'Guess it's lasagne for breakfast, then,' says Luca, heading back up the stairs. 'Bet it's not like the one Dad used to make.'

When he's gone, I can still see Marco. 'They were good days, when we'd make lasagne together, Thea, for the family,' I hear him say.

I nod. 'They were. I wish they could be again.'

There's no room in the fridge so I put the lasagne on the side and lock the back door. I turn back to the kitchen table.

'Goodnight, Marco,' I whisper, not wanting Luca to hear.

'Good night, *cara*,' I hear him say, so familiar and yet a memory. I wish I could wrap my arms around his neck, like I used to when he stayed up later than I did. He'd look up and kiss me. I wish I could feel his lips on mine, on my forehead, my neck, my body. I shiver at the memory, trying to hold on to the feeling of warmth and love as I make my way to bed, avoiding the broken step and the squeaking tap in the bathroom in case it wakes Aimee. I look in on her, Mr Fluffy still clasped tightly to her, and Luca, fast asleep, then make straight for the high double bed in the room with the wallpaper falling off and the glorious view over the hills. I pat down the pillow next to me, making an indentation for where Marco's head would be, and try to ignore the mosquitoes whining round my head.

7

The daylight wakes me. For once, I haven't been lying in bed and waiting for dawn. I throw back the covers and trot down the stairs, counting them so that I miss the broken one. To my surprise and delight, I can see Marco sitting in the kitchen, as if he's been there all night, watching over us. The sunlight streams through the windows as I push open the shutters.

'Good morning,' I say. He's drinking coffee, just as I'd known he would be. He always liked to be up first. Coffee on the go.

'*Buongiorno, cara,*' he replies, as I open the back door to let in the fresh dewy air and make myself coffee with the cafetière, walking around Marco who is on a chair, olive-skinned arms resting on the table. He's wearing his usual white T-shirt. 'Just like I showed you how to make it when we first met.' He chortles, making me smile.

I'm thinking about the day he told me he'd bought this place. He had a small inheritance from his mother and wanted to buy somewhere. I never thought he'd get a house for the little pot of money he had. At the time we could have used it on the restaurant, but it would have been only a drop in the ocean of our huge overdraft. This way, he had something to remind him of her. His home town was in Le Marche but he thought buying in Tuscany meant he was moving up in the world. I remember him sending photographs, telling me he couldn't wait to show me the place, introduce me to it and the local people.

The lasagnes have been generous gestures. I think about Marco's lasagne, from Le Marche. Not a lasagne, he would tell me, but a *vincisgrassi*, a lasagne-type dish. Seven layers of pasta, lots of béchamel sauce and a mixed-meat *ragù*. He always made it for special occasions, mixed meats, pork and beef, but it could also include chicken livers, hearts and giblets, sweetbreads, pancetta, veal, duck, lamb, goose, rabbit or mushrooms, depending on the family recipe, Marco told me.

I look at the table. Having emptied the three dishes and, yes, fed some to the cat outside the back door and buried some in the garden, I need to return the clean dishes, although I have no idea how to get them to their rightful owners. I don't know who the women were. I sigh. There's only one way I can do this.

The children are still asleep. I leave a note to say where I've gone, that they're not to answer the door, and I'll be back really soon. I step outside to be greeted by the cat weaving its way around my legs in the already hot sunshine. I carry the three heavy dishes, with the tea-towels I washed by hand, with some of our clothes, in the old sink in the kitchen and dried in the morning sun, on branches of the fig tree. The fridge is crammed with as much of the leftover lasagne as I could fit into it. Each differed slightly in flavour and texture, but they were all delicious and very filling. One had mozzarella on top, another a different type of meat, lighter than the first, and the third tasted like a darker meatier version. I'm trying to remember the order they came in as I walk up the narrow, cobbled street, to where the terraced houses face each other, at the end of the neglected buildings, shuttered and silent. It's sad to see them empty. I'm surprised more houses aren't snapped up by people wanting a slice of Italian life, although there's nothing around here, nothing at all, apart from the small shop, and practically no one. It's not the sort of thriving Tuscan village I'd imagined, with cafés and a bustling market. It seems that even in areas like wealthy Tuscany there are pockets that have been abandoned and left to run themselves into the ground. Poverty and isolation must have driven out even the most enthusiastic bargain hunter.

I pass another small house with an open door. A younger woman is hanging out washing on the little wrought-iron balcony. She smiles and I smile back, wishing her a good day. But apart from that, and the cat following me, there's no one around.

But, in the distance, in the other direction, I hear voices again, loud women's voices. They stop as soon as they start, clearly a short, sharp interaction. The quiet has returned. Except for one sound: goats. And bells.

The old man, Giuseppe, is coming towards me with his goats. He's leaning on his stick and dressed in a thick woollen jacket, two sizes too big, despite the early heat of the day. The goats are walking along the middle of the road, the one in front raising its head and bleating, tongue quivering.

'*Buongiorno.*' I nod and pass him, and he wishes me the same with a wide, toothless smile. I give the goats a wide berth and hold my breath, in case Luca was right and they were smelly. We didn't come across many goats on the school run at home.

Home. Was it home, or was it just because it was where Marco was? Where Marco and I created our business and our family, and an Italian restaurant would have an appreciative audience. Wherever we'd chosen, I don't think things would have ended up differently, with rent escalating and rising food prices. Back home, prices were going up and up and we'd had to pass that on to the customer. No wonder people had stopped going out to eat.

I walk on slowly, feeling the weight of the heavy dishes in my arms. Nearing the top of the hill, I catch my breath, inhaling the warm, pine-scented air. I turn slowly to the wooden gate of La Tavola. It's ajar. The dog slips out of the gap and runs towards me, wagging his tail and making me smile. Then, calling him to me, 'Bello, Bello?' I push open the gate and step into the shady walled garden.

'Hello? *Buongiorno?*' I call.

I walk towards the front door and knock on the peeling paintwork. It swings open further, letting in the morning sunshine.

'Hello? *Buongiorno?*' I call again, taking in the long table inside and the big kitchen beyond it. It's clean, white and surprisingly cool as I step down into the big room. The dog follows me and I have no idea if he's supposed to be there or not.

'Hey,' says Giovanni, walking out from the kitchen with a small coffee cup. 'You came back. I thought you might. Like I say, we're always looking for helping hands.' He smiles, his dark curls bouncing around his face.

I shake my head. 'Sorry, not here to help. Just come for some information really,' I say, as the young woman I saw hanging out washing comes through the door behind me.

'Ah, *caffè*! Great!' she says. '*Buongiorno* again. Would you like some coffee?' she asks, going into the kitchen and returning with a pot and two small cups. She is pouring it before I can refuse.

'I don't want to take up your time,' I say, looking between the two of them.

Giovanni is smiling. '*Buongiorno*,' he greets the younger woman.

'Time is the one thing we have here for free,' she says.

'Have a seat. Everyone is welcome,' says Giovanni. 'We're waiting for a delivery, but also, as always, planning, brainstorming, whatever you call it, trying to think of ways to make ends meet.'

They go to sit at one end of the long table on a wooden bench and beckon me to join them. There is a notepad with a pen that the woman picks up, and a long list. I sit down next to them, hoping to find out quickly what I need to know so I can leave them to it. I look outside the door to where the dog has lain down under an olive tree on the stone patio.

'I need to fix that end of the bench,' says Giovanni. 'It's been repaired more times than I can remember, but keeps going.'

'I could make cushions if we could get hold of some fabric. But it's not cheap, even at the market.'

The coffee smells good. I pick up the cup.

'This is Caterina,' he says. 'She came to the village . . .'

he glances at her for approval and she nods '. . . after leaving a difficult situation with her husband.'

'I left with nothing,' she says. 'It's hard to imagine now.'

I hold the cup and don't move. Here am I, worrying about too much lasagne, and I can't imagine what this woman went through to get here.

'I . . .' I stutter '. . . I'm so sorry. It must have been very hard.'

'Thank you. It has been difficult but this place has been a blessing. We're finding our feet again.'

Giovanni smiles his very attractive smile. 'What can I say? It's the fabulous food she comes for!'

'And the company,' she says.

'And we love her for her mending.'

'I have been making a new tablecloth too,' she pulls out a piece of patchwork from her basket and runs her hands over it, 'with all the scraps. But I'm running out.'

'It's beautiful,' I say, admiring it.

'It's good to keep busy.' She gives me a smile tinged with sadness. 'It keeps the bad dreams at bay. Making something where there was nothing. There is something good to be found in the most desperate places. These scraps were ready for burning. But they have something wonderful to offer when put together like this.'

I think about the house, the work it will take to ready it for sale as a holiday home in Tuscany. The furniture needs replacing and the walls repapering. I barely know where to start. But part of me is finding comfort in the old kitchen table and the worn plates. I check myself: I can't be sentimental about it. I have to do it up to sell it. We can't live on fresh air, however beautiful it is here.

'Have you always sewn?' I ask.

'I worked as a hairdresser at home. I had my own salon. But my husband didn't like me having my own business. It became a problem to him.' She takes a deep breath. 'I felt unsafe. I wanted the children to be safe and it wasn't safe where we were so we came here. It feels safe here.'

'And she has started working on the garden,' says Giovanni.

She smiles. 'I've never gardened before.' She gestures towards the little garden with sunflowers. 'I've always sewed, but gardening, planting seeds, that is something new.' I can't imagine what she has endured, her life turning into fear for herself and her children.

We fall into silence.

Then Giovanni points to the pile of lasagne dishes on the scrubbed table in front of me. 'I see you had more visitors.'

I wonder: 'Was this something to do with you, La Tavola, the community kitchen?'

He holds up his hands. 'Nothing to do with me, I promise. But I'm guessing you won't need a meal this evening!' He laughs and I can't help but join in. 'It's

Friday and we always deliver a meal to those who need it on Fridays. It's just a simple dish but the routine is good for people.' He tips his head back to the kitchen where rows of little tinfoil containers are lined up on the table ready to be filled.

'What's on the menu tonight, Chef?' I'm falling back into my old life, then wishing I hadn't. I don't want to be thinking about menus, costings, unpaid bills. I don't want to think about food at all.

'Not lasagne,' he says, making me laugh again. It feels good. Caterina has picked up the tablecloth and is sewing a patch into place.

I study the room from where I'm sitting: the cool whitewashed walls, the intimate but spacious dining room, the fireplace with blackened edges, suggesting it is used in winter. What an amazing restaurant it would make, filled with candles in winter, olive branches and greenery in summer. I shut down the idea straight away. I must stop thinking like that. I don't want any-thing to do with restaurants again. I am never heading back into that world.

'Are you sure you didn't initiate all these gifts to us? I know we were hungry when we got here but we really are fine now,' I say. 'We've been to the shop and I have plenty in.'

'Lots of lasagne now, too!' laughs Caterina, examin-ing her sewing, being in the moment and finding fun in it.

It feels good to laugh, to talk to people other than the children, and Marco, of course, which, now I think about it, might seem strange to people if I were to tell them.

'Although,' says Giovanni, 'food is so much more than just cooking something to eat, isn't it? It's about the experience, company, conversation, laughter, debate. It's about inclusion. It's about feeling part of something.'

I sip my coffee and gaze out of the open door to the sun-drenched patio. Once again, I experience a pang, wishing Marco was beside me. That I wasn't doing this on my own. I look between Giovanni and Caterina when a boy appears at the door, about the same age as Luca.

'This is my son, Pietro,' says Caterina.

'Hi,' I say. He points to a van pulling up outside.

'Pietro doesn't speak,' says Caterina, almost matter-of-factly. 'Not since we left our home and his father.'

My heart twists.

'My daughter.' She nods to a girl who has followed her brother. 'This is Isabella, she's eight.'

She wishes me *'Buongiorno.'*

'She is hoping to make biscuits for the meal tonight. To take to the community.'

Giovanni and Caterina get to their feet, she putting aside her tablecloth.

'The food is delivered here from the shop in the

village. We'll see what they've got and plan a pasta sauce,' says Giovanni. 'You will have met Tommaso at the shop.'

'I did. He was very kind.' I remember him giving the children lollipops.

'He's a good man. Lives with his wife who is bed-bound. He cares for her, runs the business, and brings us any food that is unsold to make into our meals for the community. Anything going to waste, he brings here.'

'That's brilliant,' I say, with a rush of excitement I haven't felt since Marco and I would sit and plan menus . . . Again, I shut down the memory. 'I have to go,' I say. 'I'll leave you to it.'

'No problem. You know where we are now. There's always a cup of coffee if nothing else.' He smiles widely again. I can't help but wonder if he has a partner in his life. Maybe he and Caterina have found each other, which makes me feel . . . hopeful: perhaps there is a life for the two of them after what she has been through.

'I just need to return these dishes and thank the ladies who made them. And tell them we're fine, that there's no need to bring us any more,' I laugh again.

'Good luck with that!' says Giovanni.

'Do you know where they live, or how I can get the dishes back to them?'

Giovanni chews his bottom lip. 'Sure. Tell you what,

why don't you swing by later when we're delivering food? You can take the dishes back and deliver a meal to them at the same time.' His green eyes are dancing with a bit of devilment. 'It's not cooking, or prepping,' he says. 'I promise. You're just returning the dishes.'

'Yes, of course, sorry. That would be great. I'll pop in with the meals and return the dishes. Thank you.' I turn to leave.

'Oh!' Giovanni calls after me as I reach the door. 'Did I mention that we sit with the people we hand out meals to? While they eat. Many won't have seen anyone all week.'

I stare at him. 'Sit with them?'

'It's company, while they eat. Because . . .'

'It's about the experience,' I repeat his words to me.

'Exactly,' He heads towards the door and the waiting van outside.

I really want to pull out, but I can't. He's right. It's just giving a little bit of time to help. I can do that. As long as I don't have to divulge too much about myself.

8

'This is Alessandro,' says Giovanni. He's standing outside the gate that leads into the walled garden when I
arrive at La Tavola with the children that evening. The
swallows and swifts are dipping and diving from the
stone walls of the deserted buildings, wheeling across
the valley and back again. I'm carrying the dishes, keen
to deliver them and get home.

Beside Giovanni, there's a young man on a mobility
scooter. Giovanni has a hand on his shoulder. 'Alessandro will show you where to return the dishes and
deliver the meals.'

'*Ciao, Alessandro.*' I hold up a hand, balancing the
heavy dishes on the other. 'Luca and Aimee.' I introduce them. Luca shakes hands with Alessandro and
Caterina, who has joined Giovanni outside the front
gate. Aimee hugs Mr Fluffy and moves closer to me.

'Good to meet you, Luca,' Caterina says. 'Perhaps you would like to go with Pietro, my son. He is delivering a meal to Francesco, an older resident in the village. No family any more. He gets a little confused. Pietro makes sure he has labels in the kitchen on things like the oven and the washing-machine, so he knows which is which. He once found a bowl of tomatoes in the washing-machine and Francesco's socks in the fridge.'

Luca smiles tentatively, as does Pietro, who joins us and stands beside his mother with a tinfoil dish, a small water bottle filled with red wine and a basket of bread.

Luca's getting taller, I realize. He's nearly as tall as me! When did that happen? Sometime between losing Marco and now. I wish time would just stand still. I'm not ready for life to move on.

'Is that okay, Mum?' he asks.

'Yes,' I reply. 'If you'd like to.'

Luca looks at Pietro and they smile nervously.

Pietro nods and points. Luca joins him, and turns to walk away with him, Pietro carrying the food and offering Luca the bottle of wine, which he takes. Suddenly he turns back to me. 'Will you be okay Mum?'

His concern brings tears to my eyes.

'Yes, yes, you go,' I say, and wonder if I should tell him that Pietro doesn't speak. But they smile at each other, wider this time, and I realize I don't need to say anything. They're finding their own way without me, or discussing where they've come from or why they're here, as they walk towards the other side of the village. Just enjoying the moment, in the lowering sun.

'Perhaps Aimee would like to help my daughter Isabella finish decorating the biscuits,' says Caterina. Aimee looks up at me, clutching Mr Fluffy.

'Would you like to? Or you can come and deliver the dishes with me. But it might be more fun to stay and make biscuits.'

She nods and smiles shyly as Caterina holds out a hand to her. 'Come on, I'll introduce you. But no eating the sprinkles! Well, not all of them!' Aimee sets off, with Mr Fluffy, clasping Caterina's hand.

'Alessandro, can you show Thea which meals to take?'

'Of course,' says Alessandro, hopping off the mobility scooter.

'Are you okay? I can get them. It's no problem.' I point towards the kitchen.

Giovanni claps a hand over his mouth, covering a smile – so much like Marco.

'What?'

Giovanni gives his head a little shake and his black curls bounce. 'It's not his scooter. It's his *nonna's*. He brings it to help with the deliveries. It's got a big basket at the front.'

I turn back to Alessandro, who is beaming at his own ingenuity and blushing with embarrassment at the same time.

'One day, I plan to take on Richard Branson at his own game,' he says. 'Today a scooter, then a fleet of tuk-tuks, buses and even aeroplanes.'

'Alessandro has big ambitions and he plans to build his empire right here.'

'Exactly! Starting with decent transport to get to and from the village. Better roads, taxis that will come here, buses . . . Everyone will want to come to our village.'

'I like your thinking,' I tell him.

'Now, climb on,' he tells me.

'I'll walk behind you. Just as long as you don't go too fast.'

9

Alessandro pulls up on the mobility scooter and points towards a house. It's at the end of a row at the bottom of the hill, not far from where I've parked the car. I remember raised voices and a heated argument over a washing line . . . I look at Alessandro anxiously. 'Here?'

He nods solemnly. 'This is Teresa.'

I get the feeling I've been set up. The newcomer, who doesn't know what lies behind the door, has been sent to deliver and sit with the resident for dinner. The resident no one else wants to visit. I don't know whether to laugh or be cross. But it's just a quick visit, I think. Drop off the meal and check they have everything they need. Make some small-talk and leave.

I straighten and see something moving outside a neighbouring house in the row. I'm sure I'm being watched, and feel a strange foreboding. But I'm just doing the village equivalent of Meals on Wheels, I think crossly. Why should I feel unsettled? I take another look at the houses.

Alessandro hands me the meal from the basket on the mobility scooter and the little plastic bottle of red wine. He nods at me, as if to give me courage. 'I'll go back to La Tavola, collect the next meal for delivery and meet you here,' he says.

I take a deep breath and walk towards the front door. I don't have to tell them about my circumstances. I don't have to say anything I'm not ready to say. I just make polite conversation. I knock at the door.

It opens slowly. A woman squints at me. '*Sì?*'

'Teresa? *Buonasera*,' I say. 'I've brought your dinner. From Giovanni, at La Tavola.' I point.

'Where is Giovanni? Is he here?'

'He sent me, with your dinner.'

She looks at what I'm holding.

'And I brought your dish back, from the delicious lasagne.'

Her face softens and she opens the door wider. 'Oh, Giovanni, he has so many to think about. He needn't think about me! He is always thinking of others.' She puts her hand to her chest for her glasses, suspended on a length of string. She pulls them onto her face and studies me. 'Ah! You are in Casa Luna?' She opens the door wide now and I smile. We're just making small-talk. 'The one with no husband.'

My spirits slump. So much for keeping my business to myself.

'Come in, come in.'

The table is laid for two in the brightly tiled, tidy kitchen. Clearly expecting someone to arrive with food.

'Come, sit!' She takes the dishes from me, and I can see Giovanni was right. She's clearly glad of the company.

I sit on the cushion on the upright kitchen chair and look around the room, the walls filled with photographs and a dresser with crockery. I put the basket with dishes to be returned under the table. Now all I need to do is work out which is whose.

It's early evening. There is a window at the back with heavy nets across it, presumably to keep insects at bay.

She puts the food on the table.

'Can I serve for you?' I hover over the seat.

'No, no. You are my guest. Sit!' she commands, waving a hand at the chair and I do as I'm told, without question.

I hear the whine of a mosquito. I itch.

'Lemon juice, squeeze,' she tells me. 'No more mosquitoes!'

'Right,' I say.

'Here.' She takes a lemon from the bowl on the table, cuts it in half and gestures for me to rub it over my skin. It stings in the bites, but I'll try anything.

'Now, *mangiamo*,' she says, putting two plates of pasta on the table.

'This is for you! Not me.'

She stops. 'There is plenty here. Eat,' she commands. It would be rude not to so I take a bite of the pasta, courgette and Parmesan. Lots of pepper and garlic. It's delicious. I eat the whole bowl, forgetting to talk, and my worries about being interrogated disappear.

'That was wonderful,' I say. 'Just like my hu—'.

'Giovanni is a good cook,' she says. 'He will make a good husband. But he would be so much better if he took advice from those who have been cooking much longer.'

'You don't like his cooking?'

She shrugs. 'It's good, but he doesn't listen. He has worked in kitchens all over the world, Michelin stars,' she waves a dismissive hand, 'but we learnt from our mothers, who taught us everything we know.' She pauses. 'Well, most things.' Her eyes narrow. 'And their mothers before them. It is not just in the recipe but in the way we cook. How we slice, chop and serve the food. It is an experience.'

'Well, I enjoyed it,' I say, indicating my empty plate.

'You ate it all!' She clasps her hands over her chest.

'Thank you.' I get up to leave.

'I will bring you dessert. My tiramisu.'

She tops up my wine glass from the little terracotta jug into which she has poured the wine. I try to refuse, to no avail: 'Oh, no . . .'

There's no stopping her. She's like a juggernaut gathering pace. I'm here for the meal, to the end.

'Just *piccolo*,' I say. 'A little bit.' I hear her laugh under her breath. She turns from the kitchen and places a glass dish in front of me.

I'm very full, but it would be rude not to eat some.

I lift my spoon. Her eyes are on me, watching intently. I put it into my mouth . . . and it is just heaven. Gorgeous. Just like I remember when we sat down after service in the restaurant, with a cold thirst-quenching beer on a hot summer's evening after a busy service, the waiters happy with their tips, and customers' promises of reviews on Tripadvisor. Or a coffee, with some brandy and a bowl of tiramisu from the fridge. A quiet time in the restaurant kitchen, like backstage in the theatre, enjoying the buzz of an appreciative audience.

'This is wonderful,' I say, after a second mouthful.

'*Buono.*' She beams. 'Now, tell me about you. What are you doing here?'

I scoop more tiramisu onto my spoon, trying to work out how much I'm prepared to say. I mustn't feel bullied. I take another mouthful of the delicious pudding. To leave any would feel like a crime, especially with Teresa watching me like a hawk.

'Well . . .' I start, taking little spoonfuls quickly, buying myself time to decide what to say '. . . I'm doing up Casa Luna.' I'd like to leave it there, but she's waiting silently, watching me. 'And I'm here with my children for the summer.' That should be enough. I put a big spoonful of cream and sponge into my mouth so I can't say any more.

'Ah, yes, Casa Luna.' She shakes her head. 'So sad she had no one to pass the house on to. All that time alone after her husband died.'

I choke a little on my big mouthful, not wanting to talk about dead husbands. I swallow quickly and drink some wine, which clears my mouth, throat and mind all in one go.

'Oh, of course,' I say, 'I brought back your dish. *Grazie mille* for the lasagne.' I lift the basket onto the table. 'But I'm not sure which is yours.' I pull out the three.

She stares at them, then up at me. Her face tightens and she purses her lips. 'I see you had some other visitors.'

Her mood has changed from friendly to frosty.

'Erm, yes, all very lovely,' I say. 'And very welcome.'

She sniffs. 'But they were all very different?'

'Yes,' I say quickly.

'Did you have a favourite?'

Suddenly I'm answering the million-pound question on *Who Wants to Be a Millionaire?*, and I'm hot, sweaty and terrified of getting it wrong. I feel the colour drain from my face. 'Er, which dish is yours?' I ask, my throat tight.

She smiles, and I think we're back on friendly terms. And then she says, 'It was the best one, of course!

My lasagne recipe has always been the best in the village. It helped me win my husband's heart. It was his mother's recipe. When he discovered I could make lasagne like her, he decided I was the woman for him.'

I stare at the dishes. Now what? 'Tell me more about your husband. Is he here?' I'm playing for time.

'He died. I am a widow.'

Gah! Back to widowhood.

I know it's not the blue dish. That was the last one and I actually took it from the woman who brought it. It's the orange one or the white one with flowers.

'And you?'

'We're doing up the house. I hope to finish by the end of the summer. My husband bought it, but we didn't have time to get out here and renovate it. Now it has to be done by the end of August. Or I'll have to pay lots more money,' I say, wishing I hadn't said that.

'Ah, yes, the housing scheme. A bargain for some who want to come and live in Italy. Maybe not so when they realize how remote this village is and how it is dying on its feet. Like its men.'

'So,' I try to move the subject along, 'I'm here and we're doing it up.'

'And your husband?' she persists.

'My husband?' Then I spot it. A matching white dish with flowers on the heavily laden dresser.

'Yes, your husband.'

'My husband is . . . Marco,' I say.

91

'Marco. Your husband?' She raises her eyebrows.

'Yes.' I smile. 'Did you meet him when he was here?'

'I did,' she says. 'A charming man.'

'Anyway,' I stand, '*grazie mille* for dinner. And here,' I hold out the dish, the one with flowers on, '*grazie* for the lasagne.'

She looks at the dish and smiles. 'My recipe is still the best in the village!' She practically blooms in front of me.

I pick up my basket with the two other dishes in it. 'I'll return these too,' I say, clearing away the empty containers from the work surface and scooping them into my basket, to return to La Tavola.

'Tell Giovanni *grazie*,' she says. 'One day we will find him the perfect woman to make him a happy man!' Again she clasps her hands over her chest, and I fear for her glasses. 'If only I were ten years younger,' she says, as I walk towards the door.

Ten years! That's optimistic but it makes me smile. What's wrong with optimism? We could all do with a little hope.

'He is a good man. If only we could find him some-one to be a husband to. What a shame you still have yours.'

And this time I have no words . . .

'I must go,' I say. 'I'll tell him you said *grazie*. And, yes, I hope he finds a wife, if that's what he wants.'

'Ah, men do not always know what they want. Like

my husband. He thought his mother made the best tiramisu . . . until he tasted mine!' She beams, and I feel full all over again.

I pull open the door, hoping for a little coolness in the air. Alessandro is waiting for me with the mobility scooter.

'*Ciao, Nonna Teresa,*' he calls.

'*Ciao, Alessandro.* How are you and your brother?'

He says they're fine.

'*Ciao* – sorry, what's your name?' asks Teresa.

'Thea,' I say.

'I will bring you another lasagne,' she says to me.

'Really, no need.'

'I insist!' she calls after me brightly, waving, as I hurry back to the scooter, where Alessandro is waiting as the bats flit in and out of the stone walls.

'Right, who's next?'

'Nonna Lucia,' he says. 'She can be scary, but she's fine once you get to know her.'

'Okay,' I say, as he leads the way on the scooter to the house next door.

10

Nonna Lucia's house is much the same as Teresa's. I knock at the door and she frowns as she opens it a crack. I explain I've come with dinner from La Tavola and Giovanni and she ushers me inside.

She asks if I'm from Casa Luna.

I say I am.

The table is laid for two. I can't eat another meal, I think.

'Please, sit,' she says, taking the food and the wine from me and pouring it into a glass. I take a sip, trying to work out how to get out of eating. But it's too late. I'm already being served.

'I have made a little *antipasti* and *salata*,' she says, as I'm faced with a platter of mixed meats, olives, cheese and beautiful ripe tomatoes. I attempt to eat the salad, hoping it will be light and not too filling, but the fig and goat's cheese in it make it far too delicious to stop at just a mouthful or two. The saltiness of the cheese and sweetness of the figs, complete opposites, are a match made in Heaven.

When I sit back, she stands, her apron tied around her ample hips, and begins to serve the pasta dish I've just had at Teresa's. Wonderful home-made pasta, with courgette, a kick of garlic and a spritz of lemon.

'Just a little, please,' I say. 'Er, watching my weight,' I add.

She turns slowly to me, looks me up and down, 'Phfff,' and serves a hefty quantity of the pasta.

I explain I'm here with my children, doing up the house by the end of the summer.

'And where is your husband?'

'He's not with us,' I manage, without feeling I have to tell a complete stranger I'm widowed and miss him every single moment of every single day. If I thought I was going to get away with leaving some of the pasta and saying I'm giving up dessert for my diet, I was mistaken. I'm handed a bowl of more fresh figs with creamy mascarpone.

'From the garden,' she tells me.

'They're delicious.'

Finally, I stand up, feeling as full as I did when I was nine months pregnant. I hand her the orange lasagne dish. She takes it, then looks at the final dish in my basket, the blue one, and sniffs. 'I see you had another visitor. My sister, no doubt.'

'Oh, your sister? Yes, it was delicious . . .'

She's waiting for me to say something about her lasagne.

'I enjoyed them all, but I could tell which one you'd made.' I try to be diplomatic. 'It was very distinctive.'

'So mine was your favourite?' She smiles triumphantly as if she's lifting a gold medal at the Olympics. 'I'm glad, though not surprised. I have worked hard to make the best lasagne in this village.'

'Of course.'

I'm keen to leave, so after we've said goodbye, I open the door. Alessandro is waiting for me. I can hardly walk.

'How was it?' he says.

'Filling!' I say quietly, with a little burp.

'Giovanni says one more to go. Nonna Rosa. And don't be put off by her. Her bark is worse than her bite.' He smiles.

With the last dish in my basket, I knock at the door. Dusk is turning to nightfall but it's still warm and muggy. More than anything I want a cold shower and to drop into bed. At least I haven't been bitten by any more mosquitoes since I doused myself in lemon juice.

I take a deep breath, hoping Luca and Aimee are

okay. I need to get back to them soon. I check my phone. They could get in touch if they needed me, but there are no messages. I'm feeling anxious, though, and want to be back with them as soon as possible.

The door opens. 'Nonna Rosa? I'm from La Tavola. I've brought dinner,' I say, immediately recognizing her from when she dropped off the lasagne at my house.

Alessandro is right. She has a very lined and hard face. She's older than the other two, her house is a little bigger, and she's twice as intimidating.

'And I brought your dish back. *Grazie*,' I say, holding out the dish and the tinfoil box of food.

She reaches out and takes both. At first I think she isn't going to invite me in but then she says, 'I suppose you want to come in.'

Part of me wants to say no, then go home to the children, and undo the top button on my trousers, but I can't. I promised Giovanni. And he helped with the electrics. It's only right that I return the favour this evening. At least I've found a way to get all the dishes back to their rightful owners.

I don't want people to think of me or the children as rude or standoffish. Marco would have wanted me to join in. He'd have been waiting at home to hear all about it when I came in.

I follow her inside. At least it's cooler in here.

The table is set as it was in the other two houses, with a colourful tablecloth, a jug of water and wine glasses.

I sit, without questioning it. I'm so full, I'm wondering if I could feign sickness and leave, or fake a phone call from the children, asking me to come home.

But before I can think of anything, another plate of pasta is put in front of me. I thank my lucky stars there is no *antipasti* as a forerunner to the main event.

I take another sip of wine and I'm feeling tired.

'*Grazie mille* for the lasagne,' I begin. 'It was very kind of you.'

'So,' she lifts a fork, and nods for me to do the same, 'you are in Casa Luna.'

I put a piece of pasta on my fork, stare at it and am determined not to be beaten.

'You are here with your children.'

'I am.'

'You said your husband he's dead?' she growls and the hairs on her chin even quiver.

I nod. I take a mouthful and chew quickly, washing the first down with a sip of water. I twist more pasta, hoping that the sooner I finish what I can, the sooner I can get away.

'I see,' she says, and encourages me to eat by nodding at the plate. I know that if I don't carry on, she'll think I don't like it and find me something else,

I take a deep breath. 'My husband . . .'

'Marco,' she confirms.

'Yes.' I brighten. 'You met him when he was here?'

'Yes,' she growls again. I eat as quickly as I can.

I finish most of the bowl and put down the fork, like a weary marathon runner crossing the finish line. I ease down the last forkful with a large gulp of wine.

Nonna Rosa stares at me. I'm hot, and very, very full. I'd like to leave. 'Your husband Marco,' she says, narrowing her eyes. 'It is a shame he's gone.'

And I'm jolted back to when he first died. The pitying looks. Here, it had been good not to be 'the young widow' and just Thea.

I take a deep breath, mostly to ease my tight waistband, but it's reached capacity and cuts into my stomach, making me wince.

'He was a nice man. I was looking forward to speaking with him.'

'Indeed,' I say, and with that, I try to stand.

'You haven't had dessert!' She's affronted.

'Perhaps,' I say bravely, 'I could take it with me, to share with the children.'

She nods curtly. 'I will give you plenty,' she says, and I'm definitely not going to insist she doesn't. This is a non-negotiable situation.

'How long will you be here for?' she asks, cutting an almond tart into slices, then putting it into a tea-towel and tying it.

'Till the end of August. I have to get the house finished. Or I have to pay the full price of the house to the previous owner.'

She nods. 'Our mayor is looking out for the community,' she says.

'Yes. We never expected it to take so long to do it up. But things got in the way.'

'They often do,' she says, handing me the tea-towel with the almond tart inside it. 'Like husbands dying when you don't expect it.'

Suddenly I don't know whether to laugh or cry. I try to focus on the job in hand to stop me doing either. I remember the baking dish. 'Well, thank you for the lasagne,' I say handing it to her. 'It was delicious.'

'My mother's recipe.' She adds, 'I will make you another.'

And my heart sinks into my very full stomach.

Outside, in darkness, the air is warm and sticky. Alessandro is waiting as I leave the house, under the light from the moon. I don't need asking twice when he offers to take me back to La Tavola on the scooter instead of walking. I'm so full, I don't think I'll ever look at or think about food again.

11

Back at La Tavola I find the children.

'And then she offered me almond tart!' I'm telling Giovanni and Caterina as we all sit under the olive tree, with small glasses of limoncello.

'For the digestion,' Giovanni tells me.

'More like indigestion,' I say.

There is a candle on the table and, despite the warm night, the mosquitoes seem still to be leaving me alone. Aimee has a box of decorated biscuits and Luca and Pietro are sharing the almond tart.

'So, you met our three *nonna*s?' says Giovanni.

'I did! You could have told me!'

'Told you what?'

'That I'd have to eat with each of them.'

'I said you had to sit with them.'

'But I couldn't turn down their offer of food. It would have been rude.'

He laughs. 'You're beginning to sound like a local already – you'll fit right in!'

'How come they eat on their own every night?'

'Like many older people here, their families have moved away so they're on their own.'

'But they're sisters? Why don't they eat together?'

'Sisters and sister-in-law. And it's a long story. But the three women fell out many years ago and now you'll never get them in the same room together.'

'How sad.'

'It is.'

'What did they fall out over?'

'That's not my story to tell. But I'm sure you'll find out, one way or another.'

'No, no . . . I won't be here long enough.' I hold up a hand and laugh. 'I'm not getting involved. It has nothing to do with me. I just have to do up the house and be back in the UK in time for school starting in September.'

'So you don't want any leftover pasta, then?' Giovanni nods to the orange light from the kitchen.

'No, thank you.' I sip the limoncello, praying it will help my digestion. It certainly loosens my tongue after the glasses of wine I've had. 'And they all wanted to hear why their lasagne was the best.'

Giovanni and Caterina laugh.

'It wasn't funny,' I say tartly, and find myself laughing

with them. 'Don't make me laugh – it hurts.' And we laugh some more, as if I've known these people for years.

'Believe me, it is never just about the recipe,' Giovanni says sagely, offering me more limoncello.

'No, thank you. I have to get to bed.' I stand up as if I might give birth at any moment.

'Would you like a biscuit, Mum?' asks Aimee. I can see Giovanni trying not to laugh.

'I would,' I say, 'but I'd love to have it in the morning.'

'With *caffè*?' she says.

'With *caffè*.'

'Okay.'

Luca bids Pietro '*Buonanotte*'.

Pietro grins and waves.

'See you tomorrow,' Luca adds. And then, suddenly serious, 'If that's all right, Mum?'

'Yes, of course.' And then I say quietly, 'It's okay to have fun, you know. We don't have to feel sad about Dad all the time. He wouldn't want that.'

I head back to the house, along the moonlit lane, with two tired children, and a soft stuffed rabbit.

With the children in bed, no complaints about washing or cleaning their teeth and fast asleep in no time, I kiss them lightly. Coming here may have been good for them: they're away from all the memories and constant reminders of Marco. A summer of being themselves with other children. Maybe Marco knew exactly what he was doing when he bought this place. Maybe it wasn't just a moment of madness.

I go downstairs, where I see him sitting at the table, arms folded, smiling up at me, telling me he knew I'd love it. I join him there, putting down the cookies, knowing he would have eaten the lot if he could. It's like when things were hard at the restaurant: we'd come home tired, sit at the table with a glass of wine and hope tomorrow would be a better day.

'Maybe tomorrow will be a better day,' I say, 'but you'll still be dead. So, really, it can't get any worse.' I sip the water I've poured.

'But I am still here, *cara*,' I hear him say.

'I know. And I'm grateful for that.'

I look at my notebook. 'Tomorrow I need to tackle some jobs . . . A couple of weeks' cleaning and painting and this place could be looking half decent. I have to do it. I can't miss the deadline, because I don't have any money to pay to the mayor. It has to be done.'

A small memory scratches at the back of my brain. What was Marco going to tell me about this place? Why he fell in love with it? Was it just the views? Why here?

'You'll understand. There is a little piece of me left behind,' he'd told me after his trip here. And I feel it too. Maybe that's why I see him sitting at the table, and why I'm talking to him: because there's a bit of him here. I don't want that ever to leave me.

I finish my water. 'Night, Marco,' I say, feeling his presence and warmth, and wondering how I'll feel when we have to leave. For now, though, I'm just taking comfort from him being here.

'Goodnight, *cara*,' he says, as I turn out the lights and climb the stairs. I check on the sleeping children, then get into bed. Once more, I push the indentation into the pillow beside me for where his head should be, enjoying him being in the house. How sad it is that the three *nonna*s I met tonight, living their own lives, have ended up alone and lonely. I wonder what happened to allow the quarrel to go on. Surely letting go of the past is a good thing. As I will one day, just not yet.

12

The following morning, after a night of mad dreams about giant cakes, I wake in a hot sweat, only to remember where I am and why I'm here. It's my only chance to get family life on an even keel and back to something like it was.

I push back the damp covers, cursing the heat of the Tuscan summer, and open the windows wider to let in the early morning sunshine. I'm determined to get the house cleared today, start working out what needs fixing and get on with painting it.

It's hot and humid. I pull on an old T-shirt and long shorts, then head to the kitchen.

Marco is sitting there, waiting for me, arms crossed, espresso in front of him.

I move to the old cooker and the cafetière, which is cold. I wish it was still warm from him having made coffee. But it isn't. He isn't real. But it doesn't stop me imagining him there.

I consider my plans for the house. 'I'm going to keep it plain and simple. I just need to sell it and get home. And make sure I hit the deadline you never told me about.'

He planned for us to do up the house and spend our retirement in the sun. I smile at the thought of him here, with me, in the kitchen, mornings with his coffee, lunches, siestas and evenings, singing, as he often did, while prepping in the kitchen, sipping red wine and cooking up a storm, his big build filling the space. I wish he was here now. I wish we'd done it sooner instead of trying to make the restaurant work against the odds. I'm sure that's why he had the heart attack. It was all too much, trying to do it all ourselves, like King Canute trying to hold back the tide.

I pick up Marco's iPad from the table, pour my coffee, open the back door, letting in a shaft of light, and take the mug to the table. I tap in his password – he was predictable with such things – and open it to his photographs, many of this place, and his messages, which I still haven't been able to face going through yet. I look at them, I know I should see if there's anything important in there, anyone I need to still contact, but no, I still can't face doing it. I'll do it another time.

I put down the iPad. I have a house to clear out. I wonder where to start. Not the kitchen. I'm not ready to erase the image of Marco I've created in my head.

I head upstairs to where the children are in bed, awake now. I pop my head around the door and am struck, again, by the tired, dated paper peeling off the walls. The children seem unaware of their surroundings. They are lying on their backs, staring at the stained ceiling.

'Mr Fluffy says let's play guess the animal,' says Aimee.

'Okay, but I go first,' says Luca, from under his rumpled sheet, where usually he would be staring at his phone, but now, without the internet, it's a different landscape.

'Mr Fluffy says you always go first,' replies Aimee, grumpily.

'I'm not playing unless I go first.'

I wonder whether I should intervene.

Aimee sighs. 'Okay. Mr Fluffy says you can go first.'

I step back from the doorway and into the shadows on the dark landing.

'Okay. I'll make the sound and you have to guess it,' says Luca.

I turn away, walk into the room where I've been sleeping and throw open the wardrobe doors to reveal the contents. It seems like as good a place as any to start.

I pull out coats and jackets, and put them on the wrought-iron-framed bed. Part of me is wondering what Marco did when he came alone to check out the house. Had it occurred to him to start making a home for us? There certainly hasn't been any work done on the place. But I knew that. When he signed for the house, he paid with all of the money he had from his mother. All that was left was the big black hole of our business bank account to pay wages, rates and rent. And a lot of hope that one day it would all come good, that the business would get back into profit and we could sell up in Cardiff with some money behind us.

I pick up, fold each item and put it into the black bag I've brought upstairs with me. These clothes were clearly kept for best: a neat woollen jacket, a dark knee-length coat. Everything smells of mothballs and a floral scent. This was someone's life, someone's home. I work steadily throughout the morning as the day gets hotter and muggier. The children entertain themselves with just a few reminders to play nicely.

'Mum, can we go back to La Tavola?' asks Luca.

'Yes, can we, Mum?'

'Giovanni said it would be fine. They'll be starting to prep for tomorrow's Sunday lunch,' says Luca.

'Please, Mum! Mr Fluffy really wants to go back and see Isabella again.'

'Er . . . we don't know she'll be there,' I say, playing for time. The one thing I said I wouldn't do was encourage the children into the world of hospitality. 'Don't you want to help me here? We can make it fun!' I say, jerking a thumb at the black sacks I've already filled.

'It's not fun!' says Luca, deadpan, folding his arms, just like his father. 'You said it was okay to have fun. This isn't it. Going to see Pietro and La Tavola is fun!'

'No, you're right.' Of course it's not fun here, but hanging out with Pietro and Isabella yesterday was. It's not like he'll suddenly announce he wants to be a Corden Bleu chef. He's eleven, I remind myself. 'Of course you can go, if it's okay with Giovanni.'

'*Yessss!*'

I could cry to see Luca so excited, even if it is about going into a kitchen.

When Marco was training to be a chef, it was hard, with long hours in dark kitchens, never seeing the light of day. He came from Le Marche to London to try to make it. It was a hard slog, living up to the chef's standards but also avoiding the knives aimed at your back by someone equally keen to earn the chef's approval. It was brutal. A bit like the world of finance. But I stood my ground, survived it, met Marco and got what I thought I'd always wanted: our own business. It was just as brutal, navigating difficult customers who threatened bad online reviews, and being responsible for others' welfare, income and security. All Marco ever wanted to do was cook. He loved it, and every night was a performance. I loved to make everything happen seamlessly, like a theatre's stage manager. Until the final curtain came down abruptly. I shake away the memory.

'*Muuum!*'

'Sorry, Luca. Yes?'

'Can we go, then? I said I'd meet Pietro.'

'Yes, yes, of course. Have fun, and look out for your sister. Come home when Giovanni or Pietro's mum tells you to. Make sure you wear hats and sun cream. Wash your hands. Have you got your phone? Is it on? Oh, no Wi-Fi. I remember. Does La Tavola have Wi-Fi?'

'Yes, Mum.' Luca sighs and takes Aimee's hand.

I watch them go up the lane from the front door, carrying water bottles and Mr Fluffy. We've come a long way from where we were: summer was for organized sports camps, and an au pair, the last of whom seemed to spend most of her time on her phone, leaving them to make their own lunch and calling it 'an activity' for them. They're growing up. I don't know if that makes me happy or sad. But time is moving on whether I like it or not. The summer is at its peak, autumn just behind it, and tomorrow will be another day without Marco. I need to hurry up with the house.

I turn away, locking the front door, then push up the sleeves of my thin shirt and go back upstairs. By mid-afternoon, I've packed nearly all of the clothes from the bedrooms and put the tied bin bags at the top of the stairs. I carry them down and put them by the front door, ready to take down to the car. I'll find a charity shop or a clothes bank, whatever they have here.

I take a breather by the back door, tilting my face

upwards, hoping for a hint of breeze to bring relief from the intense heat that's been rising all day. Suddenly a gust whips the treetops and the shutters bang, making me jump, and I run upstairs to close them. Outside, raindrops start to fall, turning quickly to a downpour. Should run up and get the children? They're probably in as safe a place as any at La Tavola. I don't want them trying to get back here in the rain.

I text Giovanni and ask him to keep the children with him until the cloudburst passes.

He replies: *Of course.*

The rain against the windows is loud. But I can hear something else: drip, drip, drip. And this time it doesn't sound as if it's outside. I follow the sound onto the landing.

Drip, drip, drip.

I look up at the ceiling above the stairwell and see a bulge. I wonder what to do about it. The drip isn't new. Another job to add to the list. But now I know it's there, I can patch up the leak.

Suddenly, there's a clap of thunder, and a flash. I find myself crouching. The rain intensifies, slapping against the window panes, and I hope there aren't any other leaks.

I go into my bedroom, sit on the bed and watch shards of lightning shooting across the sky. There's a crash and another flash, but as quickly as the rain arrived it seems to pass, grumbling and rumbling off into the distance. Soon calm is restored. I watch the storm roll away and the return of the sunshine, with fresher air. I open the windows again and drops of rain fall from the frame, quickly drying in the sun's rays.

The clouds are scurrying away, leaving a brighter, bluer sky. I imagine Marco saying, 'Blue skies after rain.'

'I hope you're right, Marco, I really do.' I push the shutters wider and turn back to the now empty bedroom, a blank canvas we can put our mark on. I glance from the bed to the brightening fields below, with the scent of wet soil in my nostrils. The rain has given the soil what it needs to nourish the plants, to allow seeds to germinate and grow into tomorrow's blooms.

I turn to the last of the bags by the bedroom door and go over to tie them up and take them to the top of the stairs. I'm hot, sweating, ready for a beer and a wash in the basic bathroom. I straighten my aching back and suddenly there's a shout from outside. Is it one of the children? Are they in trouble?

'Luca? Aimee?' I call, and drop the bags I'm carrying to navigate the stairs without them.

There's banging on the door. My heart is thundering.

'Open up!'

'I'm coming!' There's more banging, and my eyes are burning with tears from the panic rising in me. 'Coming,' I shout.

I take the stairs two at a time, avoiding the fourth, which needs repairing. 'I'm coming,' I call again.

But then I hear something that doesn't make sense and I freeze.

'Hey, Marco! Marco! Marco!' Am I imagining it, just like I've imagined him in the kitchen? I freeze.

'Marco! Where are you?' The door rattles. I'm being visited by a ghost from the past.

13

'Marco? Come on, I know you're in there. The shutters are open! Hello?' The shouts continue.

I make my way to the front door and look at the handle, rattling and turning this way and that, threatening to give way at any minute.

'Hey, Paps! I know you're here.'

The key is on the floor – where the wind must have caught it and caused it to fall. I pick it up, my hands shaking as I put it into the lock, turn it and pull at the heavy door handle. My heart is racing, as if I've downed a couple of Jäger Bombs.

I open the door to see a young woman stepping back and staring up at the house. Dark hair bundled messily on top of her head, like Amy Winehouse's. A collection of earrings in her lobes, catching the light.

Friendship bracelets around her wrists. Cut-off denim shorts, a bikini top and a tattoo of a heart just above her breast. I don't move.

The afternoon light is pouring onto her, as if she's arrived on a shaft of sun. She just needs wings to make her celestial.

'Marco! Paps!'

Why does she keep calling him that?

'I didn't know you were back! I saw the windows open! You could have messaged! No word from you at all!' Beside her is a rucksack.

I take a deep breath. Is this some kind of imaginary figure, like I've been seeing Marco in the kitchen? Has it gone too far? Are my anxiety meds not working? Or perhaps I'm heading into perimenopause and my mind is playing tricks on me.

Suddenly she looks straight at me, with dark, laughing eyes. 'Who are you?' she says, in full combat mode, narrowing her eyes.

Feeling on the back foot, I match it. 'Well, who are you?'

She says nothing and steps forward to the door. To my surprise, she crosses the threshold. She looks around the room. 'Where's Marco?' She is searching the room with her eyes, but obviously Marco is nowhere to be seen.

'How do you know him?'

'Marco!' she shouts again, taking another step into the house.

'Who are you?' I ask again.

She stops and looks straight at me. 'You first.' She juts her chin at me.

'I'm his wife,' I say slowly.

She stares straight at me, then up and down, as if she's putting me in check mate. 'I'm . . . a friend.'

And I feel as if I'm in a vortex, swirling, spinning, like heat stroke.

'Where is he?' she insists.

My vision goes blurry, my head swims. What does she mean, she's a friend? What kind of friendship?

I reach out to the door handle and take hold of it.

'Marco!' she calls again, and I feel as if my heart is being ripped out of my chest.

'Please just go!' I say, my breath shortening. She turns to me and is right in my face.

'I'm looking for Marco. Where is he? He didn't tell me he was coming! He hasn't been here for so long! He's told you about me?'

'I know nothing about you, or who you are.' My chest tightens so hard it hurts.

'Well, call Marco. He said he was going to tell you, so maybe now is a good time.'

My head is really light. I need to sit down before I fall. 'It's not a good time.'

'Why not? Where is he?' She throws her head back, laughing hollowly. 'It appears it hasn't been a good time for a while.' And I can picture Marco standing in the kitchen laughing too. The noise fills my head until it can't take any more. I put my hands over my ears.

'Marco . . . is . . . dead,' I say.

Suddenly she stops laughing. '*Scusi?*'

I drop my hands from my ears, then say slowly, 'Marco, my husband, is dead. Now, please, leave me alone.'

She glares at me. I have no idea who she is, or what kind of joke is being played on me, but it's cruel. Then she spins around, steps outside, grabs the rucksack and runs off up the hill.

'Wait!' I step out into the road. What was I supposed to say? What am I supposed to think? Is it true? Is it a joke? 'What's your name?' I call after her, questions bouncing around my aching head. 'What kind of friend? How did you know him?'

But she's gone, into the sunshine, as bright as it was before the storm.

I grab the door frame and support myself, stepping back into the cool of the house. Marco is nowhere to be seen. 'Damn you, Marco!' I shout. 'Haven't I been through enough?'

With that I take hold of the door and slam it as hard as I can, leaning against it and shutting my eyes.

I hear a loud noise.

My eyes spring open, just in time to see a large crack

opening across the ceiling, over the stairwell, where the bulge in the plaster had been, then another crack and another, as plaster start to fall, an avalanche gathering pace. All I can do is hold my arms over my head and wait for the lumps raining down on me to stop.

14

What seems like for-ever later, the room is finally quiet. I lift my hands from my head and look around. White dust covers everything. There's rubble everywhere. It's like a volcano's erupted. Marco is sitting in the kitchen, his dark curly hair covered with white dust.

'What the hell happened?' I rasp. Then, as the dust settles, the storm inside me begins to rage. 'Marco! What the hell is going on?'

But he doesn't answer.

15

I'm not sure how long I've been crouched here. I seem unable to move so I stay there because I can't see a way forward. Not even to standing. The only thing I had left has crumbled to dust. The house is ruined. And my mind is as messed up as the house. Who was that young woman? How did she know Marco? Was it an affair? Was he leaving me? Was any of this true, or was it just a fantasy?

Well after the dust has stopped falling, I'm still sitting, leaning with my back to the front door among the rubble. I feel as if my whole world has come crashing down. I'm in a daze. Suddenly I hear footsteps and shouts coming down the road. There's a bang on the door, jolting me out of trance.

'Mum! Mum!' It's Luca. I try to pull myself together.

Jo Thomas

'Giuseppe says the roof has fallen in! Mum!' He bangs on the door again.

I scrabble to my feet. 'Yes, yes, coming. I'm okay!' I hang onto the door handle to help me to my feet, then try to turn it. It's temperamental at the best of times, but try as I may to open the door, I can't. There's plaster everywhere.

'Stand back from the door.' Giovanni is clearly with them. I do as I'm told without question. He clearly takes a run at the door and shoves it open with his shoulder, pushing back with sheer force the lumps of plaster that were jamming it shut.

The children stare at me as if they've seen a ghost.

'It's all right, I'm fine,' I say, and they rush forward to hug me.

'Mum!'

'Are you sure you're okay?' Giovanni asks, concern all over his face.

'Giuseppe came to find us. He was walking the goats! He saw it happening through the windows.' Aimee starts to cry.

'I'm fine.' I crouch down to her. As I run my fingers through my hair, lumps of plaster fall from it. I realize I must look dreadful. I stand and peer into the dust-covered mirror by the door. I look like a ghost of the woman I was for all those years when life was great and Marco and I planned our life together. Our plans for coming here to live. All of my hopes and dreams in

122

ruins. I can't do this any more! I can't keep going! My knees buckle.

'Whoa,' says Giovanni, and I feel myself caught round my waist. 'Let's get you to bed. You've had quite a shock,' he says. 'It's just the plaster that's come down, so the floor upstairs will still be fine.'

A shock. That's exactly right.

He and Luca guide me upstairs, over the rubble. 'Watch the fourth step down,' I tell them despite my haze. 'It needs fixing.'

'That's the least of your worries right now,' I hear Giovanni say softly.

I flop onto the bed, and although the ceiling is still intact in here, dust particles fly up in little clouds as I land on the covers.

I stare upwards, feeling as if I'm in a parallel universe: I'm in Italy without my husband, and a young woman I've never met has just come to the door looking for him, as if he's still here, no time has passed, and as if she's known him all her life. Maybe she has. What do I know? None of this seems very real any more.

I turn my head towards the window, which Luca is pushing open, and then at the empty pillow with the indentation in it and feel wetness on my pillow. It's tears.

'Luca, get some water for your mum. It's just shock. She'll be all right.' I hear Giovanni reassuring Luca and wish I could too, but I feel as if I've been hit by a bus.

I can't move. 'She just needs a rest. She's taken on a lot to get you all here.'

Suddenly it's all there, rolling around like an Instagram video, the last few years of my life. Marco just back from Italy having signed for the house. The celebrations and plans. 'You will love it, *cara*, as much as I love you!' And then, the very next day, Marco having the heart attack, the ambulance, having to tell the children before social-media gossips spread the news and the children found out from someone else. Trying to keep the restaurant going, remortgaging the house and, finally, losing them both. And now, when I thought it couldn't get any worse, the ceiling has collapsed and I don't think I am fine any more.

'Don't worry, the children will stay with Caterina tonight. If that's okay with you. A sleepover. They'll be fine. Get some rest,' I hear Giovanni saying, but his voice is in the distance, just like when I had to call time on the restaurant. My mind couldn't take any more. It was on overload, like a too-full washing-machine, stuck, whirring, just like now.

'I . . .' is all I manage to say. I need to get up, sort out the children. But my body feels like a collection of lead weights.

'It's okay not to be fine, Thea. The children are safe. Get some rest. It's absolutely okay not to be fine,' he repeats.

'Thank you,' I croak.

*

Later . . . I'm wide wake and staring at the ceiling. The one that is still intact, not like the hall and downstairs. My pillow is sodden with tears I didn't even know I'd been shedding. I turn my head to the pillow next to mine. There's no indentation in it. Marco isn't here. He never was. He's gone. I turn my head away from it to see Mr Fluffy tucked in beside me. The tears come fast and furious now.

The following morning, when dawn arrives, I haul myself out of bed, carrying Mr Fluffy. I have a quick wash and get dressed, barely brushing my hair. Nothing matters right now.

I make my way downstairs, turn the corner and look at the mess. The plaster is still everywhere, but I notice a pathway to the front door that someone has cleared for me.

I follow it, carrying Mr Fluffy, go outside and stop to stroke the cat lying in the sun.

I close the door and start to walk, no idea where, because that's all my brain will manage. I walk away from the house, away from the images of Marco and the arrival of the young woman last night. I walk up the hill, feeling the sun on my face, the dust in my hair and eyes despite the wash. I shake it out. And then I walk around the village. I don't know where I'm walking to. I just keep going until dawn turns to morning, the day starts to warm, and I'm outside La Tavola.

Jo Thomas

I stand and look at the gate, ajar as always, letting people know they're welcome. I push it open, step into the shady garden and move towards the open door. I feel the rush of familiarity as voices from the kitchen travel across the big dining room to greet me.

'Mum!' The children appear from the kitchen, run over and hug me hard.

'We had such fun!' Luca tells me excitedly. 'We stayed up and had a firepit in the garden and drank hot chocolate and watched the stars.' He sounds like the boy he should be. 'There was a shooting star. I said it was Dad, bombing around Heaven, making everyone smile.'

'We've had such fun,' Aimee joins in. 'We made a tent out of a sheet in the bedroom and slept in it!'

'Can we stay again tonight? Can we, Mum?'

I look up at Caterina, who is beside me, smiling. 'Thank you so much for having them.' My voice is weak. I don't sound like me at all.

'Really, the pleasure was all ours. We loved having them. Such a change for the children to be themselves without all the other stuff they have to worry about.'

Someone hands me a coffee, I'm not sure who. It's hot and deliciously sweet.

'It's fine for them to stay again tonight,' she carries on. 'Really no bother. I imagine your house is going to take a bit of sorting.'

'Yes,' I say, not knowing where to begin. Where do I start to unravel all this mess?

In the kitchen, there are people, some of whom I may or may not have met before. They greet me, and are busy laying the big table. Giuseppe is the only one I recognize. A few others I don't know. One woman is in a wheelchair, with a bowl of peas she's shelling slowly. It's Sunday. They're preparing today's lunch. I don't move. I'm not sure if it's because I don't want to or can't. I don't know what I'm doing here. But being in the kitchen feels like where I need to be. Like the home I left a long time ago.

There's a shout from outside and everyone puts down what they're doing and dashes to the front door. A delivery has arrived from Alfonso. I put Mr Fluffy on the table, and go out to where everyone is taking things from Alfonso to carry them into the kitchen. He greets me with a smile and hands me a box of tomatoes. Their ripe scent is amazing, keeping me in the here and now, not letting my mind wander.

In the kitchen, the boxes are unpacked to the delight of Giovanni and the others.

'Pasta carbonara!' someone calls out.

'Pasta Norma!' says another.

A pile of onions and other vegetables sits on the kitchen island. I can feel Giovanni next to me, but he's not watching me. He slides a knife towards me on the work surface. I pick it up and begin to peel, then chop the onions. Not in a cheffy way, because I was never a chef. Marco was the chef. I just liked helping him when we were in the kitchen as a family. Organization and front-of-house were my areas but I loved being backstage, in the kitchen, the excitement before service, then relaxing at the end of a successful or stressful shift. I say nothing. I'm on autopilot. I just keep chopping.

And when I've finished chopping the onions, my eyes stinging, tears falling, he pushes something else towards me, courgettes, and I chop some more. Until . . .

'I think that's enough.' He rests a hand on my arm. And I look at the pile of onions and other vegetables in front of me.

'Oh . . . maybe a caponata?' I say suddenly, remembering it being on the menu when we had a glut of aubergines, tomatoes and courgettes from the suppliers. 'Or . . .' I put up my hand. 'Sorry, sorry . . .' The tears catch in my throat as I remember what Marco would do with a surplus of onions. I thought I knew exactly what he would be thinking and that I knew everything about him. But maybe I didn't. Now I feel I didn't know him at all. The memory of the Marco I loved has disappeared, like *gelato* on a hot, sunny day.

I put down the knife, hurry out of the kitchen and across the road, hoping the children haven't seen me. From the sounds of laughter and fun in the kitchen, I can breathe a sigh of relief that they haven't.

I lean against the wall, hug myself and gaze at the beautiful green valley below that, for a while, from the photographs Marco had shown me, I believed would be my future.

I hear footsteps behind me. 'You didn't finish your coffee,' says Giovanni.

'Thank you.' I turn to take it from him but with no intention of drinking it. I try to clear my throat. 'A young woman came to the house last night.'

'Ah,' he says.

'She said . . .' I cough and try to clear it again, but it's as tight as a coiled spring. 'She said . . .' my voice is very quiet '. . . she said she was a friend of my husband.'

He pauses, then says, 'In that case I'm gathering you have met Stella.'

I glare at him, needing to direct my fury somewhere. 'Who is she?'

He gives a sigh. 'Stella comes and goes.'

'Goes where?'

He shrugs. 'She grew up here, but doesn't have family here now. She travels and returns. Usually with stories of wild times and adventures.'

'How does she know my husband? Are they . . . were they lovers?'

He shakes his head. 'Stella is a young woman, looking for her place in the world. Like most of us. I would talk to her. Get the story straight before jumping to any conclusions.'

He's right. I don't know anything. But right now everything I thought we had, everything I believed

Jo Thomas

to be true, has gone. This was my last chance to save something of what Marco and I had worked for. But that's crumbled too.

'I can put you in touch with her if you want, so you get a chance to hear her story.'

'*Grazie* . . . but I'm not sure I'm quite ready for that.'

'Okay. When . . . if . . . you are, let me know.'

I look over the sun-baked field, breathing in the scent of the wild herbs growing there. 'The only thing I know is that I have to leave here. As soon as possible. I need to get the house finished and go.'

I turn to Giovanni. He's an attractive and kind man and, in another world at another time, I would have loved to lean against him, rest my head on his chest, breathe him in. But I won't. Of course I won't.

'I only came here to do up the house,' I say. 'This was Marco's dream for us. Not mine.'

At least, not without him. I'm sure it's a great place to be and I can see why he wanted us to come but he's not here. I have to leave, as soon as I can. I shouldn't have let my guard down, enjoying dinner and glasses of wine under the big fig tree. Or passing the time of day with Alfonso, the shopkeeper, whose wife I ask after, knowing he cares for her while running the shop. Waving to Giuseppe and the goats. Eating with women who have ended up on their own. I have enough on my plate. I need to get on and get out.

'I must find a plasterer. I know you said that if there

130

was anything you could do to help . . . I really need to get the work done, and quickly. Is it something you could do?'

He shrugs.

'As soon as the house sells, I can pay you. Just . . . not until then.'

He stays silent.

'No, of course not. That's a ridiculous idea. You don't even know me. Why would you work for me and wait to be paid? I'm sorry I asked.'

'It's fine. I understand. Getting yourself back on your feet is hard. It's hard to accept help too. I remember,' he says, gazing straight ahead at the view, 'when I found myself here. I'd been travelling, just kept moving. I didn't want to stop. If I stopped, I had to think.' He swallows. 'I lost a friend. A good friend. We worked in a kitchen together but the pressure became too much for Richie. He was younger than me, his whole life ahead of him. But the hours were torturous, as was the pressure. He took uppers to get to work and downers to try to sleep, but it all got too much for him. That was when I left. My relationship was in ruins and the kitchen was a toxic place.' He lifts his head. 'But here I've remembered why I loved the kitchen. The camaraderie. The sharing, the fun. It's okay to let others help you.'

I feel him turn to me.

I shake my head. 'I have to try to do it on my own.

I don't have the money to pay someone and I can't expect anyone to help for nothing.'

'Look, I can help with the ceiling, the plastering, but I'm needed here at La Tavola, as well as finishing jobs for some of the locals. I have painting for Alessandro's *nonna* and a garden job for Alfonso. I can't do those and your place as well.'

I nod. 'Yes, I can see that.'

'But if I could get someone to help at La Tavola, organize the food coming in and the meals, find ways of raising money to help more people, I might have time to do some plastering in return.'

He wants me to help here, in a kitchen. The last place I want to be.

He shrugs. 'I have a few other jobs on that are paying me. I can't turn those down. Putting in handrails to help Gabriella, Alessandro's *nonna*, move around the house more easily. She is in her eighties and needs support. I don't charge much, but it helps. And creating a flat patio for Alfonso so he can help his wife sit outside and enjoy the sunshine. And, like I say, painting the school.'

'There's a school here?'

He smiles. 'Just a small one. Caterina has a job there, starting in the autumn, helping with the little ones.'

'She'll be lovely, I'm sure.'

'It's good to keep it going. Some of the children from a local kids' home go there. And it's great that Caterina can settle and not feel she has to keep moving on. She feels safe here.'

I nod. 'Thank you,' and then, 'But I'll find a way to pay for the plastering. I can't let you do it for nothing.' I hand him back the coffee mug. Every part of me wants to walk away and never come back. But where would I go? I've got literally nothing left.

As I walk down the hill, in the cool shadows of the buildings, I can see a figure, outside the house. Waiting . . . for me.

16

'I hear there has been a problem with your property?'

It's the mayor.

'Yes.'

'Ah, I see,' he says, as he peers through the window. There's a silence.

'I'm sorry,' he says. 'I wish there was something I could do to help.'

'You could give me more time to do up the house . . . so I don't have to find the extra money.'

He shakes his head. 'I wish I could. But your husband had the house for a very good price. And I can't change the rules for one person. It must be done up, either to sell it at market value or live in it.'

'I understand. It wouldn't be fair,' I say, sighing.

'But if you meet the deadline, decide to live in it,' he raises an eyebrow, 'there will be no further costs. Or . . .'

'I'm going to be selling. I need to go back to the UK, with my children,' I tell him firmly.

'I see. Well, I'm sorry to hear that. The longer you stay in one place, the more it starts to feel like home.' He wishes me a good day and walks up the hill towards La Tavola.

I open the door to the house and stare at the mess.

I think about what the mayor said. I need to get help. And to leave soon.

I have a shower and wash the remaining dust from my hair and eyes. He's right: the more you stay put, the more it starts to feel like home. But this isn't my home. Not mine or Marco's. I want to leave.

Back at La Tavola, washing-up is in full swing.

'How was Sunday lunch?' I ask Giovanni, feeling refreshed after my shower.

'Good. We had a decent turn-out, not all of the residents but lots. Even the mayor came. It was busy. We nearly ran out of pasta.'

'I can see you're needed here.'

'I am. Well, La Tavola is. Without it, I don't know what many of the villagers would do. They wouldn't see anyone all week.' Giovanni is wiping his hands and I notice a burn mark across his palm. 'Even the mayor said how much it's needed,' he adds.

'That's good.'

'Well, it would be if he could do anything to help,'

Giovanni says. 'But he can't. The only thing he can do is try to sell off more houses to people who think they can find their dream life in the sun, then maybe put some money our way when they realize they can't complete the houses.'

I feel, again, as if I've been slapped.

'Sorry, I didn't mean . . . Really, I didn't mean anything by that.'

'It's fine. You're right. I think for just a little while I could see why people would want to do this, why they'd fall in love with this place, leave their worries behind and start again. A blank canvas. Marco wanted this for us when we got older, but what if he'd been alive now? I could see him wanting to be here, enjoying *la dolce vita*. Dreaming of a life away from the one we were living. He never did things slowly. He'd have wanted to up sticks and move out here.' I give a little laugh. 'But living here would have been a pipe dream. You can't run away from your problems. They have a habit of turning up when you least expect them.'

The children look at me and then at each other, as if sharing a thought.

I take a deep breath. 'I'll do it.' I nod firmly and give Giovanni a tight smile. He raises a questioning eyebrow. 'What you said earlier. If you'll still do it.' I swallow. 'I'll help here if you'll help with the plastering.'

'Okay,' he says slowly.

Again, the children look at each other.

'Just for a few weeks. For as long as it takes to sort out the house. But I need it all done by the end of August. It has to be valued and put on the market then.'

'Okay, so you'll help here at La Tavola and I'll do the plastering at Casa Luna.'

I nod. 'And help with the decorating, if possible. Also, I need to find someone who can deal with the garden.'

'Fine. And, just checking, do you have any experience in this field? Kitchens, looking after the place?'

I'm not sure if he's teasing me, but the children seem to be enjoying the exchange.

'Mum ran our restaurant, La Cucina.'

'She ran the whole shebang!' says Aimee.

'Dad did the cooking, and Mum ran the orders, business and front-of-house,' Luca continues. 'Until the rent got too high.'

'And the shit hit the fan,' says Aimee. We all stare at her and Pietro laughs.

'You sound very qualified to step in when I'm not here. There are plenty of other helping hands. But if you're happy to take up the reins?'

I take a deep breath. 'I wouldn't call it happy, but I'm happy to be getting the house sorted and if that means helping here . . . then I'll do it. I'll take in the deliveries, do the Friday dinners and Sunday lunches.'

'And be here if anyone needs just somewhere to be? A coffee, or *cacio e pepe*?' He grins.

'Or a glass of wine,' adds Luca.

'All of those things.' I manage a smile at the memory of our first day here.

'Everyone is welcome at La Tavola,' says Giovanni. Again, I think how warm he makes me feel: he's like a rejuvenating ray of early morning sunshine in the garden.

'Even the lasagne *nonnas*?' asks Luca.

'Particularly the lasagne *nonnas*. They may be lonelier than the rest of us,' says Giovanni, and something inside me shifts, softens and draws me towards this man, teaching my children an important lesson in life. But, we're just here until the house is renovated and I can sell it to get back to the UK. And look for a new job. Maybe I could manage a restaurant for someone else.

Where did that idea come from? I can't go back to doing that as a proper job. I return my attention to Giovanni.

'So, do we have a deal? You'll do the building work on the house?'

He looks at me, curly hair framing his face, and nods. 'And you'll take over here, organize the food and the menu?'

I take a huge breath. I'll be back in the kitchen, the one place I said I'd never go. I think about the staff I had to lay off when La Cucina closed, vowing I'd never put myself in that position again, that I'd never go back into a kitchen now that Marco was no longer in it. The last thing I want is to be reminded of everything we lost but I have to do this if I'm to make any of this work. 'I will,' I say. 'I can mind the shop, no problem.'

'Then we have a deal. I have to finish at Alessandro's *nonna*'s but I'll be at Casa Luna on Tuesday.'

We nod at each other.

'Right, back to work, everyone. There's lots of clearing up to be done before we have *gelato*.'

Luca and the other children cheer, apart from Pietro who smiles and jumps about with them.

17

I spend the following day, Monday, trying to clear plaster out of the house and clean the work surfaces. I'm exhausted and every movement seems an effort, but I have to be able to make coffee and find plates for the children to eat. But Stella is uppermost in my mind: how does she know Marco? What could she have to tell me about my husband that I don't know? Giovanni told me to speak to her. But I'm not sure I'm ready for anything she has to say. I thought I knew Marco as well as he knew me, totally and completely.

By evening, when the children return from their second night at Caterina's, I've washed the bedding, swept the plaster into piles to be walked around, wiped the windowsills and mopped the floors. In all my time working there, Marco is nowhere to be seen.

The children return full of stories of fun with Pietro

and Isabella. I thank Caterina and she tells me she's here to help. Just like La Tavola when she arrived in the village.

'I left a very bad situation,' she tells me, making sure the children are out of earshot. 'My husband was a bad man. I made the decision to leave and take the children. I just went. I had no idea where, just that I needed to put as much distance as I could between us. I'm so grateful for the help I found in La Tavola and from Giovanni. The past isn't forgotten, but here, we have a now and a future.'

I can't speak – the words catch in my throat. I hope she understands I'm grateful for all she's done for me.

The following morning, having slept like a log, I creep downstairs in the early morning sunlight and go outside. I can sit there and just be in the now. I'm wondering if Marco will be at the kitchen table and, if he is, how I'll feel about him now that Stella has turned up. I'm very mixed-up, trepidatious, yet hoping I can see him. I can't. He's not sitting there as he was before. My heart dips in disappointment, wishing he was still here for me, but he's finally left me, abandoned me when I needed him most, when I needed him to explain about Stella.

I wander over to the cafetière by the kettle. Suddenly I hear a noise outside the back door. A bleat. Slowly, I open the back door. A goat is standing there, staring at me. It opens its mouth. *Baaaaa!* Its long beard swings. I jump back in surprise.

Baaaaa! it says again, and steps forward. I move further back and grab a tea-towel: it seems to be attempting to come into the house.

'Shoo!' I wave the tea-towel at it. 'Shoo!'

There's another bleat, and another . . . Two more goats are in the garden, bleating at me.

'Shoo!' I say louder, even though they're making me smile.

I hear footsteps upstairs.

"What's happening?' Luca calls.

'Have we got sheep in the garden?' That's Aimee's voice.

'Goats!' Luca corrects her.

'Put your shoes on,' I shout up to them. 'Mind the fourth step! Watch out for the plaster!'

Luca and Aimee rush downstairs in their pyjamas and towards the door, sidestepping the piles of plaster as if it were the most natural thing in the world.

'What's happening? Where did they come from?' asks Luca.

'No idea,' I say, still waving the white tea-towel as if in an act of surrender. And in some ways it feels like it is. I seem not to be in control of anything going on here. All my plans to tart the place up and sell it on quickly have gone out of the window. A bit like my parenting skills: I want to tell the children to be careful, not to get dirty, don't go far, but they're outside before I can say a word.

The goat nearest the door bleats again.

The children throw back their heads and laugh.

'He's funny!'

'And tickly!' says Aimee, as the goat nibbles her pyjama top.

'Perhaps they want breakfast,' says Luca, frowning, as if he's always thinking about what needs to be done.

'Here, give him this,' I say, and hand over some stale bread from yesterday. Luca offers it to the goat, which starts to nibble it, and gives some to Aimee.

They're giggling again.

'And there's another!'

'And there!'

'Mum, they're eating everything!'

Suddenly there's a knock and I'm distracted. I sprint past the piles of plaster to the door.

'*Ciao!*' It's Giovanni.

'Giovanni, we've got goats in the garden!'

'Ah.' He smiles. '*Buono!* Good! Giuseppe dropped them off,' he says, as a goat takes a couple of steps into the kitchen. 'They're supposed to be outside.'

'Out, out!' say the children.

'Giuseppe dropped them off?'

'Well, you said the garden needed clearing. His goats are the best. He moves them around the village to keep the grass down. I told him you needed the garden

143

clearing and he said he'd drop them off. Couple of days should do it.'

'A couple of days?'

'Should be nice and clear by then.'

'We've got goats here for two whole days?' Aimee jumps up and down.

'Any longer and he'll be expecting a fee!' He laughs.

'Oh, God, is it going to cost?'

Giovanni shakes his head. 'I'm joking. Giuseppe is happy that his goats are fed well and so is he at La Tavola.'

It's a mutual agreement, helping each other.

'Like you helping at La Tavola, Mum,' says Luca. And he's back to being the sensible young adult he's been for the last two years.

'You two keep an eye on the goats,' I say, and when Luca smiles I glimpse the child he is again.

'Are you sure you don't need me to help here?' he asks.

'We'll be fine. Go and enjoy the goats. Just don't . . .'

'Don't what?'

'I don't know. What shouldn't you do with goats?'

'Don't let them go anywhere they shouldn't!' says Giovanni.

'Good plan,' I say, pleased that the children seem entertained without Wi-Fi.

'I said I'd meet Pietro later . . . if that's okay. Can he come and see the goats?' Luca asks.

I catch myself feeling surprised. It seems so long

since he's just enjoyed being a boy. I could cry for all the time he's missed and feel guilty that I've only realized this recently.

'Of course!' I sniff. I give him a little hug and he lets me.

'It'll be okay, Mum.' He gives me a little squeeze.

'Of course it will,' I say. 'It'll be—'

Luca cuts in. 'Don't say fine!'

'More than fine.' I chuckle and the children disappear outside to the goats, the cat, sitting on the table, watching them, and Giovanni's little white dog, Bello, leaping around the garden joyously, clearly thinking he's a goat, much to the goats' confusion. But they all seem happy enough.

I turn back to Giovanni, who is looking around the big room, taking in the mess. I expect a comment about it being a lot to take on, but he just says, 'Better get started. First, let's clear this plaster. There's a tractor and trailer on the way. We'll get it piled up by the door, ready to load into the trailer.'

'We?'

'I have some helpers on their way. Alessandro and his older brother, Enrico.'

'You're good to them,' I say.

'It's just Alessandro and Enrico, looking after their *nonna*. They're kind to her. But it's good they can get some work experience and skills. Alessandro started to wander down a wrong path. Enrico's been trying to hold things together at home. He's smart. He needs to work, and it's good for them to learn how to do stuff, and to keep Alesssandro busy over the summer.'

He grabs the broom I've left propped by the stairs and sweeps the piles of plaster towards the door. I pull it open and there, hand raised, on the doorstep, is a caller, standing in a plume of white dust.

'*Scusi, scusi,*' I say. She closes her eyes but stands stoically still. It's one of the *nonna*s, Teresa, I think, with the flowered white dish. I look down and see she's holding it now.

'Oh, Teresa, *scusi,*' says Giovanni, putting down his broom and rushing out to her.

'Giovanni,' she says, as he greets her warmly and apologizes. Then she turns to me. 'I brought lasagne. You said how much you liked it so I made you another.'

'Oh, that's so kind of you,' I say, holding out my hands to take the dish, knowing resistance would be futile and wondering if goats like lasagne.

She peers around me into the mess of the house. 'Terrible. It's been abandoned for so long.' Then, 'I heard you were widowed.'

'Um . . . yes.' I'm not sure how to answer. 'It's just me and children here, as I said.'

'Poor children,' she says, as shrieks of laughter float to us from the back garden.

'They're adjusting. It'll be the two year anniversary in just under six weeks, the day after he bought this place.'

Aimee's birthday . . . when we were waiting for him to get home from the restaurant to have a special tea.

There is more laughter from the garden and the dog comes running in with Mr Fluffy, Aimee and Luca chasing him, followed by a goat. They race out of the front door and round to the back. No one bats an eyelid.

'It's good to have children here,' she says, a little misty-eyed. 'I was widowed. I know your pain.'

'*Grazie,*' I say, and she turns to leave.

Giovanni is smiling as he leans on his broom. '*Ciao, Teresa, e scusi,*' he repeats. She pats his cheek. As she walks away, we watch another figure puffing up the hill, carrying an orange lasagne dish. 'Oh, please, God, not another!' I may have said it under my breath. Giovanni gives me a wicked smile, teasing me and enjoying the fun of the moment, just like Marco would have.

Nonna Lucia approaches and stands in front of Nonna Teresa. They stare at each other, give a curt nod and politely wish each other a good morning. Neither makes to move around the other.

'Just say thank you,' Giovanni whispers.

'It's okay. I've got this. *Lucia, buongiorno.*'

She lifts her chin. 'You ate all the lasagne I made, so I made you more.' She holds out the dish I recently returned. I'm feeling hot in the morning sunshine.

'I already brought lasagne,' says Nonna Teresa.

'But she ate all of mine last time, so she must prefer it.'

I can feel the heat in the air and the tension between the women. 'It's very generous of you . . .'

'You didn't like my lasagne?' Nonna Lucia raises a grey eyebrow.

'Oh, we loved it!' I say quickly, and step forward, taking the dish in my other hand. I'm now holding two heavy dishes of lasagne. 'Yours too, Teresa.' I nod to her dish.

The two women fold their arms over their chests, neither wanting to be the first to leave.

The sun is shining brightly in my eyes, and with no hands free to cover them, I don't see the other person arrive until I hear her voice . . . and feel her presence. It's practically frosty under the hot Tuscan sun.

'I can see I've been beaten to it,' says a third voice. Nonna Rosa. I can see her large silhouette against the sun, holding a lasagne dish.

Nonna Teresa is the first to speak: 'They have lasagne, I've made them one. They liked mine so much they finished it all and gave back an empty dish.'

Nonna Lucia joins in: 'They asked for more of mine. And she's a widow. I understand how she feels.'

'We all understand how she feels,' retorts Nonna Teresa.

'But I have been widowed the longest!' Nonna Lucia replies.

'Mine was the most recent,' Nonna Teresa bites back.

'I brought lasagne,' Nonna Rosa says to me. 'I heard you had a problem in the house.'

'I have. The ceiling has collapsed.'

'I thought so.' She looks smug. 'I saw Giuseppe. Very unsettling. You'll need my lasagne to recover.'

She holds it out to me. I look at the two in my hands. Giovanni takes one, and I smile gratefully, accepting the third.

'I can show you how I made mine if you like,' says Nonna Lucia.

'She won't show you – she won't tell you it all!' argues Nonna Teresa.

'And you won't, because you tried to steal my recipe!' says Nonna Rosa.

'I did not try to steal your recipe! It was our mother's,' says Nonna Teresa. 'I learnt to make my own, my husband's mother's way.'

'Still not as good as mine.'

'Mine is better. It comes from outside the family,' says Nonna Teresa.

'Mine will always be better than yours. It is our family recipe. I don't need to be told by someone else how to make Tuscan lasagne. I've been here all my life. Not an incomer.' She looks at Nonna Lucia.

'I came because I married your brother. He loved my lasagne.'

'You took him from the family, more like!'

'And my husband loved mine.'

'My husband loved mine, because it tasted just like his mother's,' says Nonna Teresa.

'He only married you for the lasagne. I turned him down first.'

'Wait!' I try to cut in, to no avail, and wish I could hold up a hand as they carry on arguing. 'Stop!' I shout. They are silent. I can hardly believe my ears. 'This can't be true. You've all fallen out over lasagne recipes?'

No one says anything and I hear Giovanni draw a sharp breath. Clearly this was a much bigger problem than my fallen ceiling.

Finally, Nonna Rosa speaks: 'It is never,' she says slowly, 'just about the lasagne recipe.' She starts back down the hill.

The other two wait their turn, Nonna Lucia first, then Nonna Teresa. 'Families. Take it from me, you're better off out of them,' she says, as she follows the others, hips swaying as they make their way home.

I stand there, holding the two very heavy lasagne dishes. Giovanni leans against the broom, holding the other. I let out a long breath. Luca and Aimee are staring at me. 'Well, I think we can agree that that could have gone better,' I say.

Giovanni laughs. 'They like you. They're pleased you're here. They want to look after you. It was the same when I first arrived.'

'Really?'

'It's their way of welcoming you and telling you they're here to help.'

'Well, what are we going to do with all these lasagnes?'

Giovanni smiles. 'Share them, of course.'

And I can't stop smiling back.

18

Later that day after all the plaster heaps have been removed, with the help of Alessandro and Enrico, I mop the work surfaces and the floors again. And then, with dust in our throats and sore eyes, we all walk up to La Tavola carrying the three lasagnes, Bello dancing at Giovanni's side.

'So, Teresa, Lucia and Rosa, why did they all fall out?' I ask Giovanni, as we prepare salad and make a dressing in the cool of La Tavola's kitchen.

Giuseppe is there, happy that his goats are content, and Francesco, who thinks it's Sunday and is enjoying the atmosphere. Caterina is in the garden, showing Luca and Pietro the vegetables she's growing.

'It was the lasagne,' says Giovanni, 'from what I've heard.'

I put down the knife and look up at him. 'It can't just be the lasagne,' I say. 'How long ago was that?'

'Oh, quite a while,' he says, dipping his head to breathe in the aroma of one of the dishes. 'This one is Lucia's, made to her mother's recipe. She married the brother of Teresa and Rosa. There was huge upset when he preferred Lucia's lasagne to his own mother's. It was seen as complete treachery. His confession came out after he'd had too much wine at the wedding. They barely spoke after that.'

I smile at his light-hearted account. Here in the kitchen I feel more relaxed and at home than I have in ages. Aimee and Caterina's daughter are playing with Bello, and Mr Fluffy has been left on the long table in the dining room.

'This one is good. It's Teresa's.' He takes a deep sniff and I do the same. 'She's worked hard to recreate her mother's recipe, but eventually learnt her mother-in-law's version. This one is Rosa's, her mother's recipe. Her Tuscan lasagne.'

'Why don't they cook the same recipe?'

Giovanni sighs. 'That's where the story gets complicated. Teresa and Rosa's mother shared her recipe only with Rosa, to woo the young man she wanted to marry. But when Teresa wasn't given it, she decided to go about things differently. She wooed the same young man's mother, got her recipe and made it for him. They married shortly after. Rosa married eventually, but the two women didn't speak and their mother's recipe was never handed on to Teresa or Lucia. It was a sign of Teresa and Rosa's mother's disapproval and favouritism, that she shared the recipe only with her elder daughter.'

'And now they're all widowed, but still don't speak?'

'Only to sling insults and argue over the washing lines,' says Giovanni.

We pick up the lasagnes and take them through to the big table, with large bowls of dressed salad, glistening with olive oil and lemon juice. I stare at the salad, lost in my own thoughts, still wondering about the young woman I met, Stella, and how she knew Marco. I wish I could stop thinking about her, and her words 'I'm a friend of Marco', but trying to block them out is getting harder.

'Tutti a tavola!' calls Giovanni, jolting me from my thoughts and everyone moves towards the table, laid with knives and forks, red and white napkins fresh from drying on the line in the sun after Sunday lunch, jugs of water, stubby glasses and a couple of small carafes of red wine that have been poured from a big box in the storeroom. Alessandro's much older brother, Enrico, has washed the dust from his face and hands and slides onto the bench next to Caterina.

'Let's eat!' says Giovanni, and Giuseppe guides Francesco to the table. Aimee and Caterina's daughter fill water glasses. Alessandro helps to cut up the lasagne while Luca and Pietro hand around the plates. I offer the salad up and down the table, and Giovanni pours wine for those who want it.

I look at Luca and Pietro helping themselves to salad, then passing it to Francesco.

'*Buon appetito,*' says Giovanni, and Alessandro raises his water glass as we all join in: '*Buon appetito.*'

I look along the table at people's faces and enjoy this moment. It was what I loved most in the restaurant: the sound of people's anticipation, good humour and delight in the food and company, as if they were sitting down to watch a film, a show, read a book. Mealtimes like this are special. To me, it's what makes Christmas special, the sound of happiness being shared. It nourishes the soul and the body. I wonder what Christmas will be like this year. I wonder where we'll be.

I take a mouthful of lasagne, chew and swallow. 'That is *sooo* good,' I say, taking another mouthful.

'But can you tell whose it is?'

'Lucia's. Her mother's recipe.'

He nods.

'I could tell by the dish,' I tell him, 'just so you don't think I've got amazing tastebuds.'

'Ah! So you had an advantage. When you have eaten enough of them you will notice subtle differences. Teresa uses more meat, and Lucia cheese.'

'And Rosa? What's her secret?'

He has another forkful of meaty *ragù*, layers of soft

pasta and creamy béchamel sauce. His lips glisten with dressing from the crunchy green salad Caterina has collected from the garden.

'She won't say . . . None of them will. They all have their own way of working, how they cut the garlic or which dish they bake it in.' He waves his fork in a little circle.

'How many years has it been since they fell out over how to make lasagne?'

He shrugs. 'I don't know exactly – twenty-five, maybe even thirty. All I know is there was an annual competition. Here in the village apparently. Giuseppe will remember.' He nods as Giuseppe smiles his tooth-less smile, rolling his hand over and over as if to say it was even further back.

'At the end of the summer, a long table was laid out, and the entries were judged.'

'Just lasagne?'

'Tuscan lasagne,' he corrects me. 'It's different, of course. Lasagne came from Emilia-Romagna. Tuscan people put their own spin on it. But, as always, each family has their own way of making it.'

'So what happened?' I say, sipping my spicy red wine. Everyone is enjoying the food and so am I.

'Well, the competitions were a thing of great pride, for the family and the individual who made a lasagne. Recipes passed down from grandmother, mother to daughter. That was when it all came to a head. The village wanted to bring the families together, and the mayor at the time thought a good way to get the women out of their homes was to organize a lasagne competition.'

'I can see that wouldn't have been a good idea.'

Giovanni laughs. 'Nonna Rosa accused Nonna Teresa of trying to steal her recipe and stealing her man, and they both accused Nonna Lucia of stealing their brother from the family. The event ended in napkins being hurled, families pitted against families, fists flying. The younger women in the families had fiery tempers, which they let rip. Finally, the event was abandoned and the women were escorted home by their battle-scarred families and husbands.'

'Oh!'

He nods. 'It was a big deal back then.'

'So it was all over a man!'

'They'd never say that. It was a matter of pride and honour . . . and the man.'

We laugh. And suddenly Stella's words pop back into my head.

'But it's so sad that they haven't spoken in all those years.'

'The accusations never went away. Rumours have a habit of hanging around if they're not brought out into the open,' he says, meeting my gaze. For a moment I wonder if he's talking about the *nonna*s or Stella. 'They all married,' he carries on, 'and had families of their own. But the families have moved away for work or for town life. As you can see, not much goes on here.'

'And they're left on their own, like whoever owned Casa Luna.'

'A lot of people are on their own here now. It's why I wanted to help. This place was here when I had my . . . difficulties. It was quiet. I could re-centre myself. Work out what was important to me.'

I notice him rub his hand.

'I didn't mean to end up here. I just did. And although they didn't know me, their lasagnes kept me going until I started to feel more myself again. That, and the stunning sunsets.'

'So you set up this place?'

'It was up for rent. I didn't really know what I was going to do. My partner and I had split and it took me a long time to get over it. I was working ridiculous hours, trying to make it in London in the big kitchens. As I'm sure you know, it can be a brutal way of life. No room for anything or anyone else. Once we'd split and after losing Richie, my friend, work got too much for me. Things were spiralling out of control. I followed in his footsteps, using substances to keep me awake in service, substances to help me sleep. It was a dreadful dark place. I knew I didn't want to go the same way as Richie. He ended his life. It was such a waste. I mean . . . it's just food. There was no way I wanted to continue in that world. I was leaving it for good.'

'But . . .' I look around.

'I didn't want to go back into fine dining. Before I got into catering I'd worked my way across Europe picking up odd jobs and skills along the way, like plastering and bricklaying. I thought this place could be a lock-up for my tools and a workshop for a carpentry business. But once I was here I felt more energized. The fog began to lift, and I wanted to say thank you to the people who had kept me going when I arrived. One Sunday I opened the doors and cooked lunch to see who would come. Lots did, but some didn't, so I took whatever was left to people who hadn't left the house. Who were inside, alone. I knew how it felt to be alone. I felt alone when I left the kitchens.'

'And you just stayed here?'

'It was a good place for me to be. It's a secure base. It was a breather in my travelling. I offered to do odd jobs, and cooked for those who wanted it at the weekends . . . away from the pressure of the commercial kitchen. I began to fall in love with cooking again and creating a space where people could enjoy food and company. Maybe I'll take the idea to other towns one day. It seems to bring people together.'

Was Stella one of those people . . . maybe Marco too? Bringing them together here at La Tavola? I feel as if I'm wading through treacle, trying to find the answer that is hidden in the darkness. He's right: food brings people together. It's what I loved about the restaurant and about Marco. It's what I miss . . . I shake myself out of my reverie. My days in hospitality are long gone. And I certainly don't want to talk shop about how hard it was to be a restaurateur in the UK.

Caterina seems to pick up on my deflated mood. 'It may feel bad now, but we have hope,' she says, 'for you, and your children. Losing your husband, you have to search for the hope. It might not be there now, but it will come.'

Her words choke me. I swig my wine. I hope she's right. There doesn't seem to be much hope right now. And now Stella, whoever she is, is muddying the waters and the memories. Maybe once I sell up here and move back, with some money in my pocket, I can think about starting again.

I watch the children, who are laughing. At least I have these two, I think. And they seem happy, sleeping better . . . Maybe it's the heat.

'You're right,' I say, and put another forkful of the delicious, creamy, meaty lasagne into my mouth. There's hope.

Suddenly the front door is pushed wide open. 'Hey! *Ciao!*' The figure cuts quite a dash in the doorway. It's Stella, whose words have been messing with my head.

'Hey! You're back,' says Giovanni, and the mood in the room changes.

'Just a flying visit. I've met some friends on their way to Greece. Thinking of joining them.'

'Why don't you have something to eat? You can tell us about it.' He turns to me and says quietly, 'Remember, everyone is welcome here.' He lays a hand on my arm. He's right. But I'm not ready for this. I feel hot and my appetite has gone. I watch her.

He stands and goes to the kitchen for another plate. Stella follows him.

Caterina watches her go. 'Stella bases herself here, but she's from nowhere. She comes when she has nowhere else to go.'

I glance in the direction of the kitchen.

'Giovanni looks out for her. Makes sure she gets fed when she's here. But when Stella is around, trouble is usually following her.' At that moment, Stella comes out of the kitchen, carrying a plate. She smiles at me – a smile that makes me uneasy . . . very uneasy.

19

Over the next few days Giovanni turns up every morning at Casa Luna, sometimes with Alessandro or Enrico, sometimes on his own. I go to La Tavola and offer coffee or pasta to anyone who needs it. I take in the deliveries when they arrive from the shop, cook and freeze vegetables ready for pasta sauces. I have coffee with Caterina, and the children enjoy days helping in the garden or cooking with me. It's a little routine I'm starting to enjoy.

Today, though, Giovanni arrives at the house with someone else. As soon as I see her, despite the heat of the day, I turn cold.

'This is Stella. You've met.'

She smiles at me.

I say nothing. Just stand and stare.

'She's come to help me today.'

'*Buongiorno*,' I try to say but my tongue is tied and I have no idea how the greeting sounds.

'It would be good for her to learn a trade. Be able to work, like Alessandro and Enrico.' Giovanni smiles but I can't.

I turn to the tap to pour water into the cafetière. It's stiff.

'Oh, you have to go first one way, then the other,' says Stella, turning the tap on for me, making me bristle. How would she know the workings of the tap in this place?

Giovanni tells her he'll be plastering the ceiling, repairing broken woodwork, including the step, and painting the walls – oh, and fixing the leaking roof.

I make coffee and put it on a little table I've positioned outside the front door where Giovanni sits for his coffee breaks, watching the world go by and chatting to the locals he knows. My hands are shaking. Giovanni joins me. 'Are you okay?' he asks.

'I'm not sure I am, actually,' I say, remembering his words: it's okay not to be okay. I glare at him. 'What's she doing here?'

'I told you, it's good to get her working, learning skills,' he says, looking me straight in the eye.

'Of all the places you could have taken her to, you brought her here. Is that really a good idea?' I say crossly.

'Stella?' He looks back inside. 'She can be a handful.

She needs to be kept occupied. I'll keep an eye on her, don't worry.'

'But—' I stop myself. So many questions are running around in my head, but do I really want to know the answers? Right now, I don't want to hear anything about how she knows Marco. I want it all to be a silly lie that got out of hand. A sick joke would be better than the truth, if there is any.

The mayor walks past and congratulates me on how I'm getting on, and for using local labour. '*Ciao, Giovanni.*' Stella comes out to join us and I bristle. The mayor nods to her, then walks on. She finishes her coffee and goes inside.

I can feel Giovanni standing next to me. 'If it wasn't for La Tavola, people like Stella would have nowhere to go.'

'I know. And I know you're doing good work there, Giovanni. I'm just not sure that this is helping me right now.'

'I needed La Tavola as much as some of the residents do. I needed to get back into the kitchen, to realize that's home for me. Just not the bullying, shouting places that call themselves professional kitchens.'

I can feel frustration in him, matching mine. It's creating hot energy between us, drawing us closer, like magnets.

'But it can't survive on charity alone. More and more people are relying on La Tavola, and we can't exist on what we get from Alfonso's shop. Money is short and rent has to be paid. And he is selling up. He's finding it hard to run the shop and look after his wife. He wants to retire. But without his donations, and without any money, I don't know how we'll keep going.'

'Whose money is short? Yours? You've been financing this?'

'Like I say, it started as a thank-you, after I arrived here, but La Tavola has taken on a life of its own. It needs more than I can give it now.'

'But you can't walk away?'

He shrugs. 'I won't leave yet. It gave me everything I needed when I needed it. I'm back on an even keel now. At some point, though, I may want to move on. But I don't think I can keep La Tavola going for those who still need it.'

'There must be a way to save it,' I find myself saying, for all the people who rely on it as a place of safety and sanctuary as much as they do for the food.

He frowns. 'If only I knew how.'

'There has to be something you can do.'

He looks straight into my eyes, and I feel something shift, as if I'm walking over quicksand.

'Nothing scares you, does it, Thea? Not falling-down houses, in foreign countries, with leaking roofs, nothing.'

'Everything scares me, Giovanni. You and I both know how scary life can get. That's why I can see how important La Tavola is to the people who need it. There must be a way to save it.'

He's running his hands through his curly hair and then throwing them up in despair. 'Do you think I haven't tried to find one?'

'What's the alternative, Giovanni? Where will Caterina go? Alessandro and Enrico, Giuseppe, Francesco and Alfonso, whose only respite is the time he spends here on a Sunday. You were there when I needed you. Still are.' We look at each other and something shifts in me again, like sand, swirling and creating patterns. I want to hold on to it and also to push it away.

'La Tavola is there for you, not just me.'

But something inside me speaks differently.

Luca is running down the hill with Pietro. 'Mum, the mayor was in La Tavola! He says La Tavola will have to be sold! Mum, you can't let it happen!'

I look at Giovanni.

'As I say, unless I can find a way to make an income to run it, I'll have to hand back the keys. The mayor will sell it, like this house, to someone who wants to commit to staying here.'

'Can't you open it as a restaurant, make it earn its keep and buy it?'

He shakes his head. 'There aren't the customers here. If there were, others would be doing just that.'

'Mum, you must help!' Aimee begins to cry. 'It's just

like when Dad died and the restaurant went. You can't let La Tavola close.'

Suddenly everything is rushing back at me. The restaurant closing. The people I had to let go.

'But,' I say, gesticulating and feeling every bit Italian, 'I don't know how!'

'Yes, you do!' says Luca. 'You ran the restaurant for years, even after Dad died.'

I really don't want to go back to that world.

I look at the children's faces. 'Okay, okay. If Giovanni wants my help . . .' I'm trying not to let myself think that the strange feeling inside me is anything but nerves at finding something to help here '. . . how about we meet at La Tavola once you've finished here for the day? We should call a meeting for anyone who has an idea about how we can save it.'

'*Grazie*,' he says, getting back to work.

In the garden I can hear the goats bleating . . .

20

Later that day at La Tavola, a group of us sit under the whitewashed domed ceiling, with a big jug of water on the table and cups of coffee, the fragrance of roasting beans filling the room.

'It's no good opening as a restaurant. There isn't the trade,' says Giovanni. 'People don't come here on holiday.'

'It's a very traditional Tuscan village,' says Alfonso. 'People came years ago but not now. They go to the better-known towns. Only someone who didn't know what they were doing would buy a place here.' He grins at me sympathetically. 'Sorry.'

'People love the authentic Italian experience, though,' I say. 'Maybe we could try for some press coverage, entice some bloggers here to see what you're doing, get them talking about La Tavola.'

Caterina nods. 'Great idea.'

But Giovanni shakes his head. 'Only trouble is, that's not going to pay the rent, which is due in four weeks.'

The same day as my deadline to have the house finished.

My iPad is pinging with messages on the table next to me.

Luca's head pops up: he's playing on his phone, clearly delighted to have Wi-Fi here, then shuffles guiltily. He's hardly used it since we arrived here but this morning, he's been glued to it. 'It was just an idea,' he says.

I open the iPad to read the messages coming in. 'What was just an idea, Luca?'

'Me and Pietro thought we'd test the water. See if we'd get any response,' he says. 'I put up a few videos on TikTok of when we're all here.'

Giovanni and Caterina pull out their phones.

'I made a page. La Tavola.'

'And what's it about?' I ask.

'Being here. La Tavola. I thought we could do a cooking school, like being back with Dad in the kitchen, making lasagne. All around the table, learning how to cook . . . and then eat together. Like we do here on Sundays. He always said food tastes better with good company.'

Giovanni is smiling at Luca. 'Well, this place was set up to help the community and for them to eat together.

I hadn't thought about passing on my skills, teaching people to cook. But you're right! Eating together and learning to cook go hand in hand. They bring people together. That's what La Tavola has always been about.'

Likes are pouring in for the newly formed page.

'I didn't know if you'd go for the idea, so I thought I'd test it. It was something Dad used to talk about. He'd say that when he gave up the restaurant he'd find a bunch of *nonna*s to come in and teach people how to cook properly because *nonna*s always know best!'

I study the post: *Want to cook in a traditional Italian kitchen and learn how to make lasagne, like Nonna's?*

'Luca! What have you done? A cookery school? It's madness! It makes no sense. We can't do this. You'll have to take the post down. I don't know why you put it up without saying anything.'

'I didn't want to make you sad, talking about one of Dad's ideas. Thought I'd see if it was any good first.'

The likes are still coming in.

'You're like your dad, thinking of this. But it would take lots of organizing. It would need advertising, marketing and planning.'

'And I have a house to plaster,' says Giovanni.

We pause.

'But it's absolutely brilliant!'

21

'Where have you posted this, Luca?' Giovanni asks.

'Facebook, Twitter, Instagram, Threads and TikTok. It's had loads of likes. And requests for images.'

'Well, that's good to hear!' He smiles. 'And it's a great idea. But we can't run this without *nonna*s to teach.'

Luca's head drops. There's a lull and everyone looks at their phones or drinks their coffee.

'What about Stella?' says Aimee. 'She said she wanted to hang around for a bit over the summer.'

'Who?' I double-take at Aimee and I'm freezing suddenly.

'Stella. Daddy's friend, who was here the other day. She's cool.'

I've no idea what to say. Who is this young woman and why is she talking to my children about Marco?

What on earth is she playing at? Whatever her game is, it's sick. I'm suddenly furious.

Giovanni is gazing at me, as if he's instructing me to take a deep breath.

'I'm not sure Stella is a cook or a *nonna*,' he says kindly, to Aimee.

'I'm happy to wash up,' says Caterina, still hanging on to the only idea we've had so far.

I chew my bottom lip and try to focus on the problem in hand, and not that Stella has been talking to my children, Marco's children, about their father.

'Even if we could find someone to teach, what sort of people would want to come and learn to cook here?' says Giovanni.

My phone pings. I look at the screen.

Hi, Thea, long time no speak. Great to hear from you!

'Luca,' I say slowly, 'did you send this link to all my contacts on my phone?'

He shrugs, half guiltily, half nonchalantly – in a thoroughly Italian way. 'That was Pietro's idea. What with all your contacts from the restaurant, we thought you might know some people who'd be interested.'

I turn to Giovanni.

'Who's that?' he asks.

'It's someone from the past.'

'Your restaurant days?'

'Someone from my old company. The headhunters

I used to work for before I set up the restaurant with Marco.'

I scroll through the message. 'It says,' I swallow, 'they're looking for a team-building trip and this looks perfect. They want to come here.'

We stare at each other, wide-eyed.

Luca slides down in his chair, clearly a little regretful.

'You should have spoken to me first, Luca. It's a great idea, but with Giovanni working on Casa Luna, and me just covering here and helping with the house, it's not feasible.'

Luca picks up my phone. 'Mum,' he says, so quietly that I barely hear him.

I sigh.

'Mum!' I feel Luca tug at my soft white shirt sleeve.

'Just a moment, Luca,' I say. 'We'll take down the post in a second.'

'But look!' he says. 'Mum, look at the rest of the message.'

'What do you mean?'

'Your old company friend. Look what they say. Their budget . . . Look what their budget is for a weekend of learning to cook in a traditional Italian kitchen.'

We stare at the screen. I show it to Giovanni. He stares back at me. 'Really?'

'That would sort out the rent!' I say, my throat a little tight with shock.

'It would solve everything,' he says. 'For now.'

I nod slowly. 'But how? I can't teach people to cook. You're working at Casa Luna. And they're expecting an Italian *nonna*!'

'You need someone who's been cooking Tuscan food all their lives. We can do the rest, set it up, help wash up. But you need a cook,' says Caterina.

'Or three,' I hear myself say.

22

'They would never agree to help together and it'll take more than one for it to work, with the number of people your friend wants to bring,' says Giovanni.

I can already see how the weekend would proceed: preparing food for the locals on Friday, market in the neighbouring town on Saturday, a fun-filled Saturday night and a big lunch on Sunday, all pulling together.

I'm sure my eyes are sparkling. This is like when Marco and I made plans, him in the kitchen, us working side by side . . . the excitement of the adventure. But this is just a one-off. A thank-you to Giovanni. He's not Marco and I'm not looking for a relationship. I just want to help and say thank you before we leave. If it wasn't for him, there's no way the house would be anywhere near sorted. I'm doing this for the village.

Are you? says a voice in my head.

Yes, I tell myself firmly.

And a fight back for all those who lost their jobs in catering. *People need community kitchens*, I hear myself saying. *It's about so much more than the food. It's the experience. It's about being part of a community that cares.*

Giovanni shakes his head. 'The three *nonna*s? They'd never come here, especially not together. They haven't been in the same room as each other for thirty years, not since the lasagne competition.'

'But if we could get them to understand how important this is to the village . . .'

'I agree.' His shoulders are starting to sag. 'But they won't do it. Maybe one on her own, but there's no way you could get them all in the room together.'

'There might be one way.' My mind is turning over. 'You said the reason they fell out was over whose lasagne recipe was the best.'

'Yes,' he says slowly.

'*Sooo* we hold a lasagne contest. It will get them into the same room together and then we can talk to them about the cookery-school weekend.'

'*What?*'

Luca and Caterina are clapping their hands in excitement.

'This place deserves it, Giovanni. At least let's try,' Caterina says.

'The last lasagne competition blew the village apart. They won't go for it.'

'But if we don't try, if La Tavola fails and closes, the village will struggle more than ever.'

We're quiet, until Giovanni says slowly, 'One thing we know about the *nonna*s is that they have their pride. They will each think they have the best lasagne recipe. They will want to settle old scores and all be proved right.'

'We have to try!' I plead.

We hold each other's eyes for just a moment longer than I'm expecting. My stomach flips.

'For La Tavola's sake,' I add.

'For La Tavola's sake,' he echoes.

23

'So it's lasagne for lunch on Sunday,' Giovanni says, writing it up on the whiteboard in the kitchen.

'Just one thing,' I say. 'How will we choose a winner?'

'We will ask the mayor to judge. It can be on his head!'

We're all in agreement.

'Let's get everyone to spread the word. Friday suppers, tell everyone about the lasagne contest.'

We've put up signs around the village. Giovanni and I are visiting each of the three *nonna*s with their Friday-evening meals.

'Well, this is a surprise. Two guests!' says Nonna Teresa when we visit her first and tell her of our idea

Then on to Nonna Lucia. 'What a lovely pair you make!' says Nonna Lucia.

'Oh, no, we're not . . .' We speak in unison, and see disappointment on her face.

'Well, not officially,' I say. Beside me, Giovanni practically chokes on his coffee and I nudge him. 'We're planning a party, for when the house is finished.'

'An engagement party?'

'No!' we say.

'More of a summer celebration,' I say, 'inviting people to join in with what the village has to offer. Cooking at La Tavola and enjoying the company.'

'A *festa*,' Giovanni puts in, and we wish we'd rehearsed what we were going to say.

Lucia's eyes twinkle. 'But it could be an engagement party?' She smiles naughtily.

I say nothing.

'We want to choose the best meal for the party,' Giovanni says.

'Lasagne, of course!'

'Yes . . . but which one?'

'Well, mine has always gone down well, like my tiramisu.' She looks down at the *fritto misto* we've delivered. 'This fish needs more salt. And a little less time in the pan.'

'We'd love to try your lasagne.'

'On Sunday at La Tavola?'

She sniffs and even gives a small smile.

*

'A lasagne competition, you say?' Nonna Rosa's competitive streak is apparent as soon as we mention it.

'Like I say, we're choosing a lasagne for a summer party. We thought everyone should get the chance to put forward their recipe.'

'It's all in the sauce,' she says. 'A chance to show that mine was the original and the best!'

We leave the final house as it's getting dark. We put all the empty dishes into the basket to return to La Tavola. We walk up through the cobbled streets under the bright white moon, which seems to hang over Casa Luna.

'Would you ever do it again?'

'What? Make lasagne?'

'No, get married. You seem to have your life sorted.' I tilt my head. 'The *nonna*s sound pretty keen to find you a match!' I smile. 'Maybe you and Caterina.'

'No. We're friends, good friends.'

'Ah, okay.' Again my thoughts turn to Stella.

'Once burnt, twice shy!' he says. 'What about you?'

'Oh, I'm not looking for a partner right now. That's the last thing I need.'

We carry on walking up through the village, watching the bats flit in the lamplight.

'I have the children to think of. And, besides, I don't know if I'm angry about Marco dying and leaving me, or just so sad that he did. Or sad for the future we didn't get. I couldn't bear to have his memory trampled on right now.' I swallow, my mind wandering back to what on earth Stella had meant by her and Marco being 'friends'. 'He was the love of my life. I could never see myself with anyone again. Especially not someone . . .' I stop, not knowing where that came from.

'Who worked in a kitchen, reminding you of him. Not wanting to put yourself through it again.' He turns to me, and my insides fizz with excitement that I try hard to extinguish.

I clear my throat. 'Something like that.'

And we walk on in silence, lost in our thoughts.

Back at La Tavola Giovanni pushes open the wooden door into the courtyard, and Bello rushes to meet him. The soft orange glow of the lights draws us into the kitchen where everyone is tidying up after Friday-night deliveries.

They turn, practically as one, to us.

'Well?' says the mayor, who is there, shirt sleeves pushed up and elbow deep in soap suds at the sink, 'What did they say?'

We stand in the doorway, and then, together, we smile.

'They said sì!'

Everyone cheers and whoops. It's like we've had a lottery win! Giovanni tries to manage expectations, but everyone is buzzing with delight.

'Look, all we've managed to get them to do is turn

up to the lasagne competition on Sunday,' he says, trying to calm things. 'They know nothing about the cookery weekend yet. They think they're coming just to defend their recipes and honour.'

'And so they are!' says the mayor. 'We want them to share those recipes and help keep this place going. It's the heart of the village.'

'It's a start!' I say cheerfully. 'We'll get them to share their food and hopefully agree to help us.'

'I wouldn't like to be in your shoes.' Giuseppe gives a throaty laugh, patting the mayor's shoulder. The poor man looks as if he's carrying the weight of the world on it.

And now the big day is here, Sunday. The church bells are ringing, signalling the end of Mass and the beginning of lunch in the village. The thin congregation files down the steps, stopping to talk to each other. There is a buzz in the air in anticipation of the lasagne competition. Everyone is talking about it. Who will enter? Who will win? Will it come to blows like last time? I'm nervous. All we can do is hope that the *nonna*s turn up . . . and that it doesn't end in a brawl.

Everything is prepared. The salads are made, with fresh green leaves and herbs that Caterina has grown in the borders and the pots in the garden at La Tavola. The table is laid, with jugs of wine and water. The bread is in the kitchen, waiting to be sliced, alongside baskets.

Giovanni made it that morning, Luca helping – he got up especially early to join Giovanni in the kitchen. It's been so good to see him want to be involved.

Now, nervously, we're standing in La Tavola with the doors wide open. We look at each other anxiously, myself, Giovanni, Caterina, Enrico, Alessandro, Giuseppe and the mayor, who seems more worried than anyone else.

'One of them wanted to marry me once,' says Giuseppe. 'I decided to stick to goats. Much more predictable.'

'Look!' shouts Alessandro, pointing down the road from his lookout position standing on the wall. 'She's coming. Nonna Lucia is coming!' he shouts to us.

We hurry out into the road, to see her walking up the road, carrying a basket.

'Go and help her with her basket,' I tell Luca and Pietro. They race down the hill and relieve her of her heavy load.

'*Buongiorno!*' we call to her and wave. She's happy to be here by the look of it.

We usher her inside. She sits and accepts the glass of water she's offered. The weather is hot but she's in her Sunday best. Gold earrings and matching necklace. A blue dress covered with sunflowers, pop socks to her knees and smart court shoes.

We offer to help unpack her bag, but she shakes her head and pulls the basket closer to her, clearly protecting her ingredients and favourite kitchen utensils.

She soon realizes she is the first *nonna* to have arrived, sips her water and waits.

Soon there is another shout from Alessandro. 'Nonna Teresa!' he calls.

Nonna Lucia bristles, straightens, and checks her lightweight blue cardigan and her brooch.

Nonna Teresa is just as smartly dressed, with bags that Luca and Pietro are carrying in for her. She and Nonna Lucia offer each other a stiff greeting, and she directs Luca and Pietro to put her bags on the work surface at the furthest end of the kitchen. She sits and takes a glass of water.

The clock ticks slowly round to ten.

'*Mamma*,' Aimee calls, a change from her usual 'Mum' but I don't say anything. 'It's not much of a contest with only two people.'

'We could enter?' says Luca.

'I don't think so,' I say, trying to hide my disappointment that Nonna Rosa hasn't come.

Luca is warming to his theme. 'Dad used to make a sort of lasagne all the time,' he says. 'The customers loved his *vincisgrassi* from Le Marche.'

'Not a lasagne, though,' the children and I say.

'Seven layers of pasta, always!' says Luca, in an impersonation of Marco, and we laugh.

'We used to make it for birthdays,' says Aimee.

She's remembering the good times, not the day Marco didn't come back from the restaurant and her birthday tea was abandoned.

'Yes, we did,' I murmur. I see a lasagne dish being slid across the counter and look up to see Giovanni smiling.

'It's about the experience,' he says. 'Plenty of ingredients from the delivery this morning from the supermarket. Might not have the meat, though . . .'

'It's okay,' I say.

'We could do a veggie version.' Luca nods and smiles widely.

'I'm not sure,' I say, feeling hot. This wasn't what I was expecting. But none of this has been quite what I was expecting.

The clock slips past ten and a shadow appears in the doorway. It is Nonna Rosa. I feel a flood of relief and I'm not sure if it's because she's here, and things are going according to plan, or that I don't have to make Marco's version of lasagne. Somehow, I'm not ready to do that, even though I can see how keen the children are.

Nonna Rosa is still standing in the doorway. 'You weren't thinking of starting without me, were you?'

Giovanni greets her warmly. 'We wouldn't have dreamt of it!'

'Good. Because we all know who makes the best lasagne in this village.'

The other two *nonna*s sniff. 'Phfffff.'

Giovanni and I smile. They're here. All three of them.

'Perhaps we could help the *nonna*s,' I say, to Luca and Pietro. 'We'll work in teams.' My mind is whirring, seeing how this could work for the cookery weekend. They nod enthusiastically.

'It'll be like helping Dad make his,' I tell Luca. But it won't be the same without him. 'Let's make a start, shall we?' I call. 'Oven on?' Then to everyone, I say, 'Put yourselves into teams with your *nonna*s.'

Luca goes to Nonna Lucia and I hear her say, 'I'll tell you some of the secret but not all of it!' Pietro stands next to him. Aimee and Caterina's daughter join Nonna Teresa, and I go to Nonna Rosa, although I'm not sure I'll be much help. Alessandro, Enrico, Caterina and the mayor wait nervously in the archway into the dining area, watching.

'Let's cook!' says Giovanni, clapping his hands together.

The big kitchen turns into a hive of activity, with the three *nonna*s overseeing their own cooking, as well as each other's.

'No, no, not like that!' Nonna Rosa calls to Nonna Teresa.

'Madam, pay attention to your own cooking. I've been making this lasagne for years!'

'Trying to copy mine . . .'

'It is my recipe! It may look similar but I can assure you that it tastes very different! I had to make it up myself, remember? Until I found another woman prepared to share her recipe.'

'It's not authentic. This is the real lasagne. Our mother's mother's mother passed it down the family. Not like an outsider's.' She sniffs at Nonna Teresa's and then at Nonna Lucia's.

'This is authentic! My mother-in-law learnt it from her maternal grandmother.'

'But it's not traditional Tuscan lasagne, is it? Not like mine!'

The argument erupts, like volleys in a table-tennis match, the insults slung back and forth. But somehow in the chaos, sauces are made, pasta is rolled, flour flies into the air, béchamel thickens and the lasagnes are layered into dishes, like *bambini* being tucked snugly into bed. And as the dishes are slid into the oven, with some jostling over who has which shelf, resolved by pulling straws, the tension in the usually cool kitchen is almost palpable.

I organize myself and the children into helping the *nonna*s with the clean-up. Work surfaces are scrubbed, and even that seems like a competition for the cleanest space.

'If that's a reflection of her cleanliness at home, I wouldn't eat there ...' says Nonna Teresa to Nonna Rosa.

'I can see my face in the shine on this worktop!' barks Nonna Lucia.

'Don't scare the young ones,' says Nonna Rosa. 'They won't sleep tonight.'

When the work surfaces are done, and glasses of water have been passed around, the kitchen fills with the most delicious aromas. The bread is put into baskets and bowls of salad placed on the table. The room fills with chatter and expectation.

Slowly the oven's door is opened.

'Don't open it! The hot air will escape!'

'There's so much hot air coming from you that that won't be a problem!'

'Madam, do not touch my lasagne! It has to be cooked in the very centre of the oven.'

'I haven't moved it.'

'I saw you touch it when you reached in to check yours.'

'I didn't go near it, you silly woman.'

'I am not a silly woman! How dare you?'

'You're just scared you won't win.'

'We'll see about that!'

The dining room starts to fill with locals. Pietro has gone to get Francesco. And Alfonso arrives with his wife, in a wheelchair: she is clearly delighted to be out and about and in company.

I hand round glasses of wine from one of the jugs on the table and offer small plates of *antipasti*: marinated olives and little cubes of carrot from jars in the store cupboard, squares of goat's cheese from Giuseppe, and Caterina's home-grown small, sweet tomatoes that burst with flavour when you bite into them.

The excitement is building. Everyone is keeping an eye on the kitchen door and an ear to the exchanges taking place in there: will things bubble up and boil over between the three women, just like the rising temperature?

Finally, the three big lasagne dishes are taken ceremoniously from the oven, with a flourish, and carried into the dining room. A hush settles among the room's occupants. Each lasagne is golden brown, bubbling with molten sauce. One is topped with breadcrumbs, another a sprinkling of cheese, and all undulate, like the rolling hills around us.

Everyone in the dining room stands and stares, gripping their glasses and the *antipasti* plates, stopping in mid-conversation. It's as if they're in the presence of great works of art and their creators. No one speaks and I'm hoping this will put an end to the years of arguing, each appreciating the others' hard work. Until Nonna Rosa lifts her head and declares, 'Anyone can see mine is the better lasagne.' She points at it on the table.

'Clearly not!' says Nonna Lucia.

'And yours looks nothing like a traditional Tuscan lasagne,' says Nonna Teresa.

'That's because the recipe is from my family's home! Remember? I left to be with your brother, who brought me here so he would have a decent meal every evening,' Nonna Lucia bites back.

'Madam! May I remind you that I won the

189

competition all those years ago and I will win again today,' Nonna Rosa snarls.

As one, they turn to the mayor, who looks terrified and I don't blame him. This was a dreadful idea. What were we thinking? I glance at Giovanni, whose face tells me this may not be turning out as we'd hoped.

'I think, really, you're all winners today,' the mayor says nervously. He is visibly shaking.

'But what about the taste test?' demands Nonna Teresa, determined to have her revenge.

'Really, you're all winners,' the mayor repeats.

'How can you choose without tasting?' Nonna Rosa frowns at him.

'You mean you cannot decide?' says Nonna Lucia, folding her arms across her chest.

'Or are you not man enough?' Nonna Teresa purses her lips.

'We were promised one winner.' Nonna Rosa slaps the table, making the mayor jump.

'For a summer festival!' Nonna Lucia unwittingly sides with Nonna Rosa, and Nonna Teresa joins in, narrowing her eyes at the mayor.

'Perhaps we have been lured here under false pretences!'

Nonna Rosa turns on Giovanni. 'I think the world of you, but what is this sham of a competition?'

'Shame on you!' Nonna Teresa says indignantly.

'Yes, shame on you,' Nonna Lucia joins in.

One by one, the women huff and strip off their aprons, stuff them into their baskets, collect up their favourite utensils, including Nonna Teresa's pasta machine, and strut towards the door.

'No, wait! Please.' I try to stop them. 'Really, we want you all to be winners, to be a part of this. Let me explain.'

'Help yourselves,' says Nonna Lucia to the waiting crowd, gesturing at the bubbling lasagnes.

'Lucia, won't you eat with us?' I plead.

She looks in the direction of the other *nonnas*, leaving through the gate. 'I'd better go,' she says, then smiles and makes for the door, clearly not going to break ranks against the new common enemy, the mayor. He is evidently shaken and is being given more wine, as he dabs his forehead with a napkin.

'Wait!' I catch up with her just as she's leaving through the gate.

'Lucia, we need you. All three of you,' I blurt out. 'It's Alfonso. He's closing the shop. Giovanni can't keep La Tavola going without it and we're trying to find a way to save it. We might be able to, if we can run cookery weekends for tourists to learn how to make Tuscan recipes in the kitchen.'

'Why would they come here to cook in this kitchen?' She frowns.

'Because this is about team-building, working together to create good food. It's an experience.'

Slowly her expression softens as she thinks about it.

'It's a wonderful idea,' she says. 'I know that at one time my sister, my sister-in-law and I would have loved to be a part of it. Probably still would.'

Thank goodness. 'Then you think it might work?'

She places a hand on my forearm. 'If we can't find a way to overcome our own differences, we are hardly going to be of any use to you in a team-building weekend. I'm sorry,' she says. 'I wish it were different.' She looks back at La Tavola. 'I shall be very sad to see it go.'

The last breath of wind has just left my sails. All the fight goes out of me.

24

For the next few days I help Giovanni in the house, keeping the buckets of plaster topped up. The heat is my punishment for imagining that the lasagne competition could ever have worked. I feel stupid, and I've let Giovanni down. La Tavola doesn't have a future now.

'I've been to deliver the dishes back,' I tell him, 'but they were too busy arguing over their washing lines again to notice me. I wanted to talk to Rosa. If only we could have got her onside, I'm sure the others would have joined in.'

'You're right. I think they might. But she's the eldest, the scariest, and the one to keep this feud going. I don't think she ever forgave Teresa for marrying the man she loved. And they both felt Lucia took their brother.'

'So sad to be left with no one,' I muse, glancing at the bags of photographs no one wants and the Sunday-best clothes that won't see another Sunday. 'Sad that their happy memories of life growing up will be gone.'

The house is starting to shape up. The walls are newly plastered and the stairs mended. Everything feels fresh and clean, like a blank canvas, a new beginning for the house. 'This is looking great, Giovanni. I'm going to call the estate agent. Get an appointment to have the place valued and on the market. I'm just sorry I couldn't repay you by pulling off the cookery school.'

'It wasn't your fault. You honoured your side of the bargain and helped keep La Tavola running while I was working here.' And then he looks at me with gentle concern in his eyes and says, 'Tell me, have you taken some time to talk with Stella yet? I mean, it would be good, before you put this place on the market.'

'Why, Giovanni? Why should I talk to her?'

He says softly, 'She said she was a friend of Marco's. Did he ever mention her?'

I sigh. 'Marco had been out a few times to see the house and oversee the paperwork. The day it was finalized, he was in great spirits. He came home with stories of the house and the village. The dreams he had for our quieter life here. The following day was Aimee's birthday. He said the house was the best present he could give her. A place to run free in the summer.' Just as she and Luca are now, I think. 'A place where we could be family.' And then, having kissed the three of us, he left for work. 'He'd promised to make his lasagne that afternoon for her birthday dinner. But, he didn't come home. The washer-up rang me to say an ambulance had been called. But he was pronounced dead before I got to the restaurant.'

'I'm so sorry.' Giovanni is looking at the floor.

'Giovanni, is there something I should know about Stella and Marco? Please, tell me if there is.'

I swallow and he looks slowly up at me.

'Giovanni! Giovanni!' We swing round to the door. Nonna Lucia is bright red in the face and out of breath.

'Lucia!' He runs over to her. 'Are you okay? Come and sit!'

'What's happened?' I join him and take her other arm to support her.

'It's Rosa. She climbed on a chair to push Teresa's washing back, claiming it was on her side. Now she has fallen. Stupid woman. All over some undergarments.'

'I'm coming,' says Giovanni, grabbing his phone and dialling for help as he runs out of the door.

'I'll come too!' I say.

'The medics are on their way,' Giovanni says, as we arrive at the house where Nonna Teresa is sitting by Nonna Rosa's head, stroking it.

'Not so hard. I'll have to put my rollers back in at this rate!'

'Well, sounds like she's still angry so that's a good sign!' Giovanni whispers, relieved.

'I'll go down to the road and point the medics this way,' I say. 'I know how hard it can be to get here . . .'

And to leave. I hear a small voice in my head and wonder if it's Marco. What was Giovanni going to tell me about Marco and Stella? Please, God, not an affair. Anything but that. Or was it something she did? Something he hasn't told me. If only you were here to tell me yourself, Marco, I think, as I stomp crossly towards the main road.

'Well, madam, from where I'm standing you're not going to be doing much cooking or looking after yourself.'

The medics have patched up Nonna Rosa's ankle, telling her to keep it raised and to keep her weight off it. They've also given her some painkillers.

I've been back to La Tavola to check on things there and returned to the house to find Giovanni, with Nonnas Teresa and Lucia, in Nonna Rosa's kitchen. She is sitting on one chair, her foot raised on another.

'I've been looking after myself for as many years as I can remember. I shan't stop now,' she snaps.

No one says anything. I can almost smell the sunshine on the warm cobbles outside.

'You have to keep your foot up,' says Giovanni.

'The weight off it,' Nonna Teresa says.

And then Nonna Lucia says quietly, 'So it's help from us or nothing.'

'I'll take nothing!'

'Very well,' says Nonna Teresa, and turns to leave.

'No, wait . . . I need the bathroom and I haven't eaten for hours. They wanted me to go to the hospital, but I know the food there is dreadful. Even your lasagnes would be better than that.'

There is huffing and puffing all round.

'Perhaps you would like Giuseppe to call in and help you to the bathroom,' says Nonna Teresa.

Nonna Rosa sucks in her lips, as if she's sucking a lemon. And I think Nonna Lucia may have chuckled.

'You cannot insult our food, then expect us to look after you and cook for you.'

'I'm not expecting it.' She folds her arms and lifts her chin.

'Well, how will you cope?'

'Perhaps I'll ask one of the young people to show me how to use my telephone and order my food on an appé.'

I can't help but laugh, as does Giovannni.

'It's an app, Rosa, not an appé,' I say. 'In the meantime, I brought you pasta.'

'What? One of theirs? Did no one eat it on Sunday? Too afraid of food poisoning.'

'Actually it's *cacio e pepi*. I went to La Tavola and made it.'

No one says anything. They look down at the big foil dish I've brought. There are so many unsaid words in the air and a feeling of tension, as if we're all daring each other to be the first to speak. I'm holding my breath. Finally Nonna Rosa looks up from the dish, then at the other two women and says, 'This is what we have come to? The three of us relying on pasta made by outsiders?'

They stare at each other and suddenly, with no warning, they throw back their heads and laugh. They laugh until tears run down their cheeks. Giovanni and I join in. Call it a release, a moment of madness, a line drawn in the sand. Whatever it was, it seemed to work. As they wipe the tears from their eyes, and their shoulders stop shuddering, Nonna Rosa gives instructions: 'Teresa, get the plates. Lucia, you get the forks. I'm starving,' she says, bossing them around. Although they haven't been in each other's houses for decades, they seem to move seamlessly around Nonna Rosa's, laying the table and serving the pasta.

Each of them digs in a fork and twirls, lifts it to her mouth and bites, strands of pasta smacking at her cheeks. They look at each other, then dig in their forks for more. And Nonna Rosa says, 'Well, for a newcomer to the village it is very good.'

'I agree!' says Lucia. I created the sauce with the pasta water, which mixed with the cheese, making it creamy.

Nonna Teresa leans in and says, 'Tell me, what's your secret?'

'Well, I made it with the children . . . like Marco and I used to do. I haven't done it for a very long time.'

'Then it's made with love, and that's why it tastes so good.'

We all raise a glass.

'It's not what you put into the pasta as much as who you share it with.' Nonna Rosa sips the red wine. She puts her glass on the Formica table as we clear the plates. 'This has made me think,' she says pensively. 'La Tavola has kept us all company over the past few years, while we have been too pig-headed to put our differences behind us.'

The other women nod.

'We should be very grateful to you, Giovanni,' she says, looking up at him.

I realize I have a lot to thank him for, too, and grab my moment with both hands: life's too short not to. 'The truth is, there is no summer festival happening like we told you. We just wanted to get you all in the same room so we could ask for your help.'

'No party?'

'No engagement?'

'Er, no . . .'

'Well, there should be. You two were made for each other,' says Nonna Teresa.

I catch Giovanni's eye and blush, but carry on quickly: 'But La Tavola will have to close if we can't make some money to keep it open and find a way to make it pay for itself. I'm not staying here, but I did want to thank Giovanni for all the help he has given me at Casa Luna, and La Tavola. Like you, when I needed it, it was there.'

For a moment there's silence, then Nonna Lucia says, 'So, what can we do, three old women?'

'There is a chance we could raise the money needed to pay the rent on the building, but we need your help. We could run a cookery class over a weekend ending in a Sunday lunch together. A company I know will pay a lot of money for some of its people to come and stay in the village and learn to cook authentic Italian food.'

'But we don't have any authentic Italian chefs here.'

'No,' I say slowly, 'but we do have you three. And that's about as authentic as it gets.'

'But we're not teachers, just home cooks.'

'Brilliant ones at that!' I say. I see them look at each other and their chests swell with pride.

Nonna Teresa is the first to speak. 'And La Tavola needs us to cook for it?'

'Or, if what you say is true, we're going to lose it for ever?' Nonna Rosa says.

'It is a lifeline for people,' says Nonna Lucia. 'We shouldn't be fighting with each other. We are here, on our own. We have only each other left. It is the way of the world right now. People are having to leave their homes and move to bigger towns to find work. It breaks up families, meaning they no longer stay together, eat together or pass on the skill of cooking. Food costs are rising. Processed and cheap convenience foods are the devil. It's like you say. It's who you share the food with that makes it special. If La Tavola folds, the people in this village will be deserted, like Casa Luna, because there is no one left to care.'

The three *nonna*s look at each other, and it's like no time has passed, as if they are three young girls knowing exactly what the others are thinking.

'I mean, Giovanni's a good cook. He needs more pepper in his *cacio e pepe* . . .'

'And he sometimes undercooks his broccoli in broccoli carbonara.'

'But his caponata is really very good. You can tell an Italian grandmother taught him that.'

'I will be sad to see what he has done turn to nothing.'

'He has helped us all when we've needed it.'

They nod.

'When my drains were blocked.'

'Oh, the stench!'

'And when I locked myself out and he climbed in through the window.'

'Only way you'll get a man climbing in through your window . . .'

And they cackle.

'And every week, whether we want it or not, he makes sure someone is here with a meal for us, and sits to keep us company.'

'We were too stubborn to get together and cook for each other.'

'It is time to say thank you.'

They nod in agreement. Nonna Rosa speaks for them all: 'Contact your company. We will run the cookery school for the weekend.'

My eyes widen.

'Are you sure? With no arguing?'

'That's not a certainty. What can you expect when three *nonna*s get in the kitchen?'

I can't help but smile.

After Giovanni and I leave, we stop a little way from the house and hug. And then we pull back a little and drink in each other's faces, our eyes darting from each other's eyes to lips. I'm being drawn to his, like I've wanted this for weeks, like I need to feel them on mine.

'We did it, *cara*! We did it!' he says softly, his eyes dancing with excitement, his head tilting and leaning in to meet mine.

I freeze and pull back from the embrace. 'What did you just call me?' I feel as if I've had a bucket of ice poured over me.

25

'It's just a term of affection,' says Giovanni, as I release myself from our joyous hug. I'm in shock, berating myself. No one has called me *cara*, no one except Marco. What was I thinking? I'm hugging a man, who is calling me the same name. How could I have let this happen? I can't just wipe out the memory of Marco and replace him with another man. And not just any man . . .

He's a friend, someone who's helping me and I'm helping him too. He's not Marco, despite the similarities, the generous spirit, the big build and the way everything feels better when he's around. Guilt washes through me. I can't replace Marco with him. He's not Marco. Marco isn't here, where he should be. I've crossed a line and I shouldn't have.

I step away and start walking back up the hill towards Casa Luna on the way to La Tavola.

'Thea, I'm sorry. Honestly, it's just a friendly term. I wasn't trying to . . .' he says, as he follows me. 'I thought you wanted it too. I misread things.'

I know I overreacted, but hearing someone other than Marco call me *cara* makes me feel that somehow I've just walked all over Marco's and my memories. Careered into them, like an eight-year-old in charge of a double-decker bus.

How could I do that to him, to the children?

'It's fine!' I call to Giovanni. 'But I have to get back now!' But none of this is fine. It's really not. I've been foolish, letting down my guard. I've fallen into the comfort and safety of Giovanni's arms, letting him think that's where I want to be. How could I? I'm not here for a relationship! I had one, which I treasured . . . still treasure. I can't allow another man to step into Marco's place, no matter how good it felt, how reassuring, how I wanted him. I can't have him. I'm not free to fall for anyone else. I'm still Marco's wife. I feel I've betrayed him. Tears spring to my eyes.

I break into a run towards Casa Luna.

Really, I'm happy on my own. It's where my heart is safest, for the children's and my sake. Even if I did want to be with someone else, I could never be with a man like Giovanni. He's too much like Marco. I couldn't put myself through the highs and lows of that again.

I turn the handle, shove open the door and run

upstairs to the bedroom, still skipping over the fourth step even though it's no longer broken.

I shut my bedroom door and throw myself onto the bed. I can hear the children outside playing on the rope swing Giuseppe helped them put up this afternoon, making it secure, now the goats have cleared the garden.

I turn on my back. *Cara*. That name.

I remember Stella and sit bolt upright. Was I the only one Marco was calling *cara*? After all, it's just a term of affection.

I have to leave here. Just as soon as the cookery weekend is over. I shouldn't have started to enjoy this place so much. It was never going to be for ever. I let my guard down. I shouldn't have. For the children's sake. I look around the room. The walls have been plastered, the woodwork repaired. Next Giovanni, Alessandro and Enrico will paint it and then the place will be ready to sell. I sit up slowly and look out of the window. The goats are trimming the lawn as the sun starts to set. I wonder what the garden will look like this time next year.

Who will buy the house? Who will sit here? I have to remind myself it won't be me. But there's one thing I need to do before I go. Giovanni's right: I have to find Stella and speak to her. Find out exactly how friendly she and Marco were.

26

'Argh! *Mamma!* Quick! *Mamma!*' There's a shriek from the garden.

I throw myself off the bed and out onto the landing, then take the stairs two at a time. 'Luca! Aimee!'

'*Mammaaaaa!*' squeals Aimee.

I run to the back door, but can't see them.

'Where are you?' I shout. 'Luca? Aimee?'

'Over here!' says a stranger's voice, from behind a clump of trees at the end of the garden, making my heart lurch.

'Who's that?' But I know who it is. It's as if I've conjured her up, some sort of spectre that's been hiding in a corner of my mind since I first set eyes on her.

'Brush! Brush!' She's giving out commands. I run to the clump where Stella is holding Aimee's arm and slapping her shins! Luca is looking on, stamping his feet!

'Hey!' I rush forward, push Stella away and shout, 'Leave them alone!' I grab her arm and pull her further from the children. 'Get away from my children!'

'Mum, we've been stung,' cries Luca, stamping and brushing at his legs.

'Red ants,' says Stella, pointing at their legs. 'You have to brush them off quickly, or they will inflame.'

I follow her command.

'*Spazzolata!* Brush, brush!' She waves her hands in downward sweeping motions.

And I do. I brush at their legs, as the children hop and yelp. And as they calm down, their shouts become sobs. I am out of breath, with exertion and emotion, as the children turn to me for a hug.

'There is always a nest of them here.' Stella is equally out of breath. 'You have to be careful.'

I nod slowly.

'Thank you.' I nod some more. 'I must get the children inside and give them some antihistamine.' I know now is not the time to ask all the questions I want to fire at her, like who is she, how does she know my husband, did they have an affair, was he going to leave me, and what was she doing in my garden? I walk towards the house, stop and turn back. 'Have you been stung too?'

She shrugs. 'Just a little. It's fine.' She waves a hand,

and her bangles jingle on her wrist. She wears a little silver ring on each finger, including the thumb.

That word again. When everything is all but fine. I know now that fine is not fine.

'Well, *grazie*,' I say to the young woman, her midriff showing and a tattoo twisting its way up from around her hip. She has red flashes of dye in her hair, and a nose ring. She looks like she did when I first saw her, as if she's travelling, or just leaving, with a rucksack she picks up and slings over her shoulder. She eyes me carefully. And I do the same to her.

'I'd better get the children inside,' I say again, with one hand on each shoulder and direct them towards the house.

'So,' she calls after me, 'what happened to Marco?'

I turn back to her. 'Marco?'

'Yes. Did he tell you about me?'

I swallow the huge ball that has risen in my throat and finally say the words to which I'm dreading the answer. 'How do you know him?'

'Stella is Papa's friend. She told me,' says Aimee.

I look at Stella, panicked, terrified of what I might hear, of what it will do to my memories of the man I love. I try to speak, the words sticking in my throat, my mind whirring, and wishing I didn't want to know. But I have to. 'You'd better come in.'

27

The children are bathed, with cream on their stings, and are playing Happy Families on one of their beds.

I walk slowly down the stairs. Stella is wandering around the house, as if she's inspecting the work. 'This place is looking great. A big difference,' she says approvingly.

'You've been here before?' I ask tentatively, heading towards the kitchen and pulling out an onion to start chopping, with no real idea of what I'm making for dinner.

'Uh-huh. I lived here.'

I stop chopping, my thoughts racing, like an out-of-control horse, cantering and gathering speed into a gallop.

'You lived here?' I ask, hoping it will be a

straightforward answer. 'Grew up here? Was it your family's home?'

She shakes her head. 'No.' She laughs. 'My "family",' she uses two fingers to make inverted commas, 'didn't really do conventional living. My mother moved from place to place, with friends, wherever the next festival might be.'

'Festival?'

She nods and shrugs at the same time. 'Festivals, concerts. She was part of a band. I grew up on the road. I guess that's where I still am.'

'And when did you first meet my . . . Marco?' I put down the onion and pour some wine into a small stubby glass. I should offer Stella a drink but, right now, this is not a social visit, and the wine is giving me the courage I need.

'A couple of years ago.'

'A couple of years ago?' I'm trying to process the information. ' You lived here a couple of years ago?'

'A few months before he bought this place.'

'He . . .' I feel hot. 'He bought this place after he met you?'

'Yes.'

'And how did you meet?' I pick up the knife and start chopping the onion again, putting all my energy into it.

'Online,' she says casually, pulling up a chair at the table.

'You met online?' I'm gripping the knife in my hand like a lethal weapon. I put it down quickly and pick up the wine.

'Well, I contacted him.' She reaches over to the bottle and helps herself, pouring wine into one of the children's water glasses.

'So let me get this straight. You contacted my husband online. You got in touch and the pair of you met.'

'Pretty much, yup.'

'More than once?'

She nods, casually again, making my hackles rise and my eyeballs burn with a red mist rising.

'And then he bought this place,' I say, picking up the knife again and slashing the onion with it.

'It was a really good buy. Said he planned to see out his days here.'

'Well, he did that!' I say, furious at his untimely death all over again.

'What did he die of?'

'A heart attack. Who told you he died?'

'You did. When you arrived.'

I narrow my eyes. 'And you didn't know before then?'

There's a moment when I feel for her: two years without knowing, having been ghosted. And then I check myself. Why am I feeling sorry for this woman? She was clearly planning to take my husband from me.

'Why Marco?' I ask.

211

'You tell me. You fell in love with him!' She gives a little laugh.

'I did. I gave up my life to be with him. He was everything to me. I thought I was to him too . . .'

'He told me all about you. And the children.'

'Did he?' I say, feeling sick and pulling out a chair to sit down before my legs give way.

'Everything. Did he ever say anything about me?'

I look at her. Really? The audacity. 'No.'

'He said he was going to tell you about me. He emailed.'

'Well, I guess we were just too busy keeping the house and business together for him to get around to telling me about his secret life in Italy. Too busy selling me an idea of easier days in the sunshine, when all along . . .'

For a moment, she says nothing. Then, 'I'm sorry.' She drops her head. 'He said he'd tell you.'

'What? That he was going to leave me? Me and the children?' I hiss quietly.

'He was never going to leave you! He wouldn't have done that. He loved you!'

'And you?'

'Oh, I don't know about that. I didn't really know him. We'd only just met.'

'So, how would you describe yourself? As his lover?' I practically spit the words.

'No! We were still getting to know each other. It was more like friends.'

'Well, that's something.' A sense of relief washes over me. 'A one-night stand?'

'No, I promise. Nothing like that. I swear.' She's looking less self-assured now. She stands quickly to leave. 'I swear . . .'

'Then why were you messaging my husband? What did you want him to tell me? Were you blackmailing him?' Now I'm feeling angry again, as if molten lava is rising within me.

We glare at each other.

'He didn't tell you . . . He said he'd tell you! He said everything would be okay when the house was sold to him. And then I hear nothing. For two years!'

'Tell me what?' I shout.

She glares at me. 'I'm his daughter. I'm Marco's daughter!' We stare wide-eyed at each other. I can't think of a single word to say. She can't be more than about eighteen or maybe nineteen. And then she gets up and rushes out of the front door, slamming it behind her. This time, the ceiling stays put. It's just my world that comes crashing down all over again.

I feel the knife being moved from beside me. And the onion. It's Luca. 'What are you doing?' I ask him.

'I'm making us pasta, like Dad used to,' says Luca. 'With Parmigiano,' he adds, and somehow among this tsunami, it's the most natural and comforting thing in the world. Because the new knowledge hurts as if Marco's died all over again.

28

I'm cleaning the kitchen surfaces again after a night of no sleep. I tossed and turned and tried to conjure up the image of Marco to ask him everything that is running around my head, tormenting me. How, when, where? Why didn't he tell me? How long had he known?'

I look for signs of Marco, but he's not here. It's not the same house. It's different, with a new beginning ahead of it, not one with me in it.

'*Buongiorno*,' Giovanni calls as he arrives, opening the front door with a cursory knock, as he has most mornings. It's pattern of familiarity I've come to enjoy, but even this will end soon. Bello comes galloping in to say good morning too.

'*Buongiorno*,' I say, and try not to look him in the eye.

'Everything okay?' he asks.

'Uh-huh,' I say, still not looking at him, not wanting him to see my red eyes from the crying I've done all night. Not wanting to feel as I do when I see him, which lifts me. And I can't let myself have feelings for him. Because that would mean . . . Well, I don't know what it would mean but it would certainly mean Marco and I were in the past. But maybe, having found out what I did last night, that's exactly where we are, in a big sorry mess in the past, without the glorious memories of our life together, no matter how tough it got.

'*Caffè?*' I say, putting the cafetière on the hob, knowing the answer already.

A silence hangs in the air, as usual these days.

'You doing okay?' he says.

'I am. *Grazie.*'

'Okay . . . Well, we'll finish the plastering today and then we can start painting. Maybe we should have a painting party, get everyone to help.'

'Yay,' says Luca, coming down the stairs. 'I can help. So can Pietro,'

'And me.' Aimee has followed him.

Giovanni smiles and turns to me, but when he sees I'm not smiling he frowns. 'Thea, what's happened?'

For a moment I say nothing. Then, 'I spoke to Stella last night.'

'Ah,' he says. 'Do you want to talk about it?'

'Not really. There's a lot to get my head around,' I say, turning my forefinger at my temple.

He nods. 'And her too, I'm sure.'

I'm stopped in my tracks. He's right. None of this is her fault, but I have no idea how to make that better.

'I'm going to La Tavola, to start getting ready for the cookery class,' I say.

'*Mamma?*'

'Yes, Aimee?'

'Does this mean Stella's our sister? I've always wanted an older sister!'

There's a knock at the door.

'Stella!' says Aimee and throws herself at her. I'm at a loss to know how to handle the situation,

'Hey, how's things?'

Aimee slides her hand into Stella's. 'Are you my new sister? I've always wanted a big sister! Now I have you!'

No one else says a word.

'You told them, then?' she says at last, her usual sass not in evidence.

'We heard you and *Mamma* talking last night,' Luca says.

Stella looks at me. And it's almost as if I'm looking at Marco. It's all so . . . messed up. Where is he when I need him?

Stella smiles at Aimee. 'I am . . . if you'd like me to be. Actually, I brought you a present.'

'Yay!' says Aimee, and even Luca, although he's standing back warily, is intrigued.

'I just wanted to say,' she looks at me again, 'I know

this was all a bit of a shock. I'm sorry you found out like this.'

There are so many things I should be saying right now, like no, I'm sorry she had to find out about Marco this way, and asking so many questions.

When Stella smiles, it could be Marco's smile. She pulls open the basket she's carrying, puts her hand into it and scoops out a little white kitten.

'Ooooh!' Aimee's in raptures. 'Can we keep him? Is he for me?' She reaches forward and takes the kitten before I can step in, and it's love at first sight. Mr Fluffy drops to the floor.

I rush over and pick him up.

'*Mamma*, look! He's beautiful! I love him!' She holds him to her face. I hold Mr Fluffy to mine as frustration swells in me.

'No, Aimee, sorry, we can't. Not with us going back to Cardiff. It wouldn't be fair!'

I'm furious that I'm now having to take the little furry bundle from my daughter.

'We can't!' I say, feeling wretched.

'I thought it would help with the Mr Fluffy thing.' Stella nods to the sad, worn-out rabbit I'm holding. 'I found him in the hedge. The mother gave birth but she seems to have moved on.'

'You can't just give people pets! They're not toys. They mean responsibility. We're not going to be here.'

'I was just trying to do something nice!' she shouts.

217

Jo Thomas

'Can I keep him, *Mamma, pleeeease*?'

Stella looks between Aimee and me. 'Look after him for now, yeah? I'll look after him once you've gone.'

I give a huge sigh of relief. Once we're gone. 'I have to get to La Tavola, to confirm everything for the workshop next week,' I say. 'I've got accommodation to find, and a taxi company. Come on, guys. You can come too,' I say to Luca and Aimee.

'And Snowy!' Aimee says, holding the kitten with one hand, the other in Stella's. I don't want my daughter's heart to be broken all over again. I have to work out how to do the right thing for all of them.

29

A week to the day, and a week after the kitten arrived into our lives, and I'm up early. I push open the shutters to lose myself in the view. The orange sun is rising over the fields and cypress trees, perhaps a little lazier than the past few weeks, as if taking the pressure off, signalling the start of late summer. The cicadas are singing and I have butterflies in my stomach. In a good way. It's the workshop. And once I've shown Giovanni how this can work, I'll be leaving here knowing I did the best I can.

I hurry to dress, dropping in on the children, who are still in bed, and putting a kiss on each of their heads, then telling them to dress and come with me to La Tavola.

I head downstairs into the brightly painted living room, clean and fresh, then straight out of the back door, into the morning, lifting my face to the sun. Then I go back into the kitchen to make and drink coffee as the children get ready without argument. Gathered by the newly painted front door, we walk outside. I close it behind me and step onto the cobbles, heading up the hill. The warming stones under the soles of my shoes are becoming familiar. A familiarity I like. I look back at the little house, cleared of the weeds at the front, shutters open, cleaned and painted by Enrico. It is a very different house from the sad, closed-up one we encountered when we first arrived. A lot has changed since then.

I haven't seen Stella. I've asked Giovanni.

'It's best to wait and let her come to you,' he told me.

Tonight is the Friday dinner and the *nonna*s will work in three teams, making the food for the village and delivering it. Each student will visit a village resident with dinner. Tomorrow will be a market visit to the neighbouring town and the guests will have lunch there, enjoying the cafés, the street food on sale, and pizza at La Tavola in the evening.

And on Sunday, there is lunch, with one last important decision to make: whose lasagne recipe shall we use?

I unlock La Tavola's door and leave it ajar so that anyone can come in to join me for coffee and a chat.

The place is spotlessly clean because I scrubbed and scrubbed all week. All I need to do is lay out what's needed at three different work stations. I put my bag on the table, and it's only then that I realize I'm still carrying Mr Fluffy around in my bag. Exhausted and finally retired, he looks as if he deserves a good rest and now needs to be put into a darkened drawer to recover.

I smile at him. 'Thank you, Mr Fluffy. You've been amazing.'

Outside I can hear Aimee showing Isabella the kitten, taking it in turns to hug, kiss and love it.

I head into the kitchen and make straight for the coffee pot.

'Can I help?' I jump and spin round to see Stella standing there.

I falter. 'I really have to get on. We have students arriving,' I say, trying to put off the conversation. But she doesn't move. 'I'm sorry for how I reacted last week. It was a shock. It's all been a bit of a shock,' I say.

'You're right, I shouldn't have brought the kitten. It was irresponsible. I'm sorry. So stupid.'

She sighs, drops her head and, with it, her guard. She starts to cry.

'It was impulsive, not stupid. It was a kind thing to do.' I point to a stool at the work station. 'Come on, sit,' I tell her.

'Impulsive. Yes. I am.'

'Well, at least I know where you get that from!'

She chuckles, and sniffs.

I make the coffee and put a cup in front of her. Its steam rises, a phoenix from the ashes, spreading its reviving roasted-coffee-bean scent, and she lifts her head slowly. 'I wish I'd known him more.'

'You're very much like him in many ways. You probably just need to look at yourself to know who Marco was. He gave his all to whatever his plan was at the time.'

She smiles again and goes to wipe her tears on her sleeve. I reach for the kitchen roll instinctively and hand it to her. 'I'm sorry I didn't know about you. But that night, after you'd gone, I went through his emails. I know you'd only just met. And he planned to introduce us, here, once we came out together to see the house. I see that now. We just never had that moment.'

She blows her nose, loudly.

'And it's just that—'

'You want to know how I happened? If he cheated on you with my mother?'

I nod. 'Yes, I do. I want to know if my memories of us are still special.'

'He didn't,'

A heavy weight has just lifted off me. 'Please don't say it to save my feelings. If anyone should be having their feelings saved, it's you. You thought you'd been abandoned and now you find out the father you'd only just met is dead.'

'Really, I promise. I'm not bullshitting you. Sorry.'

'It's fine.' I smile as we try to navigate the situation as best we can. We're like a couple of rookie dodgem drivers, bumping into each other.

'My mother told me. She was totally into him. They met at a festival. She was in a band. He was cheffing for the acts. She thought he was the one. But then, after the festival, he went to London. He arranged to meet her. She thought he was going to propose, and she planned to tell him she was pregnant. Instead, he told her he'd met someone else, the love of his life, and he couldn't see her any more. He was honest about it. He never strung her along. But she wanted a clean break. So she never told him she was pregnant. She never badmouthed him. Just said they'd split before I was born and he had found happiness. Just like she did eventually with my stepdad before she died. When I was sixteen. She stayed here. She'd got into a bad crowd and Giovanni helped her when she was trying to stay clean. But she couldn't stop living the life she lived, on the road, with people she knew. This village became a safe place for me. Giovanni has been here for me. And I looked up Marco online when I was old enough. Facebook is a great thing!'

'That's debatable!'

'He wanted to tell you. But he said he wanted to meet me first. Take things carefully. He had a family to think of. He came here to meet me, and saw the house. He told me he was going to buy it, and wanted to bring you here, for us to meet in person.'

223

'That's what he said in the emails . . .' Tears fill my eyes. 'And now we have.'

'Just without him.'

'What about you? Where did you go when you didn't hear from him?'

'Here and there, staying in Casa Luna when I was in the area. It felt the closest thing to a home I'd had.'

'You were staying in the house! So that's why it wasn't in as bad a state as I was expecting.'

'I tried to keep it nice for when he finally came back.'

'Oh, Stella.' This time I can't help but put my hand over hers, and she lets me.

'But he didn't come back. His family did. A family I wasn't a part of. And he wasn't here.'

'But,' it catches in my throat, 'a little piece of him is here, in you, Aimee, Luca . . . in this place, where he had a dream of us all getting to know each other.'

She drops her head again.

'And we can still do that . . .'

She rubs her nose. Her hard mask has all but gone, leaving in its place a vulnerable young woman, who looks exactly like the man I loved. 'You mean you don't hate me?'

'Why would I?'

'It seemed that way when I told you,' she says quietly.

I put out my hand, wanting to make this better. 'I'm sorry. I was in shock.'

She looks up at me. 'And I wasn't exactly making it easy for you!'

I shake my head and we smile.

'No . . . but that's what teenagers do. And I have all this to come with Aimee and Luca.'

She laughs. 'They're lovely children. I'd like to stay in touch if I can.'

I nod firmly. 'Of course!'

'And, again, I'm sorry about the kitten. I'll find a way of looking after it and letting Aimee know.'

I pat her hand. 'If Marco's death has taught me one thing, it's about living for today. And we have today. And . . . there's no reason why we can't do what Marco intended, for us all to get to know each other. It's taken me a long time to stop thinking about him every minute of every day. It was all so sad. Anniversaries, birthdays, first days of school . . . I tried to carry on for the children's sake, but since I've been here, I've felt different. Not so sad. I'm still thinking about him, but I also feel lighter. He's part of the family, even if he's not here any more, but it's not all sad. It's okay to be happy too . . .'

'Giovanni once told me, when I'd got into some sort of trouble,' Stella says, 'that that's why cars have bigger windows at the front and smaller ones at the back. It's so you can look forward and see the future and not look back so much.'

'Giovanni is a wise man,' I say.

'He is.'

'Well, I'm going to make today the best I can to try to repay him for how he's helped both of us.'

I move towards one of the tables in the kitchen and Luca moves to its other end. Together, we start to create three distinct working areas.

'Team work is how kitchens function,' I tell Luca. It's as if I've slipped into a pair of comfortable shoes, not the old pair: new ones that are twice as nice.

He giggles. 'Try telling the *nonna*s that!'

Suddenly I'm nervous again about today. Even though I've had the deposit from Harris Headhunters' bank, a list of arrival times, I've passed on accommodation details and the minibus is booked, I'm still on edge about pulling this off.

I pick up a piece of chalk next to the painted wall that acts like a blackboard for recipe ideas. I'd have liked a printout of the recipes for everyone, but there's no way the *nonna*s were going to tell me that much . . . or maybe they can't. After all, Nonna Lucia reckons her lasagne is all about the dish she makes it in. And Nonna Teresa whispered to me that it's the way she cuts the garlic with a razor blade. As for Nonna Rosa, it's down to the order in which she adds the ingredients.

So, I write up the plan for today, and leave blanks where the *nonna*s will tell me what we're cooking.

Welcome to La Tavola Cookery School.

    Friday – Venerdi

    Primo

    Secondo

    Dolce

I just hope I can trust the *nonna*s to work together. I gaze around the dining room, with the hanging vines of cherry tomatoes, the red and green chillies Giuseppe grew on his smallholding and delivered for the weekend. And the bunting Caterina made – she's been sewing all week with the clothes she's been repurposing from Casa Luna. And the big arched doorway is wide open. I go outside, through the courtyard, out of the gate, across the cobbled road and swing my legs over the low wall in front of the blanket of fields that runs away from the village. Giuseppe's goats are happily grazing. I give them a pat and bend to pick some wild rosemary and oregano. Back in the cool of La Tavola, Luca has found some empty jars and we put the herbs and greenery I've gathered from the field into them, then place them on the three different work stations. The room smells amazing.

Having set everything up, I look around, just as I used to do before service in the restaurant, enjoying the peace before the performance, before the curtain goes up. The company has paid a lot of money for this weekend. I know how important team-building is to big businesses, even more so now that so many people work from home. It's important they get together, let their hair down, work as a team. I have everything crossed that it goes as planned, that the *nonna*s behave, that they don't fall out and refuse to cook with each other. I look at the time on my phone. What if the *nonna*s don't come? What if they come and refuse to cook? What if this was all a terrible idea?

Suddenly I hear voices.

'Come on, Teresa. You have the speed of an old mule!'

My heart lurches and I hold my breath.

And there, in the arched doorway, stand the silhouettes of the three *nonna*s. They're here! I start to breathe again. In the middle, taller than the other two, with turned-out feet, in a smart navy-blue dress, is Nonna Rosa. Next to her, shorter, her hair pinned up neatly, a pasta rolling pin under her arm, is Nonna Lucia, and then, leaning gently on Rosa, is Nonna Teresa, bent over and catching her breath.

'You're here!' I throw my arms open. Luca and Aimee appear beside me, smiling.

'Of course!'

'We gave our word.'

'Your word is worse than nothing.'

'Madam, my word is my badge of honour.'

'Honour, what honour?'

Suddenly, I'm worrying again, but then they laugh.

'Just friendly banter,' says Nonna Rosa.

They're here, and now I can relax. It's all going to be fine. Just as I've planned.

'Come on, come in,' I say, smiling. 'Would you like coffee?'

'Depends who's making it.'

'Nonna Lucia's coffee tastes like tar.'

'It hasn't stopped you coming round to drink it . . .'

'I do so out of politeness.'

'Politeness, ha!'

'Come this way, to the kitchen.' I'm herding them, like small children.

'And this is where we will cook?'

'You cooked here once already, remember? Or are you getting forgetful?' Nonna Teresa says to Nonna Rosa.

They look around, reacquainting themselves with the kitchen.

'I shall take that area!' Nonna Teresa points.

'No, that would be a better place for me to have my pasta machine.'

'I need to be in the middle so I can see what is happening around me,' says Nonna Rosa.

'Poking your nose into everything, more like!'

I hold up my hands. 'I'll let you get settled in.' I back out of the kitchen, wondering if I should intervene or not.

'Hello? *Ciao?*' The voice makes me jump. It's the guests and I spin round to the open front door. For a moment, I experience *déjà vu* with two of my worlds colliding. I stitch on my welcome smile. This is all going to be fine, I think, as the three *nonna*s lay territorial claim to their work stations and noisily unpack the baskets of equipment they've brought with them, clearly preferring their own tools of the trade to anything we can provide.

'Come in, come in!' I turn from the kitchen where the *nonna*s have stopped bickering and are now laughing.

The guests are filing into the dining room, taking it all in: the cherry tomatoes, the chillies and Caterina's bunting, cushions, and a huge patchwork wall hanging, now in pride of place.

'Good morning, welcome to La Tavola,' I say, slipping back into my hospitality shoes and finding them as comfortable as they always were, perhaps even more so now that I've had a rest from them. It feels good to be back, just for this one time.

I stretch out an arm, with a wide smile. And stop in my tracks, frozen to the spot as the past rushes up to meet me again, as if my life is playing to me backwards.

'Hello, Thea! I bet you didn't expect to see me here!'

30

And suddenly I'm not this Thea, aged forty-three and widowed with two children, her only money in a holiday home that was in need of repair. All of a sudden I'm twenty-five-year-old Thea, living life in the fast lane. Working in London, drinking in pubs after work, eating in Michelin-starred restaurants, and enjoying weekends away with friends in the country.

'Seb!' I manage to say, as if it was only yesterday we were working hard and playing hard. 'What are you doing here? I didn't know you were coming too.'

Pietro, Luca and Aimee follow him in from outside and stare at me.

The man, in a colourful, Hawaiian shirt, knee-length shorts, a Panama and boating shoes, smiles back at me. It's a very familiar smile.

'I couldn't not come. Once I got the pitch through on my phone!'

I look at Luca who grins back at me.

'I thought it couldn't be you at first, but a team-building event in Tuscany? Brilliant! I passed it on to HR, got the go-ahead, and thought I should try a bit of team-building myself. Haven't done one in years. Couldn't resist a jolly, especially when you said you were running it. Never could resist a fun trip away, as you know! Nothing changes!' He flings out his arms. 'How are you?' He kisses me on both cheeks, knocking off his Panama. We laugh, as the rest of the group is peering around.

'This is so cool!'

'Literally!'

'Rustic and authentic!'

'Too early for a drink?'

I hear the general chatter but am staring at one person. 'I . . .' I'm in shock. Sebastian Thornberry is here, in Italy. 'I'm fine. This is so weird!' I laugh.

'Isn't it? It's been a while.'

I see Giovanni arrive at the back of the group and make his way towards me.

'*Buongiorno, ciao,*' he greets everyone. 'Hey,' he says, 'just thought I'd check on how you're doing. That you don't need me.'

'Checking I'm up to the job.' I smile back, still flustered by Sebastian's arrival in rural Italy.

'Bit different from our trip to Venice, eh?'

'Yes.' Then, facing Giovanni, I draw a deep breath to calm myself.

'You've got this,' he says. 'I know you have.' And his eyes tell me he really thinks I have. Just for a moment, I want to stay there, with him looking at me, believing in me.

Then I remember what I'm supposed to be doing rather than admiring Giovanni's soft green eyes, or staring at Sebastian's familiar face. Despite the extra lines, the thinner hair, it's still the same Sebastian. The man I met by the photocopier. The same Sebastian who wined and dined me, took me to his family home in the countryside and to Paris to propose. All of this BM, Before Marco.

I try to refocus on the rest of the group, but my eyes are drawn back to Sebastian, who is looking around the dining room.

'I'll leave you to it and get back to Casa Luna. I have painting to get done,' Giovanni says, and surprises me by kissing me gently on the cheek. 'Thank you, Thea.' He makes his way out of the dining room and I watch him go.

'So, is this your and Marco's new place?' Sebastian interrupts my thoughts.

I swallow. 'Marco died, just over two years ago now.'

His face falls. 'Oh, Theally.' It's his nickname for me – and I'm right back there, twenty-something with life

233

stretching ahead of me. Sebastian and I had had so many plans – buying our first home, a family home in Wimbledon or Wandsworth, wedding in his parents' village, honeymoon in the Maldives, three children, a black Labrador and a golden retriever. We'd spend Sundays on the common and have lunch at a gastro pub. Private schools for the children, early retirement to the family home and weekends by the sea. 'I'm so sorry,' he says.

I gather myself and try to slow down the images scrolling through my mind, like a flip book we made at school on the corners of our workbook pages, making the images move.

'It's okay. I'm fine, really. I'm fine.' I focus on my customers and put myself back in hospitality mode. I know where I am there. The same can't be said of me outside it. I don't know where I fit any more. Here and back home, I'm not Marco's wife now, but I'm not the Thea from Before Marco either. But front of house, with food, I know where I am and it feels good. 'Come in, please. Help yourselves to water.' I point to the glasses and jugs on the table and pick up a glass with shaking hands, pour for myself and down it.

'So, you're living out here?' I hear Sebastian ask.

I shake my head. 'Just here until the end of the summer. A couple more weeks. Helping out . . .' I can't think how to describe Giovanni: a stranger who helped me when I needed it, '. . . a friend,' I say finally. 'And you?'

'Happily divorced. Paying out shedloads in the settlement. See the kids every other weekend and alternate holidays.'

My heart twists. None of this is where we thought we'd end up back then. We had it all mapped out. And then I met Marco and everything changed.

'I'm sorry to hear that.'

'Ah, it could've been so different.' He laughs, still the jovial good-natured Sebastian, but I think I detect a real tinge of regret in him. I turn back to the gathered group, all taking selfies. I put my hands together and the room quietens.

'Okay, when do we open the wine?' one of the younger members of the group pipes up. 'I've come to Tuscany to eat and drink!'

'And bond. That's what we're supposed to be doing,' says Sebastian.

'I could bond better with a drink!'

'This place is so quaint,' says one of the women, making me wince. But I pull back my hospitality smile.

'So, yes.' I clear my throat. 'As you might have realized, I used to work where you do.'

'And you're an old friend of Sebastian?'

'More than friends by the sound of it.'

'Enough,' says Sebastian. 'This is about team building, not insulting your boss and getting your P45!'

There's a good-humoured ripple of laughter. I blush and glance at Sebastian, who smiles fondly. Same old

Sebastian. Good-natured, and dependable. Not like Marco! I mean, who comes home having bought a cheap house in Italy, in a village we don't know? The same man who wanted to buy a rabbit for Aimee's first birthday so they could grow up together, but hasn't thought through buying a hutch or looking after it. The same Marco who took me out to dinner and his card was declined. He was friends with the owner and went back to pay cash the next day. Wild, impetuous, impulsive Marco. He was different from anyone I had ever met. Until I met Giovanni, I think. And pull myself up. What has Giovanni got to do with any of this?

'Reminds me of myself,' I hear Marco's voice. And I think of Stella . . . Suddenly the door opens and she's standing there, in cut-off ripped jeans, her dark hair piled on top of her head, friendship bracelets around both wrists, and I wonder who gave them to her, where she's been in life and who's been there for her. She's so like Marco. Wild, impetuous, impulsive Stella.

'Thought you might like some help,' she says, without pleasantries. There's a murmur among the young men, and a young woman executive.

'*Grazie mille.*' I smile at her, and she walks through the group, coming to stand by me.

'Welcome to La Tavola,' I begin, and the room hushes. 'Here at La Tavola, everyone is welcome. We treat everyone with respect, kindness and understanding. It's where we gather to support each other, because eating is about so much more than just the food we put on the table. It's about the experience and the people we share it with.'

'No, no! You've taken my flour!' I hear from the kitchen. 'Yours is over there!'

'You moved it!'

'I didn't move it, silly woman!'

Stella and I smile.

'I think it's time you met your tutors for the weekend,' I say. Stella and I lead them into the kitchen, where flour is flying everywhere. 'This is *la cucina*, the kitchen, where you will cook with your tutors, work together and prepare dinner for each other. As I say' – I try to keep a straight face, but struggle – 'it's all about working together.'

'*Buongiorno*,' say the three *nonna*s politely, boldly riding out their appearance: they have flour all over themselves, their hair, over their aprons and on their bottoms, where they've wiped their hands.

'Perhaps you should introduce yourselves and split into three teams,' I suggest.

'This is going to be amazing!' Sebastian whispers, from where he's standing behind me. I can feel his breath on my neck. It's not unpleasant. In fact, it's quite nice. 'Good job, Theally. I knew this weekend would be the real deal with you behind it. You always did give a hundred and ten per cent! Real *nonna*s.' He chortles. 'Inspired!'

'I'm Walt, here for the wine,' says tall, blond, good-looking Walt. 'And the ladies.' He looks at Stella, who doesn't return his smile, and gives him her resting bitch face, which seems to pour cold water on his over-confidence as intended.

'You can be with me, Walt. We are making panzanella. With ripe tomatoes, cucumber and bread. Smell!' Nonna Teresa thrusts a tomato under Walt's nose. 'It will be the best you've ever had.'

'It will be the best if he makes it and not Teresa!' says Nonna Rosa, and the room laughs. Walt goes to stand by Nonna Teresa.

'I'm Daisy, also here for the ladies.' She gives Stella a smile and gets the same resting bitch face. She gives Walt a look – there's clearly rivalry between them.

'I'm thinking you two should be together,' I say.

'No, no, not a good idea,' they respond. 'That'll never work.'

'I'd be better on desserts,' says Daisy.

'Okay, but tomorrow you'll all be swapping around,' I say, and make a note to put those two together and watch the flour fly between them. I glance at Sebastian, who clearly knows what I'm thinking and grins.

'I'm Charlie, here for the eating.' He's in a T-shirt, long shorts, straw trilby and sunglasses. He rubs his wobbly tummy and the group laugh.

'You come with me. I'll make sure you are never hungry,' says Nonna Lucia, pulling him into her team.

'Glenda,' says a woman with glasses, her hair tied back. She's in a suit and smart trainers and is clearly hot. 'Here because I was told to be! And I can't afford the time away from my desk.'

Eventually each *nonna* has two team members. Just Sebastian is left.

'You can work with Stella and me,' I say. 'We're on *antipasti*.'

'My favourite.' He smiles and it feels nice. He rolls up his sleeves, and the rest of the groups are being given a flurry of instructions.

We're standing side by side in the kitchen while Stella gets the *antipasti* ingredients from the pantry, the sunlight streaming in through the window and the sounds of the children in the courtyard. I suddenly feel completely at peace.

'It's nice to see you again, Seb,' I find myself saying.

'It's nice to be here, Theally.' I glance up in time to see the *nonna*s, no matter that they're busy, give each other a look.

31

'I hope you save some for us.' Giovanni smiles as he arrives in the cool of the dining room, just as we're all finding seats and laying out the *antipasti*.

'Of course!' Stella turns quickly to the dresser for cutlery and plates, and lays an extra three places at the table for him, Alessandro and Enrico, who makes a beeline for Caterina and sits next to her. I notice how keen Stella is to be a part of this. I wonder what Marco would have made of it. I wonder how it would have been if he'd been here.

But I know how he would feel: he'd be proud. He'd want Stella to be part of the family. It would have been so much easier if he was here. But he's not. It's just me. It's not Stella's fault, although from the sound of it she hasn't made it easy for people to get close to her. She's grieving too, I remind myself. She's lost the father she never had, twice. Once when she'd never met him, and now when she'd hoped to get to know him.

'Sit, sit!' Nonna Lucia is on her feet.

'Eat, *mangiamo*,' Nonna Rosa says, from the other end of the table.

'Try my *primo*, panzanella salad,' says Nonna Teresa 'It is very good. I had good students.' She smiles at the pair she was matched with. 'Very attentive.'

'You must learn to relax.' Nonna Rosa pats Glenda's arm. 'Food is a serious business, but you have to be relaxed to do it at its best,' I hear her say. Glenda takes another slug of wine and slides off her jacket, hanging on Nonna Rosa's every word.

'Sebastian, some more salad?' Nonna Teresa offers.

'I'll be too full for the *secondo*,' laughs Sebastian, as she ignores him and loads his plate. I can't help smiling. Sebastian, kind, thoughtful and steady, I think.

Nonna Teresa leans into me. 'You look to be enjoying yourself. Something tells me you may be ready to find love again. Let someone into your life to share it.'

'What? *Scusi?*' I clear my throat. 'I'm not . . .' I hadn't realized I was thinking about Sebastian in that way.

'I think you may be. Time moves on. Why not think about love again?'

Giovanni smiles at me from the other end of the table, helping himself to the salad.

I try to clear my tight throat. Is that what I was thinking about? Finding love. I never thought I'd ever consider it. I thought it would be just me and the children, who are enjoying their new-found friendships, and chatting with the students. Everyone is mixing, everyone welcome. What would a new future look like if I was with someone again? I take a sneaky look at Sebastian, who has clearly charmed Nonna Teresa. Would I be happy? Would the children? He's a good man, solid, dependable. I look again at Giovanni, who is being fussed over by Nonna Lucia.

Maybe there is another chance of happiness for me. A different life, without Marco in it. It would have to be completely different.

I regard the chattering, laughing table, and Giovanni is looking at me from the far end. My stomach flips over and back again. Oh, no . . . Definitely not that. I put down my wine. What was I thinking? The children and I are fine as we are. I don't need to be with anyone else. I'm absolutely fine. I gulp my water. There is no way I can go to a man who is just like Marco, who even called me *cara*. I can't work in a kitchen with a partner again. I can't go back there.

Sebastian refills my wine glass.

'Thank you,' I say.

'You're welcome.'

We clear away the *secondo*. Nonna Rosa is enjoying the compliments on her tortelli, filled with mashed potato, garlic and spinach and served in a rich tomato sauce, comforting and very tasty. When the plates have been wiped clean with chunks of bread and cleared away, Stella and Aimee carry through the bowls for dessert. Pietro and Luca are laughing, as they seem to be most of the time, these days.

I'm keeping my head down, confused by what happened to me when I looked along the table. The memory of what it was like to fall in love. My mind's playing tricks on me. It's being here, with memories of Marco, while Sebastian is staying too. I'm happy on my own. I have the children to consider. I should be thinking about them, not about life with Sebastian before I met Marco, and what might have been if I hadn't met him. Or what life might be like with Sebastian, now we're older, wiser, enjoying a comfortable partnership. Someone to share meals with. A sunset. A crossword clue.

Now I'm sounding really old. I smile to myself.

'Just like the old times.' Sebastian is standing next to me at the sink, looking out at the setting sun, holding a pile of plates from the table.

And for a moment, it's how it feels, just like old times, when crowds of us would go out for long dinners after work. Only then there weren't children to get up for, or an empty bank account, or the continual worry about what to do next that dogged me, my feet paddling like a duck's under water, as I tried to keep us afloat.

'It's a lifetime ago,' I say to Sebastian, as he puts down the plates.

'Not to me it isn't, Thea,' he says softly. 'Seems like yesterday.'

My cheeks colour. I stare into the sink and try to come up with a means of escape from the conversation. I need time to think. Is he saying what I think he's saying? Maybe we could . . .

Nonna Teresa's words ring in my ears.

I grab more dessert bowls from the work surface and spin towards the dining room, right into Giovanni, who is clutching two wine jugs for refilling.

'Woah!' he says, and laughs as I career straight into him. Immediately I remember his smile and look back at the table, at something we had created here this evening, something to be proud of, like Marco did with family meals in the restaurant, when we made the time.

I look back at Sebastian and, my thoughts spinning and twisting like the Waltzers ride at the fair, I smile and he smiles at me. It seems like a safe place. One in which I know I won't get hurt. Maybe it's a place I could revisit, if I was going to dip my toe into the dating pool . . . maybe.

32

The following morning, after a warm, restless night, I'm in the kitchen at Casa Luna, putting the coffee on before Giovanni arrives. As soon as he's here, I want to go straight up to La Tavola. For some reason, I'm keen not to spend time alone with him. Something inside me has shifted. I don't know what it is, but a wall has crumbled and light is coming in: a possibility, a chink of a new life, the other side of the grief. A possibility of finding comfort in Sebastian's company maybe. Back to where I was when life was mapped out. A safe and comfortable place to land.

I feed the kitten by the back door and stroke him as I breathe in the morning air, as welcome as the first cup of coffee.

'*Buongiorno.*' I jump at the sound of his voice, which is ridiculous because I was expecting him and he's letting himself in, as he has done every morning since he started putting Casa Luna back together for me. What on earth is wrong with you? I ask myself. But Marco is no longer in the house and I no longer feel like his widow. I'm Thea, a single woman with children, and that's a very different landscape, a shifting one, as the sun rises slower in the sky, the heat not so intense. Summer will soon be retreating to make way for autumn. Nothing stays the same for ever. Everything changes. Like the seasons, time moves on.

'Okay, I have to go,' I say, wiping the work surfaces needlessly – I've already done them half a dozen times. 'I'm going up to La Tavola to check everything is cleared away and get ready for tonight.'

'La Tavola will be fine. Everyone helped tidy up last night.' Giovanni chuckles. 'Have a coffee.'

'No, really, I should go.'

'Thea, I'm grateful to you for making this weekend happen, but I don't want you to run yourself into the ground.'

He takes hold of my shoulders and my nerve endings are standing to attention, like sparklers that have just been lit. 'You should take some time to enjoy what you've done.'

He's right. I can't go back to how I was when Marco and I had the restaurant, the pressure it put on us, and we put on ourselves. I can't lose myself in the kitchen again. I can't do that to the children.

'Sit. Let me pour the coffee. I'll join you outside.'

I do as I'm told.

'The boys will be here soon,' he says, carrying two cups of strong coffee to the little table outside where the garden is looking trimmed and ready for some love. When we arrived, it was a jungle of long grass. Now the grass is short, there's the swing and the kitten is lazily swiping at a passing butterfly.

I breathe in deeply. There's that feeling again, which has been constant since the day I got here. It's a cocktail of the earth warming up, the cobwebs glistening with dew, and the scent of coffee drifting on a passing breeze. I hold my face to the sun and the breeze, loving what they bring to the party, the sun for its warmth, the breeze for the fragrances it carries, printing this place on my mind. A memory of it. A memory of when life turned a corner for me. I'm not going home the same Thea who came here, still with images of Marco everywhere. I'm going home with Marco as part of my past, but with the possibility of a future, maybe with someone else in it.

Giovanni sits next to me at the table, gazing out over the rolling hills. 'So, the cookery course is going well.'

'Better than I could have expected, really,' I say, breathing in the coffee. 'And the house, will it be ready in time?'

He nods. 'Don't worry. A big push over this weekend and we'll meet your deadline.'

'Two years exactly,' I say. 'From the moment he

bought it. Two years from when he died.' There's a pause when we're both lost in our thoughts. It's Giovanni who speaks first but doesn't look at me.

'So Sebastian. Seems like a nice man.'

'He is.'

'You worked together,' he says, rather than asks.

I nod. 'I didn't realize he'd be coming when I booked the company in.'

'You didn't say that Sebastian was an ex . . .'

We're staring straight ahead, looking out over the early morning mist rolling around the undulating fields and around the trees.

'Yes. How did you . . . ?'

'Just got a feeling last night. Unfinished business.' He sips his coffee, his leg slung casually over his knee. 'And Nonna Teresa told me.'

'Well, yes. We were together. But it didn't work out. You know how it is.'

'Yes. You could say that. Part of why I ended up out here. My . . . partner didn't like the hours I worked. She didn't like the amount of time I spent at the restaurant. In a way, she was jealous of the time I was there. She didn't understand how hard I was working to try to make it in that world. Trying to climb the ladder, to get the chef's attention. People scrambled over each other to get his approval.'

His fist, resting on the table next to his coffee cup, suddenly clenches.

'And the burn on your hand?' I ask.

He rubs it with the other as if back there, in the moment. 'A new boy's initiation. Kitchen life can be brutal.'

I turn to him. 'That's awful!'

'It is. And then you find yourself doing anything to stand up to these guys, get one over, be better. You eat sitting on the floor. Sleep hardly at all, live off cigarettes and anything else you can get your hands on to keep going, stay awake, alert.'

'And your partner?'

He shakes his head. 'I decided I'd had enough of kitchens, living with the other kitchen rats. It was no life. So I gave notice and went home early to find her in bed with someone else. A kitchen colleague of mine. He was on a day off.'

'I . . . I'm sorry.' That's all I can think to say, unable to imagine the betrayal.

'And then I needed to get out, get away. I packed a bag and hit the road, working for various builders on the way to make money. It was like cooking. Following instructions. Measuring, mixing, spreading. I caught on quickly. One job led to another . . . until I found myself making my way through Europe and landed here. I didn't plan it. I didn't want to go back to Rome where my family were from. No one was left there. By the time I got here, I had no idea who I was or where I was going. I was in the middle of a thick fog. But, gradually, I found the sort of peace I needed. The *nonna*s fed me, and sat with me when I needed it. That was when I decided to stay and repay them. Once the mist lifted, I saw it wasn't food I'd fallen out of love with but kitchen life. Fine dining. Food is much more than something pretty on the plate.'

'It is,' I agree. 'It's somewhere safe,' I find myself saying. 'It was the glue that held Marco and me together, but things started to unravel when the bills went up. Then Marco died and meals were the last thing on my mind. Just making the business wash its face was all that mattered. Until I couldn't any more. But, here, the glue has started to stick us together again as a family.'

He nods and we look out, the church bells ringing.

'I should get off,' I say. 'We need to go to market to buy the pizza topping ingredients for tonight. I have the minibus coming.'

We stand up close to each other, as if a bit of the wall between us has been chipped away. And then he says, 'Is Sebastian going?'

'To the market? I think so. Why?'

He smiles. 'Just . . .' He pauses.

'What?'

'Have a nice time. Enjoy it. You deserve it.'

I stop in my tracks. Was he going to say something else? Or does he mean it? As if he's read my mind, he says, 'Take some time to soak up the sun and catch up. We're nearly done here,' he says. 'We should be finished. You can just put your finishing touches on it.'

'Giovanni . . . I . . .' He turns to me. Why do I feel the atmosphere between us has changed? Something has shifted: where my wall has crumbled, he's building his up again.

There's a knock at the door, and Alessandro arrives with Enrico. They let themselves in.

'*Buongiorno*, Thea,' Alessandro smiles.

'*Buongiorno*, Alessandro.' I smile back.

'You're going to the market?' he asks politely.

'Yes. And tonight there will be pizza!'

'I love pizza!'

'Then I will make sure you have one all to yourself,' I say.

'*Grazie mille!*' and he sets to work, whistling.

'He'll like that,' says Giovanni. 'He and his brother are doing really well. It's just them and their *nonna*. It's good for him to have fun and not feel responsible for her all the time. For Enrico too . . . It's good he can spend time feeling like a young man, not a parent and carer.'

La Tavola is about so much more than just food on a plate.

I head for the door, then turn back to Giovanni. He looks up at me at the same time.

'See you tonight for pizza!' He grins. 'Hopefully the

house will be done by the time you get back. You'll be ready to sell.'

'*Grazie*,' I say, and there's a pause. I pick up my basket and turn to leave.

'Thea,' he says, 'I should be saying thank you to you. You have saved La Tavola.'

'For now,' I say.

'Yes, for now. And that is all we have. The here and now. And we should grab those chances when they come along.' I wonder if he's talking about La Tavola or possibly Sebastian.

I stare at him, as if something has been lost between us.

'Come on, children,' I call upstairs. 'Time to go to the market.'

The market, although quite a drive away along narrow country roads, bumpy and uneven, is everything I hoped it would be. As a group we wander the streets, perusing the stalls in the slightly less punishing heat. It's bearable, like a warm bath that you want to wallow in. We choose cold meats, mozzarella from a local farmer, who tells us where his farm is and the process for making the cheese, bags of olives and glistening anchovies.

With the shopping for the pizzas in bulging bags, we go our separate ways to look around the clothes stalls and kitchenware. Tablecloths hang and ripple in the lightest of breezes. Handbags, scarves and brightly coloured underwear are piled next to overalls, and a shoe stall is heaped with stilettos and slippers.

'This has been wonderful,' says Sebastian, walking next to me as the children hurry off in search of *gelati*.

'It's certainly seems to be turning out how I wanted it to. I'm glad I could set this up before I leave.'

'Will that be soon?' he asks.

I find myself sighing. 'Not long. The house is ready to go on the market. I needed to get it sorted and ready to sell. And I need to be back for the children to start school again.'

'I was thinking, Theally ... Is there a chance we could meet up when you're home?'

'I ...' Part of me is terrified, but another is excited. A future, moving forwards. Suddenly life seems full of possibilities, maybe even love, and a shiver runs up and down my spine. 'Maybe that would be nice,' I say, doing exactly what Giovanni told me to do, relaxing and enjoying this time.

'Just take it gently, do some of the things we used to enjoy doing together? We could go back to that pub on the Thames, near Richmond.'

'Where we got stranded in the beer garden when the water flooded it?'

'And we had to wait it out until it receded . . .'

We laugh.

'Or fish and chips at the coast.'

'There's a water theme here.'

'Actually, I'm thinking of moving there.'

'Where?'

'West Wales, where we spent Christmas in the cottage.'

'When the heating wouldn't work and we just had the wood-burner to keep us warm.'

'Yes, by the sea. I loved it there.'

'It was beautiful, if cold! But if you're thinking of moving there, does that mean . . . ?'

He nods. 'I'm leaving the company. I've done my time. I've put enough away. I want a new beginning while there's still time. It was thinking about you that showed me what I wanted, when I read about your idea for the cooking school here. I know that marrying Elizabeth, after you and I finished, was a mistake. But I tried to make it work. Somehow, though, however hard I tried, I was never going to be good enough. You were brave enough to realize what you wanted . . . and what you didn't.' He looks at me with a sad expression, like the young man he was back then. Just thinner hair and lines, as we pass a couple of noisy market-sellers, shouting over each other to catch buyers' attention.

I did know. I knew as soon as I met Marco that life was never going to be the same. It was a roller-coaster of a ride. But now?

'How about coffee?' I point to an outdoor table and

chairs. The children are nearby with their *gelati*, and a couple of students pull up seats beside them.

'This might seem like I'm taking a leaf out of your book, grabbing life when I can, but . . . I wondered if there might be another chance for you and me, and the children too, of course.'

At the next table, the children are playing Rock, Scissors, Paper with Walt and Glenda, who has let her hair down, quite literally, and is wearing a baggy shirt that may or may not be one of Walt's.

'It's . . . certainly something to think about.' I can't give an answer there and then. 'I don't know how I'd feel about that yet.'

'Of course not. Sorry, just got caught up in the heat of it all, so to speak.' He takes off his hat and wipes his brow. 'Silly of me, rushing in like that. I wanted to be impulsive. Go for what you want!'

'And we should. If I've learnt nothing else over the past couple of years, it's that there are no certainties in life. We have to go with what will make us happy in the here and now. Forget coffee. Let's have something stronger!'

Once again I think of Giovanni, encouraging me to enjoy myself. And I am. I could do this more often, I think, sipping the Aperol Spritz I've ordered, while Sebastian has a beer. I've come a long way in the last year or so and I'm finally climbing out of a black hole into the sunshine and it feels very good – very good indeed.

'Really, I didn't mean to rush at that. I feel clumsy, just wanted to grab the moment.'

'I know. And thank you.'

'Just think about it,' he says gently. 'It could be a very happy solution for both of us.'

And isn't that what I want, what I've wanted all this time, just to be happy and content again? For life's roller-coaster to slow down and turn into a scenic train ride, rocking through pleasing countryside?

'Just think about it. I'll say no more.'

'I will, Seb,' I say, and sip my drink, wishing I could stay in this moment, enjoying the what-if. What if I did?

33

Back at Casa Luna, Giovanni and the boys are clearing up. The house is finished.

'It looks . . . amazing!' I say, dazzled by the blank-canvas white walls, ready to have the new owner's personal touches added when someone buys it. I run my hands over the newly painted window frames. The light is pouring in. And now that just the essential furniture is in here, not all of the stuff that littered the place when we arrived, it feels airy and much bigger.

'Just these last few chairs and the table to take up to La Tavola, if you're still happy for that?' says Giovanni.

'Yes,' I say. 'We could use them tonight, eat outside. What do you think?'

'Perfect.'

Summer is coming to an end, like my time here. The

257

house has had a facelift and is ready for a new begin-ning. For new hopes and dreams.

We leave the house, Enrico and I each picking up a chair while Giovanni and Alessandro carry the table between them. At La Tavola we arrange them under the big olive tree.

'I made more bunting,' says Caterina, 'from the old clothes at Casa Luna, and cushions!' Stella is there, admiring Caterina's handiwork.

'Oh, wow! That's fantastic!' I say, fingering the lovely cushions. 'Let's get this place looking its best.' Right now, I could do with the distraction rather than contemplating Sebastian and his suggestion. But it's there, turning over in the back of my mind as we all work together to string the bunting across the courtyard and arrange tables, can-dles stuck into bottles, Stella taking charge. How proud Marco would have been. I'm doing everything I can not to think about Sebastian and his offer, though I know I should, when suddenly he's there, in the courtyard.

'This looks amazing!' he says, gazing at the bunting strung from the olive tree.

'It does,' I say, with a sense of shared pride in the place.

'Hey!' says Giovanni. 'Good time at the market?'

'Great,' Sebastian answers. 'I thought I'd come over and give you a hand setting up for this evening. The youngsters are sitting by the pool, having a siesta. Thought I could make myself useful.'

'You certainly can,' says Giovanni. 'We have a few more tables and chairs to bring up from Casa Luna.'

'Of course,' says Sebastian. 'Happy to help.' He smiles at me and I smile back. Giovanni gives me the merest wink, making my insides flip, which isn't helping me make my decision.

Giovanni directs Sebastian out of the gate.

'So, you and Thea were once together?' I hear Giovanni say. 'It's great you have stayed good friends.' And I have no idea why he's asking.

'Yes, before she dumped me, went off with the massively more charismatic Marco and gave up the life we'd planned . . . I guess the four-bed house, the Labrador and skiing holidays just weren't tempting enough – or the pensions and yearly bonuses.' He laughs but I can hear regret in it.

Is that what I could have again? Is this my second chance at life, to give the children a fresh start and a stable life. Maybe it is. Maybe coming here, setting up the cookery school, was all part of the journey to take me back to a more settled way of life with Sebastian, in Wales, by the sea. Seeing the children settling into a new school and home, where I'm not always rushing, juggling childcare arrangements and crying into my pillow at night, wishing Marco was still there. I need to talk to Sebastian, see if he really thinks we could make it work. And I should talk to the children, but maybe, I think, with a smile, this is exactly what we need to do. Sebastian, the children and I, a new beginning for us all. Another thought strikes me: what about Stella? What will happen to her after we leave? Where will she go?

As the afternoon wears on, La Tavola gets busy and it's a good feeling. Alessandro's brother Enrico is there, helping Caterina pick the tomatoes from the hanging baskets outside for dinner.

The three *nonna*s arrive, ready to make pizza dough. Giovanni is showing off his pizza-throwing skills to the delight of the children and Walt, who insists they have a dough-throwing competition, 'Just to make things really interesting.'

The outdoor pizza oven is lit. Smoke billows out of the chimney as it gets started and Giovanni feeds the fire with wood.

Then the table outside is laid. Everyone joins in, the children, the students, Francesco and Giuseppe. The *nonna*s issue the instructions and we carry them out. For once, they seem to be singing from the same song sheet. Glasses of wine are handed around, bowls of glistening olives, coated in olive oil and dried wild herbs, and the late-afternoon air is heating up rather than cooling down. The courtyard is filling and every time I think to take Sebastian to one side, something distracts me. Fun and happiness are filling the air, which feels heavier by the moment.

Pizzas are cooked on the open fire, everyone taking

a turn to be *pizzaiolo* under Giovanni's guidance. There are triumphs and disasters as we all applaud the varying degrees of success. We raise a glass to all of the chefs as the pizzas are placed on the tables under the olive tree, where the bunting is swinging enthusiastically in the wind that has picked up. The candles flicker and blow out but, regardless, spirits at La Tavola are rising.

'This is the best team-building weekend I've ever been on,' says Sebastian, sitting next to me. 'Really brilliant!' He beams.

'Thank you,' I say. 'I've actually enjoyed it. I didn't know if I would. I haven't had the heart to go anywhere near a kitchen since Marco died. But here, at La Tavola, I seem to have made peace with kitchens and hospitality. This place has a way of working its magic.'

'I can see that.'

And I wonder if I could let myself fall back in love with him. After all, I was in love with him once. What if we could find that again? The wind whips up and more candles go out, leaving just the tea lights in the jam jars on the tables and hanging from the branches of the olive tree among the bunting.

'Pizza,' says Walt, passing another – hot, freshly made – down the table. It smells delicious. Golden, semolina-dusted base, bubbling around the edge, with richly seasoned tomato sauce, topped with oozing, stringy mozzarella, a shower of Parmesan and freshly ripped basil leaves. Some have shreds of salami, shining with spicy red oil, and a scattering of olives. Others have artichoke hearts and caramelized red peppers from the market. The selection is as varied as the people gathered around the table at La Tavola.

We pass pizzas between us and bowls of salad. Everyone is helping themselves and others to the food, topping up plates with extra slices or spoonfuls of greenery. Glasses are refreshed with wine, water for the younger ones. Everyone is smiling and I haven't been so happy in a very long time.

Giovanni is sitting next to Glenda, who is staring at him adoringly as he laughs. I feel something I haven't experienced in a long time, a little stab of . . . jealousy.

'So, if you were thinking about it at all, I thought we could set the wheels in motion, so to speak.'

'Sorry, Seb, I wasn't . . .' I shake myself out of whatever I was thinking. He looks down the table to where my eyes were fixed and back at me. 'Tell me, what were you saying?'

He takes a deep breath. 'I was—'

'Actually . . .' I stop him. It's me that needs to take action. Do what Giovanni says, enjoy the moment. Live for the now '. . . I've been thinking about what you were saying, Seb.'

He smiles tentatively. 'And?'

'And . . .' Suddenly I'm feeling really hot. Perhaps Marco is looking out for me, bringing Sebastian here. No, that's mumbo-jumbo. But this is a very good option for me and the children. Press reset and go back to life before Marco. The wind is blowing up. There is a strong smell of soil and the ground warming—

A huge thunderclap crashes overhead, accompanied by a flash of lightning. Everyone jumps and some scream. And then, as if someone was throwing huge handfuls of water, raindrops are falling.

We jump up, grab plates and cushions, as people start to run inside La Tavola, Stella shouting instructions. Pietro and Luca are helping the *nonna*s to their feet. Aimee is guiding Francesco, who doesn't know which way to go.

'Get everyone inside, kids,' Stella shouts, and they do as she says.

Another crack opens up overhead and a huge electric flash lights the sky.

'Grab the rest of the cushions,' calls Giovanni to me.

Bottles holding candles fall over and begin to roll. We see one heading towards the edge of the table and make a dive for it. The rain is pelting down, so my eyes are screwed up against it. We grab the bottle.

'I've got it!'

'Got it!'

Our hands collide and there might almost have been streak of lightning, though not in the sky. We stand still, holding the bottle, rain pounding down on us, our breath fast and furious, the water seeping into our clothes, which are clinging to our bodies. I can feel a pull like I haven't felt in a long time, dragging my body, thrusting me against him, and we're there, alone, in the courtyard, the rain hammering down on us. The only thing I can see is him. The only thing I can feel is his closeness. The only thing I can hear is his heavy breathing and the sound of my heart pounding in my chest.

There's another clap of thunder and more lightning.

'*Mamma!* Hurry!' It's Luca, calling me in.

'I have to go,' I say, my feet not moving. I see him nod. One hand brushing the water from his face, the other grabbing my free hand and holding it as we run together into La Tavola's dining room where the candles have been lit. Everyone is wet, but laughing.

'*Gelato!*' calls Nonna Lucia to cheers.

I look at Giovanni, rivulets of water running down his face, both of us breathing heavily, then laughing. All three *nonna*s are staring at us, and I feel I've taken a very different direction from the one I was travelling in hardly any time ago.

Someone puts on some music, bowls of homemade *gelato* are passed around, and now the tables, under Stella's guidance, are being pushed back and there is dancing while the storm whips around outside. Giovanni grabs me for a dance, before he's hijacked by Glenda, to his surprise and my amusement, and Sebastian steps in to dance with me. It's fun, but it's not magnetic. It's not how I felt with Giovanni, and I'm not sure I could settle for living without that sensation.

By the time the minibus comes to take the students back to their villa, the storm has passed, and everywhere outside is soggy and wet. We hear the toot from the driver on the square and show the students out.

Sebastian is beside me as we step out of the gates and walk up towards the main square. 'We were interrupted, before the storm came,' he says. 'You were about to tell me what you thought of my suggestion. Hopefully what I'd like to hear.'

I open my mouth to speak when Nonna Lucia is suddenly between the two of us.

'It has been a wonderful day,' she says, linking arms with Sebastian. 'I am so looking forward to tomorrow. We have so much to prepare for Sunday's lunch. Promise you'll be on my team, Sebastian,' she says, flirting outrageously.

'I saw him first! I have seen how he can stir sauce. I will have him for my team,' says Nonna Rosa.

'We should take it in turns,' says Nonna Teresa, coming up the hill. 'He can choose whose team he wants to be on.'

Sebastian is evidently bemused, almost scared. I can't help laughing as they escort him to the minibus waiting there.

'*Grazie*, Leonardo!' I wave to the driver. 'Join us for lunch tomorrow.'

He waves and nods.

'See you tomorrow,' I say to Sebastian, as he's escorted to the steps by the *nonna*s.

He attempts to kiss my cheek but misses and kisses my ear.

'Oh, sorry, sorry,' I say, embarrassed. 'We'll see you tomorrow.' I step back, flanked by the *nonna*s and wave as everyone pours onto the minibus.

As it leaves, we turn and wander down the hill towards La Tavola.

'Would anyone like a drink? I think you deserve one. A limoncello, perhaps, ladies?'

'That sounds lovely,' I say. The children are playing with the kitten and Stella in the courtyard, in and around the puddles left there from the storm.

'No, no. I'm very tired,' says Nonna Teresa, stretching and yawning.

'I would love some limoncello!' says Nonna Lucia.

'No, we have a big day tomorrow. You need your beauty sleep!'

'But—'

'Believe me, you need it!' says Nonna Rosa, nudging her.

Nonna Lucia looks from her to Nonna Teresa. 'Ah, yes . . . of course. My beauty sleep!'

'You two, enjoy!' says Nonna Rosa. She stops and turns back. 'It was a very good day,' she says, and a brief smile illumines her usually stern, lined face.

'Can I walk you home?' Giovanni calls after her.

'No, we'll be fine!' she says, linking arms with the other two *nonna*s and they walk down the narrow cobbled street together, bouncing off each other's hips, heads together, deep in conversation.

'Don't worry, I'll see they get home,' says Stella, hurrying after them, making me smile.

I breathe in the night air.

'So, limoncello?' Giovanni asks.

'I'd love that.'

We step into the courtyard where the bunting is sodden and the jars hanging from the tree are filled with water.

'Shame about the weather,' I say.

He laughs as we head back into the kitchen. 'They had the full Tuscan experience!' He takes a bottle of limoncello from the dresser and pours two glasses. 'It was good to see Stella here tonight,' he says, putting the bottle on the table and handing me a glass.

'It was.' I accept it from him. I can smell the lemons before I've tasted it. I take a sip of the sweet, zingy liqueur.

'And they seemed to have enjoyed it?' he says.

'I'm sure they'll want to book more events. Luca's filmed some of the workshops so we can make a reel and put it on social media. You'll be inundated with students –work outings, hen weekends, big celebration birthdays . . .'

He looks down. '*Grazie*, Thea.'

'No, thank you, Giovanni. Now I have a house I can sell.'

He sips. 'And you and Sebastian, you have made a connection again?'

I stop mid-sip, in the simple orange glow of the under-cupboard lights in the kitchen.

'Yes . . . It's . . . good to see him again.'

'And he is very pleased to see you. He told me you and he were together before you married your husband.'

'Yes, we were. A lifetime ago!'

We fall into a silence.

And then, 'And now?'

I swallow the limoncello.

'Seems he would like you back in his life.' He tilts his head.

'He said as much.'

'And what are you thinking?'

'I . . . I don't know.'

'It's good to have people in your life to love you, isn't it?'

'It is.'

'It's what we all want? No?'

He's right. 'He's a kind man, I can see that.'

'He is.'

'And what about you?' I ask.

He lets out a long sigh. 'I know I don't want to go back to where I was, who I was, who I was with. This place has been good to me. But who knows? Maybe it's not the end of the journey.'

'*Mamma*, can we go to bed now? Snowy is sleepy,' says Aimee, coming in with the kitten under an arm.

'Of course, sweetheart.' I stand up and, as I do, Stella arrives back at La Tavola. 'All safe and sound,' she says and, with her free arm, Aimee clasps her waist.

'You were great today, Stella,' I say. 'Really great. You have a career in hospitality if you want one. Although it's a hard life,' I add.

'I enjoyed it,' she says, beside Aimee, her hands on my daughter's shoulders.

'Can you tuck me into bed?' says Aimee, gazing up at her pleadingly, and Stella looks at me.

'It's getting late,' she says, surprising me. From what I've experienced of Stella so far, she acts first, asks later. 'Maybe another night, if it's okay with your *mamma*.'

'Is it, *Mamma*?'

'Of course!'

'Er . . . where are you staying, Stella?'

She waggles her head from side to side. 'I'm sofa-surfing right now.'

I frown, wondering again what will happen to her when we go. 'But you must have had somewhere to live when you were here.'

'I did.' She raises an eyebrow.

'Of course! You were staying at Casa Luna.'

She lifts an eyebrow. 'I said I'd keep an eye on it for Marco. Be an unpaid caretaker, so to speak. Just until he got back . . .' She trails off.

'And now?' I say.

She shrugs. 'I'm not sure. Back to sofa-surfing, I guess. I'll be fine.'

Although it was never Stella's house, for a time it was her home. A place to come back to, anchoring her. And now it's gone. The estate agent will be here tomorrow. And I'm worried about where she will go, despite her assurances that she'll be fine.

Aimee yawns. 'We'd better go,' I say.

'*Buonanotte, Aimee*,' says Stella, bending to kiss her on each cheek.

'*Buonanotte*,' Aimee says, and I do too. Stella ruffles Luca's hair. He pulls away from her, laughing. Then he and Pietro perform an extravagant handshake and hug, making me smile.

'*Buonanotte*,' I say, to Giovanni, who smiles, making my stomach flip in a way that Sebastian doesn't. I wish he did . . .

34

'Ping!' It's a text the following morning, from Giovanni, making my stomach flip again,. Why can't Sebastian do that? He's asking me to meet him early at La Tavola.

I push open the wooden gate and move into the small courtyard. The bunting from last night has already dried out and is looking much perkier. The smell of pizza hangs in the air. The morning is fresher, not so intense. Clearer and cleaner somehow.

I walk across the courtyard to the kitchen door. It's ajar. I open it wide.

'*Ciao?*' I call. But I can't see anyone. '*Ciao?*'

A table is laid just outside the kitchen door at the back of the building with just enough space for two.

'Giovanni, are you there? Did you want to talk to me?'

On the table there is a coffee pot, with a basket of bread, freshly squeezed orange juice and a small jug of olive branches and rosemary, smelling lovely.

'Hello? Giovanni?' I call up the stairs to his apartment. By the bottom of the stairs I notice a rucksack. I'm assuming it's Stella's and my heart twists.

'Hey, *ciao*,' he says, coming through the front gate and lightly kissing me on both cheeks. 'I got your message.'

'Oh, hey,' I say, not sure which one. I'm confused as I'd sent only a quick reply to his.

'Just out for his walk.' He gestures towards Bello.

'Ah. How's Stella?' I ask.

'Still asleep on my sofa when I last looked.'

A wave of guilt washes over me again. What will happen to her once we go? We won't be here. The house will sell.

'So,' he says, glancing at the back door and then at the little table for two, 'this looks nice.'

'Doesn't it?' I say, wondering why he would go to so much effort, wondering what he wants to tell me.

'Shall we?' He holds out a hand to the wrought-iron table and chairs.

We sit. The coffee in the pot is hot and suddenly I'm as nervous as if I was on a date.

'Here.' I switch into hosting mode and pour coffee for us both, the sun warming our faces as it rises. He's smiling – and it's as if a thunderbolt has struck me.

I pass him his coffee, as well as I can with a shaking hand.

He offers me the basket of bread and I take a piece, feeling anything but hungry.

'Good marmalade,' he says. He sniffs it. 'I think it's Nonna Teresa's.'

I could have sworn I heard a rustle from the kitchen, perhaps the storeroom.

'It was kind of you to do this,' he says. 'You didn't need to thank me. I've already told you, it's me who should be thanking you. With the money from this weekend, La Tavola should be able to keep going for a good while longer. And if we can run more of these weekends . . .'

'I – I didn't do this.'

He laughs. 'Well, whoever you got to do it, it was kind of you and unnecessary.'

'No, really, you texted me!'

He stops spooning marmalade from its little terra-cotta pot onto his plate, still smiling his lazy, lopsided smile . . . He frowns and puts down his knife. 'Only to say I'd meet you, replying to you.'

He looks sideways and the other way.

Something feels amiss. Giovanni hadn't asked to meet me. And I was excited that maybe he wanted to talk to me about something other than the house or La Tavola. How stupid am I? What else is there to talk about?

Does he still think I'm going with Sebastian? Considering returning to the UK to live by the sea with my two children, three stepchildren and a black Labrador called Bert?

'You did text me to talk to me, didn't you?' I say slowly.

He shakes his head. 'You texted me!'

We narrow our eyes and, suddenly, hear a sneeze.

And a load of shushing, followed by a very quiet 'Bless you.'

We stare at each other, then jump out of our seats, abandoning the coffee and bread in the sun. We run into the kitchen and pull open the pantry door where everyone is hugging and kissing and smiling.

'It was Pietro! He spoke!' says Caterina, with tears in her eyes.

'Pietro, was that you?' Giovanni grins widely.

'Bless you,' he repeats, and we all hug him in the cold confines of the pantry, tears now rolling down Caterina's face.

'It'll be okay. We have hope,' she says, and I can feel tears forming in my eyes as I hug her.

And when we stop hugging, and sniffing: 'It's time you all came out of the pantry now, isn't it?'

They shuffle their feet, contrite. The three *nonna*s, Caterina, Stella, Pietro, Luca and Aimee file into the kitchen, like naughty schoolchildren.

'Sorry, Mum. Like you said, it's okay to enjoy yourself. We just wanted—'

I cut him off: 'I know, lovely. But sometimes you can't have what you want. You have to let people make up their own minds.'

'But there's always hope,' he says, and beams at me.

'I know, yes, there is. But we'll be leaving soon.'

'But we don't want to go!' says Aimee. 'We want to live here!'

I'm taken aback. I wasn't expecting this. 'What about school? Your friends? Going back to how things were? I can afford to buy us somewhere when we've sold Casa Luna.'

'We don't want to. We want to stay here,' Luca says. 'They have schools here too! Pietro is going to be starting and I could too. We thought if you and Giovanni got together, you'd have to stay. Nonna Rosa said so!'

Nonna Rosa shrugs, downcast.

'And I want to see Snowy grow. And what about Stella? We can't leave her behind! We've only just found her! She's our sister!'

Luca is plainly in agreement. 'Dad would have wanted us all to be together.'

Stella's eyes are fixed on the ground. 'I'll be okay, guys. I'll come and visit.' She looks at me. 'If that's okay?'

'Of course!' My heart feels like it's breaking all over

again at the prospect of leaving this young woman behind, taking her new-found family from her.

'Well, we need to get ready for the class today.' I pull myself up straight. 'We need to decide about the lasagne for today's lunch. Whose recipe are we going to use? I've been thinking about how we can do this fairly . . .'

Nonna Rosa flaps an arthritic hand at me. 'There's no need,' she says breezily.

'There's every need. We have to work together to keep what's important here going. This place.'

'We know,' says Nonna Teresa.

I remind myself that after today we need a conversation about them trying to match-make me with Giovanni and getting the children's hopes up.

'And it has to be done fairly. Not creating more divisions, like that stunt in the garden just now,' I say firmly.

Giovanni's hands are on his hips, and the pair of us are like cross teachers, scowling at the three *nonna*s.

Nonna Rosa takes a deep breath and pulls herself up to her full height, only an inch or so above the other two, but it makes a difference. She lifts her chin defiantly.

'We have made a decision!' she announces, ignoring my comments about the unsuccessful match-making.

'Being forced to spend time in a small pantry makes you see things differently,' says Nonna Lucia.

'Actually, it was Stella who made us realize,' says Nonna Teresa.

I fold my arms and cock my head.

'Locked in the pantry, when you were trying to match-make Giovanni and me.'

They nod as one, unabashed.

'You would make the perfect pair.' Nonna Lucia is sidetracked for a moment.

Nonna Teresa clasps her hands, misty-eyed. 'We want you to be happy.'

'You are so right for each other,' they all say in unison, nodding.

I cough, blushing and embarrassed for Giovanni.

'However, two people have to feel the same way about each other. You can't just hope that your feelings will be shared,' I say. Am I wearing my heart on my sleeve? I wish there was somewhere to hide. 'So, the lasagne?' I clap my hands together. 'Whose are we making?'

Nonna Rosa straightens again. 'I have offered to share the lasagne recipe with my sister and sister-in-law. You're right. Perhaps I needed to remember that we can't make ourselves feel better by denying others. It's about team work.'

'Well, that's great news!' I'm grateful that this hasn't turned into some ugly scene about whose lasagne recipe we'll use. 'So we're making your family lasagne?'

'No,' they declare.

Luca and Aimee are giggling.

'We will not be making any of our lasagnes today,' Nonna Rosa informs me.

My spirits plummet.

I stare at Giovanni. Was all this hard work for nothing? They're not going to make the lasagne. How can we finish the cookery course without teaching the dish that people have paid to learn?

35

'So, that's it!' I throw up my hands up in despair. 'You're going to let La Tavola go under. Don't you see the hard work that Giovanni has put into this place? How can you? If we don't pull off a big Sunday lunch for our final day, the company won't pay! We won't get the money to save La Tavola! Don't you see what you've all got right in front of you?' Suddenly, every bit of frustration bubbles up in me and boils over, like milk on the stove.

'No, *Mamma*, it's fine!' Luca puts a hand on one of my arms.

'It's not, Luca,' I explain. 'Giovanni is a good, big-hearted man. He's impulsive and he came to care for this place. For all of you. As we have done. Making it feel like home when we needed it. You have everything that everybody is searching for here, a community based on love. You all love each other, even if you find it hard to show it. We all do.' I catch Giovanni's eye. 'It's hard when you've been hurt. You don't want to go there again. You don't want to repeat the same patterns, so you keep your heart safe, wanting to hold on to the memories of the past, which make you feel you were special. But time moves on. Your heart will heal if you let it. There is still a place for the memories, but don't let the memories, good or bad, ruin the chance of a happy future. Don't end up lonely and not following your heart because you're scared of being happy again. Don't let everything we want for this place be ruined over lasagne. This was never about lasagne. It was about so much more. Vying for your mother's attention, feeling let down by your sister who married the man you loved, and trying to stop change happening, which you can't do, because everything changes! It just does! And you have to change with it or get left behind, sad and alone. It takes bravery, but sometimes you have to listen to your heart and hear what it's telling you. Ignore your head!'

I find myself staring straight at Giovanni and him at me, as if, for a moment, no one else is in the room, which is silent. I clear my throat. I may have said more than I intended, telling myself exactly what I needed to hear and what's in my heart. I give another little cough to try to bring my thoughts back to what I wanted to say. 'We're here to save what matters to us all, where we have all been made welcome. La Tavola. To leave hurt in the past and celebrate those we love.' I'm still gazing at Giovanni.

'Nothing says love like lasagne does,' says Pietro, quietly. We all turn to him and smile. There's a tear at the corner of my eye that spills.

'You're right,' I say, and finally turn away from Giovanni. I may not have him in my life. There is so much unsaid between us. When the *nonna*s set us up, he wasn't here looking for a date with me. But maybe the problem was me: perhaps he understood I wasn't ready to move on from Marco. But the one thing I do know is that my children have never been happier in the last couple of years than they have been here, with Giovanni and Stella in their lives. With all of the village in their lives.

Nonna Rosa speaks: 'Like we said, we've made a decision on today's menu.'

I raise my eyebrows and shake my head at her, frustrated.

'But I've promised them lasagne. I can't change it now!' I throw up my hands. 'Like Pietro told us, nothing says love like lasagne.'

'We can all change if we try,' Nonna Rosa says. The other two *nonna*s smile and nod.

I look at Giovanni, wondering what's going on, but he seems as much in the dark as I am, but he's smiling at the *nonna*s who have finally come together again.

'We have decided, together,' says Nonna Teresa, 'that we want to make your lasagne!'

'What?' I'm stuck for words.

'Yours and Marco's. The one you made with the children's father. His memory. Your lasagne, made with love.'

My chin moves up and down but no words come out.

Nonna Lucia says, 'It's not about the dish you serve it in.'

'Or how you slice the garlic,' adds Nonna Rosa, her eyes filling with tears.

Nonna Teresa sniffs and blows her nose.

'It's about the memories you make, to keep safe, for always,' says Nonna Lucia, with a crack in her voice.

'It's okay to have the good memories. About how it made you feel.'

'And it's okay to create new ones too.'

'Not get stuck in the past!' Nonna Lucia says.

'So stuck we never thought we'd see this day!' Nonna Rosa practically growls, looking at the other two.

The children are grinning, as is Stella. And through the tears building in my eyes, I smile. They're right and all I can think of saying is, 'Grab an apron, everyone. We need to be ready to cook when our students get here.'

The *nonna*s are moving around the kitchen, giving orders and creating work stations for each element of the dish.

'We need a *primo* and *dolce* too!'

'*Gelato!*' says Pietro, and we hug him all over again.

'*Salata* for *primo*. You need to leave room for the lasagne!'

'You need to tell us your ingredients,' Nonna Rosa says to me.

'Only if you promise not to sniff at them!'

The three shrug playfully. 'We can't promise, but we'll try!' They all laugh, their eyes watery. Luca and Aimee are joining in with the *nonna*s and Stella, carrying bowls from the pantry to the table, as if this was the most natural thing in the world. That is exactly how it feels. I'm doing the one thing I've tried not to do since Marco died. I've been avoiding the kitchen, not wanting to cook, not wanting to go back and remember how it felt. And the one thing I should have been doing all along is cooking with love.

The students start to arrive. Glenda and Walt appear hand in hand, while he and Daisy look as if they've put their differences behind them.

'*Buongiorno*, everyone! Today, as you can hear,' the church bells are ringing in the distance, 'it's Sunday. And we're all here to share one last meal together. A meal cooked with love. So, everyone, grab an apron and let's get ready to cook!'

'Sebastian, you come with me,' says Nonna Rosa, and he seems thrilled by his popularity, if still a little nervous.

The students split into groups, Daisy and Walt together, laughing and teasing one another.

At one corner of the kitchen Caterina is making lemon *gelato* while Isabella and Aimee are producing biscuits. The pasta machine is screwed to the work surface and flour is being liberally tossed around by Nonna Lucia, smiling as pasta balls are created and kneaded.

And then there is the sauce, Luca, Stella and myself: I explain the ingredients that Marco would put in, telling us about Le Marche where he grew up with his parents and sisters. The stories he would tell us from his home town, stories that Luca and Aimee have heard before but Stella is hearing for the first time. The long summers when Marco worked in his father's friend's restaurant and hated returning to school. When he left school and got his first job in a kitchen. He'd travelled to the UK without a coat because he'd never known weather so bad, and I told them about the stars he cooked for when he was a chef on the touring circuit. And how he and I had met, a story Luca takes up: how everything I thought I was and wanted changed in that moment. And how the restaurant was born, along with Luca and Aimee. That's where we leave it. The happy stories we want to remember as we make the sauce, ready for layering with Marco's twists, our family lasagne.

When lunchtime comes, and the church bells are

still ringing, the kitchen smells of something very special: it smells of home. In the courtyard and the dining room, practically the whole village is there, having heard that the *nonna*s are cooking lasagne and no doubt expecting them to be duelling with rolling pins.

What they find is a joyful kitchen.

We open the front door and extend the table, with those from Casa Luna, into the courtyard. We put jugs of wine on it, with water, forks and spoons. The salads are dotted down the table, with platters of homemade focaccia, in squares, with rosemary from the garden, garlic, drizzled with olive oil.

Then comes the lasagne.

It's served and passed down the table, Luca and Stella looking very pleased with themselves.

As am I.

When we have served everyone, I regard the table. Sebastian has been hijacked by one of the *nonna*s. He lifts his glass to me. We haven't had time to talk, and I know we must before he leaves later that afternoon. I have to let him know how I'm feeling. I have to make up my mind about what I'm going to do . . . and I may have done that. It was all down to the lasagne.

I lift my glass to him too.

I pick up my fork and see the children sitting between new friends, local residents and cookery-school students, happier than I've seen them in a very long time. I breathe in the scent of the lasagne, transporting me to

Sundays after the restaurant had closed, in our kitchen, cooking it together. When life was good. The memory is there clear as day. As is Marco. I put my fork into the lasagne, through the layers of pasta and béchamel sauce, the meat *ragù*, made with Le Marche ingredients. We may not have got them all exactly right, but it felt the same when we cooked it and, frankly, it tastes the same. Made with love and laughter. I lift the fork to my mouth, smell the herbs and garlic, chew and close my eyes. I'm right back there: I feel warm, happy, loved. Slowly I open my eyes and look straight ahead, to see Giovanni smiling.

Sebastian is now between two *nonna*s, who are making sure his plate is never empty.

I look at Aimee, next to Stella, and there, among them all, I can see Marco, eating and drinking. He turns to me, lifts his wine glass and smiles. He didn't leave. He'll never leave. He is part of our past and our present. He will always have a place at the table and in our hearts, in our future. It's okay to have a future, I realize. It's okay to have fun. I look at Sebastian, who looks back across the crowded table at me, as if he's hoping I'll save him from the *nonna*s . . . I find myself smiling.

We finish our plates of lasagne, mop them with freshly baked bread and wash it down with glasses of spicy red wine. It's delicious.

Slowly, I stand, collect plates and move towards the

kitchen. People are talking and laughing and I don't want to interrupt that. I head to the sink.

'Thea!'

It's Sebastian. He looks exhausted and rather too full.

'It's all I could do to get away from the *nonna*s. I have a feeling they're trying to keep you and me apart. But, really, I need to speak to you.'

I smirk inwardly at the thought of the *nonna*s, still trying to stage an intervention between me and Sebastian, to match-make Giovanni and me.

'Come with me,' I say, leading him to the pantry. 'We'll say we're getting dessert.'

In the cool of the whitewashed room Sebastian loosens his tie and lets out a little burp. 'Excuse me. It was excellent lasagne. Just rather a lot of it. Do you mind if I sit?' He points to the chair that is used for reaching high shelves . . . or for Nonna Teresa to sit on when they're hiding in here, I think, with a smile, remembering them all squashed in when they tried to set up Giovanni and me. We still need to clear the air on that one.

'The weather is lovely now. Much more settled. The storm seems to have cleared the air,' Sebastian remarks.

How very British of him. And Sebastian is wonderfully British. 'It has. Both in the weather and for me too,' I say softly.

'It has?' he asks.

'I have . . .' I falter as I remember what I'm giving up.

The chance to be with a good man, a solid man . . . but not my man, I think.

In the background I can hear the children laughing. This may not be what I planned. But it is an adventure. A new beginning in a place full of love, and that feels like a good place to start.

'I'm sorry, Sebastian. Thank you, but I've come to realize the past is a place I shouldn't go back to. La Tavola has shown me that. The past is a wonderful place, with beautiful memories.'

'Like the pub when we got stranded.' We laugh.

'Exactly. But it's not a place to stay. Time moves on. And there is a new beginning out there for both of us. A whole new future.'

He looks down.

'That's not to say we can't be a part of that . . . just not the whole of it,' I say. 'I want to know all about your adventure and your move to Wales. I just can't come.'

He nods. 'Where will you go?'

'I don't know . . . but I know it's to the future, and this time I really am fine!'

He stands up. 'Be happy, Thea!' he says.

'And you, Sebastian. Thank you for making me realize that, well, this is just the start of a new journey.'

He holds out his arms and hugs me. It's a comforting hug. A safe place. But it's not the place I want to be.

I hear shuffling in the kitchen, crockery being put down.

'We'd better help clear up or people will wonder where we are.'

'Hiding out in the pantry!' He opens the door, smiling now.

I see Giovanni turning away and walking back into the dining room. 'Giovanni! Wait! I need to . . .'

But he doesn't stop walking.

'So, it is goodbye, then?' says Sebastian.

'Yes, it was good to see you again, but I'm not going back. In fact, I'm not going back at all. I may even stay here.' A whole new idea is hatching in my head.

'For good?'

'For as long as this place feels like home.'

36

We wave off the minibus and somehow, after turning down Sebastian, I feel freer. I know I don't want to go backwards. But I still don't know which way is forwards.

I think about the *nonna*s and the children, trying to match-make Giovanni and me, no doubt in the hope that I'll stay on here, and that they can too. I absorb the view. And it occurs to me that I don't need to have a man to stay here. If it's right for us as a family, why take the children back to Cardiff? What is it that makes it home? Home is the people you're with, isn't it? Wherever it may be. Why couldn't it be here? What if we were to stay?

In the kitchen at La Tavola most of the clearing up has been done. The *nonna*s are in the garden under the olive tree enjoying a well-earned glass of wine and congratulating themselves.

'Of course, my tiramisu was a triumph.'

'It could have done with more coffee.'

'More coffee? Your tastebuds were pickled in the wine you drank!'

'Next time I'll do my almond cake.'

'Next time? Who said anything about next time?'

'I can't wait!'

'Me neither!'

They laugh.

'I can't help thinking Giuseppe looked rather smart at lunch . . .'

'I did too!'

'You both have sand in your eyes! But he complimented me on my dress!'

'He said my hair looked nice.'

'I think I'll make him a lasagne . . .'

'I'll make him a tiramisu.'

'I'll make him one of mine. My mother gave me the recipe.'

In the kitchen, Luca and Aimee are crying.

'Hey, you two! What's happened? We had such a nice lunch. What's the matter?'

Giovanni is beside me. 'Are you hurt?'

They shake their heads. 'It's Stella!'

'What about her?'

'She's gone.'

'Gone?'

'Gone where?'

They shrug. 'She doesn't know. She just said it was time to move on. The house is being sold and we're leaving so it was time for her to move on too.'

The one thing I know for sure is that we have to find her. 'Stay here. Don't go anywhere.'

'Are you going to find her?' Giovanni looks at me.

'I'll try.'

He nods.

'Please, *Mamma*, get her to come home!'

And there it is: home. Not where we are, but who we're with, and Stella, I know now, is a part of that. I have to find her.

'Look after Bello,' Giovanni tells the children.

'And the *nonna*s! Don't let them stand on any chairs!'

'Let's take my bike, much easier,' says Giovanni, handing me a helmet. I don't think twice, just put it on. 'Here, climb aboard,' he says, and holds out a hand to me. I grip it and swing my leg over the seat. He takes the bike off its stand and climbs on in front. He starts the engine,

'Hold on!' he says, and I don't need telling twice. We head down the narrow cobbled street, swinging this way and that to avoid the big bumps. With every swing, my body shifts closer to his. My arms reach around him and my body is up against his, my head to his shoulders. My legs are wrapped around his thighs and there is nothing I can do except go with the movement, our two bodies moulded together as one.

'Where are we going?'

'She'll be heading for the main road. It's the only route out of here.'

We head down the lane and steer around the bend onto the main road, and there, just a short distance away, is a lone figure on the side of the road, sticking out a thumb. My heart rips in two just a little more.

We pull over.

'Stella!' I say, tearing off the helmet.

'I didn't think I'd see you riding a bike!' She giggles.

'Well, sometimes you have to take a little risk . . . maybe a big one to do what your heart is telling you,' I say.

'I didn't take anything from the house if that's what you're thinking.' She's back on the defensive.

'Of course not.' I put up my hands. 'That's not why I'm here.'

'Oh, it's the kitten then. I know I said I'd look after him when you left, but maybe Giuseppe will, or even Francesco. He seemed to like him.'

'Stella, it's not the kitten.' I know I need to get my thoughts together quickly. I glance at Giovanni, who gives me a reassuring nod.

'Look, I don't really know how this would work or where I'll find a job. But how would you feel if we decided to stay on? Me, Luca and Aimee.'

She looks at me. 'Stay on? For another week, a

month? Nice holiday.' She's back to her prickly self, all her barriers up.

'For good,' I say. Giovanni is gawping at me. This is news to him. It's sort of still news to me, really. It settled as an idea after the storm blew through, letting me see things clearly.

She stares at me. 'You, Luca and Aimee?'

'Yes.'

'But what about you and Giovanni? I thought you said you weren't going to be together. We shouldn't have tried to match-make you.'

'No, you shouldn't.' I have no idea what Giovanni's thinking.

'I thought you and Sebastian were going to get it on,' Stella says.

'Is there a better way to say that?'

Giovanni tuts and folds his arms.

'Okay, get together,' she says, with attitude.

'Well, he asked me.' I can hear a bus coming up the road. I watch Stella as she gestures to flag it down. 'But I said no. I want to stay here. In the house. I want you all to be happy. The three of you.'

'What?'

The bus pulls up and the doors open. The driver looks at us through his reflective sunglasses. Stella picks up her rucksack and steps forward.

'I'm not going anywhere, Stella. And Casa Luna is as much your home as it is Luca and Aimee's.'

The driver calls to her.

She looks at Giovanni. 'She's shitting me, right?!"

He straightens from leaning against the bike. 'If I know one thing about Thea, it's that she's not someone to mess you around. She says what she means. She's not going with Sebastian, and she's staying here. I believe her.'

'And our home is your home,' I add.

She looks between us. 'I'd love that.' She hurls herself at me and hugs me hard, nearly knocking me off my feet.

The driver tuts, then smiles and shuts the door. He and I wave to each other.

'Come on, let's go home,' I say, picking up her rucksack, and the three of us walk back towards the village, Giovanni pushing the bike.

At Casa Luna, Stella's is rucksack propped against the wooden pillar in the living room, a big bright space, The children, all three of them, are sitting in front of me at the table.

'I should go,' says Giovanni.

'Are you sure?' I say. 'Can't I offer you something to eat or drink?'

He laughs. 'Spoken like a true Italian! Looks like this village has adopted you and made it your home.'

'I hope so.'

'I'll leave you to it.' He turns to go. 'If I don't get a

chance to say it, *grazie mille* again. For finding a way to keep La Tavola going. I know it's in safe hands.'

'Well, between us all, I'm sure it'll have a good chance now. But, like the kitchen, it was team work.'

He says no more and leaves.

'So, where to begin?' I turn back to the table. 'How would you feel if . . .'

I stare at the faces in front of me, feeling the weight of responsibility as I finish telling them my plan.

'*Mamma?*' says Luca, slowly, as if letting things settle in his mind. 'Do you mean it? We can stay?'

'We can stay!' yells Aimee, and hugs Stella around the neck. 'And Stella is moving in!'

'Well, now the house is finished, it's ours to do what we like with. Sell it or live in it.'

'And we get to stay and go to school here, with Pietro! And can we carry on helping at La Tavola? What about pasta-making weekends? All different types of pasta. And cheese weekends, all different types of cheese and recipes and maybe Christmas recipes. We could put the *nonna*s on TikTok too!' Luca gabbles.

'Wait!' I laugh. 'Sometimes it's better to get on with what you have than want more.' And Luca looks crestfallen. 'But yes! We can do other things at the cookery school. I'm sure there are lots of people who want to come and enjoy a slice of real Italian life. And that way we can still help the people who need it.'

*

With the children helping Stella to settle back into the bedroom she has been sleeping in for the last couple of years, now cleared of junk and having been given a fresh coat of paint, I head up to La Tavola.

When I arrive, I step over the lip and in through the wooden gate. The courtyard is looking wonderful. The barrels and pots Caterina planted when she first arrived are blooming and thriving with the care she's lavished on them.

'*Ciao?* Giovanni?'

I walk through the dining room, following the smell from the kitchen at the back. As I do, I pass a rucksack. I'm confused: I'm sure we left Stella's rucksack at Casa Luna's. But I must have been mistaken. It's been a long day.

'Hey,' he says, as I walk into the kitchen where he's cooking.

'Hey,' is all I can say. I'm feeling exhausted, but seeing him lifts my spirits. He pours wine into a short stubby glass and hands it to me. 'Here,' he says. 'And I'm making you pasta.'

'Thank you. But you don't need to cook for me.'

'You've been looking out for everyone else today so I think I can cook for you.'

I pull up a stool at the counter. 'It's you who needs to remember to eat!' And my heart swells at the same time as my stomach flips. My whole body feels alive, very much so, with this man.

He puts a big bowl of pasta in front of me.

'*Cacio e pepe!*' I smile. 'Just like when I first arrived!'

He gives me a fork.

'Are you having some? There's loads!'

'Okay,' he says, 'but I'm saving on washing-up.' He grabs another fork and pulls up a stool at the corner of the kitchen island.

All my nerve endings stand to attention. 'Thank you for this.'

'It's fine.' He has twisted the fork in the soft tangle of pasta and put it into his mouth.

I do the same. It tastes delicious. Creamy, peppery, comforting. Just like it did on that first day. 'Giovanni, I don't want things to be awkward, me staying here, but we'll make it work.' I don't want to add that I'm sorry about the *nonna*s match-making us, and I wish I could tell him I've moved on. That there is room for him in my life, as well as my past, which is Marco. But I don't know how.

'I don't want it to be awkward either,' he says.

And we have both forked the same piece of pasta, sucking it into our lips like the Lady and the Tramp. I could bite or . . . I could suck some more until our lips finally meet. And they nearly do, but he bites the spaghetti, setting me free. I slurp and stop, my lips trembling, swollen, wanting his on them.

'What I mean is,' he says, 'maybe I did need a nudge out of my comfort zone, which is La Tavola. It needs to be run better than I've been running it. It needs to be the cookery school you've started. It needs you. I need you.'

I blush and cough.

'To run more cookery weekends.'

He smiles, but not the full Giovanni smile.

'There I go messing it up again.' He waves his fork around.

He reaches for the wine bottle and refills my glass. I wish time would stand still and let me stay in this happy place. Here, in a village I've come to love, with a man I find very attractive, a bowl of pasta and a glass of wine. It doesn't get much better. He puts a fork into the pasta, twirls it again and puts it into his mouth, sucking at the loose ends.

'So that's why I'm leaving.'

'What?'

He puts down the fork and dabs his mouth with the napkin he's placed in front of the two of us. 'It's time for me to move on. Like I say, you nudged me out of my comfort zone. I'd got stuck here, playing it safe, too scared to venture out into the world of food again. Too scared of being burnt. A bit like with love.'

He looks at me. 'But . . . I can't be second best again. And I can't stay here, if it's not with you.'

'You know I'm not going to be seeing Sebastian again, not romantically anyway.'

'I see.' He sips the wine.

I look sideways at the rucksack. Of course it's not Stella's. It's Giovanni's.

'We're going to stay friends, but I can't go back to the past,' I say, sipping my wine. My cheeks are flushing and I'm not sure if that's from the wine or how I'm feeling about Giovanni.

'I don't think Sebastian is the problem here,' he says, looking straight at me. 'I'm not Marco, Thea. I'm just Giovanni. A burnt-out chef whose fire has been reignited since you've been around. You've lit up the whole place. But I can't stay to watch you be here and me not able to love you. It's best I move on. La Tavola is safe in your hands. I'd like to try to tell other towns how they can set up a community kitchen. Roll the idea out.'

'So that's it? You're leaving?'

He gives a little nod.

'But . . .'

'I know that's not easy for you. But if it helps, we're all about the experiences we've had, where we've come from. The past is a part of who we are now, and where we'll go in the future. I won't forget this time.'

He moves towards the door, picking up his rucksack.

'Wait!'

He turns back slowly. I don't know what I'm going to say, but I do know what Marco would tell me to say. Not to lose someone important in my life. To seize the day. To enjoy the moment, and the journey, for as long as it lasts. And he'd say I made the right decision last time, choosing him, that I should follow my instincts this time too. And he'd be right. What am I scared of? Of loving again? Marco is part of my past, my children's life, but he's not here now. I am, and so is Giovanni. A lot has changed. Having Stella in our lives for starters.

'Your pasta. It's . . . too salty!'

He turns further towards me. 'Too salty?'

I'm gathering confidence. 'It needs more pepper!'

'More pepper, you say?' A smile is tugging at the corners of his mouth. 'Let me try it again.' He marches back into the kitchen and picks up a fork. 'The pasta is not too salty, and it has just the right amount of pepper. Here, try!' He twirls a forkful and holds it out to me. Slowly I open my mouth, put my hand over his, and I'm trembling. This is me taking a gamble, a chance . . . a second chance on love.

He feeds the pasta to me. I close my mouth. He slides out the fork and watches me eat.

Slowly I chew. 'You're right. I can taste it now.'

'My secret ingredient?'

My eyes are filling with tears.

'It's made with love.'

And a single teardrop spills, a teardrop of surprise, trepidation, excitement, and the thought of losing something that I never thought would come my way again: love.

'I know you're not Marco.'

'He was your husband, Thea. He's part of your life. But that doesn't mean you're not allowed a future too.'

He's not Marco, and he's definitely not Sebastian. It's not a safe, secure future.

'I think we could run courses here for people, carers, and patients who suffer from dementia so that food can take them back to their happy place. And for young people too, young men like Alessandro, who are going down a wrong path. Food can help them find their way back on track. And for the bereaved, to remember their past and let it be part of their now, celebrate what they had and who they are today.'

'You're quite something, Thea. It's exactly what this place should be about. Sharing the recipes and love. It's not about the food on the table.'

'It's about who you share it with. And I can't think of anyone else I'd rather be sharing it with than you,' I say, suddenly feeling as if I'm standing in front of him completely naked, as vulnerable as I'll ever be. 'This works, the two of us together. Sharing our skills and our past . . .'

He looks down at me. 'You and me, together?' He smiles slowly.

I nod, matching his smile.

'A new beginning for all of us, here, at La Tavola, where our past and our future met. I don't want to do this without you, Giovanni. You are the heart of this place. But we could do it together.'

He steps even closer and I can feel him, smell him, almost hear the beat of his heart. And then he steps forward and takes my face in his hands. 'I think we could,' he smiles slowly, 'as long as you remember always to cut the garlic with a razor blade when you're making lasagne.' His head is slowly dipping towards mine. 'Oh, and you remember to use the blue lasagne dish because it'll taste better. Always,' he says, and slides his hand around the back of my head. 'But I prefer sauce first, then pasta.'

'That's something we'll have to argue about.'

'Of course, for as long as you like.' Finally his lips are on mine and they're everything I want them to be. Not like Marco's, not like the past, like a whole new exciting future.

His fingers entwine with mine, and I feel exactly where I should be right now. Home.

We pull away from each other, still holding each other's hands.

'Let's take things slowly. Keep things to ourselves for a while, allow us time to get used to being with each other,' says Giovanni. 'I don't want you to feel rushed.'

'I agree. This is our secret.'

'Like a family recipe we're creating,' he says, moving in to kiss me again, and I like the idea of a recipe for which we're still finding the ingredients. But the most important one is love.

'It has too much coffee!'

There is a clatter as we turn from where we're standing, against each other, holding hands, the abandoned rucksack on the floor.

'Giovanni, try this tiramisu!'

'It has too much coffee, try mine, it's much better!'

'I've made a different version from my home town!'

'It's not even real tiramisu!!'

They stare at us. The three *nonna*s all clutching dishes in front of them are suddenly silent. And then they explode.

'They are together!'

'I knew all along that they were right for each other!'

'You said we should try to get her with Sebastian!'

'Until I realized how they felt about each other!'

'I noticed it first!'

'I think you'll find I nudged you!'

'Ladies, please.' Giovanni holds up a hand, silencing them. 'We're just starting out. We're taking things very slowly.'

They put their tiramisus on the table and rush forward as one to embrace us. It's like being hugged by a huge duvet, warm, comforting and suffocating all at the same time.

'We should throw a party!'

'Yes, a celebration!'

'A new family in the village!'

'It could be a celebration-of-love party!'

'An engagement party!'

'An engagement party!' they agree and, try as we might, we can't get a word in edgeways.

'I can bake the cake!'

'I have a family recipe!'

'We could make three cakes, like tiers!'

'Excellent idea!'

'Mine will go on the top!'

'Why will yours go on the top?'

'People will taste it first!'

'I don't know why yours will go on the top. It's bound to be denser than the other two!'

'Okay, a competition, a cake competition,' says Nonna Lucia. 'A tiramisu competition.'

'Who will judge it?'

We're sliding towards the door, without them noticing.

'Giuseppe, of course.'

'He's always loved my tiramisu.'

'You've been taking him tiramisu?'

'So have I!'

'We've all been taking him tiramisu!'

'He probably fed yours to the goats.'

'I don't fancy Giuseppe's chances on this one,' says Giovanni, quietly.

'Perhaps,' says Nonna Teresa, 'we could make a new recipe, between us.'

'A new one?'

'Yes.'

'Get the children to help.'

'A Tavola recipe.'

'Yes.'

'I like that.'

And after a pause. 'Yes, I do too.'

'Now we just have to work out what to make.'

'I have an idea.'

'So do I.'

'No, listen, I think I do.'

'I'd like Luca on my team. He has very good ideas.'

'He learnt them from me.'

'I met him first.'

'He will make an excellent chef one day.'

'I can see it in his eyes. He has the love for it.'

'I'm sure I noticed it first.'

'He's a lovely boy.'

'A lovely family.'

'So good to have them as part of our family.'

'That lasagne recipe will be passed on for years to come.'

'I thought I might ask for the recipe myself . . .'

We slip out of the front door, and across the road, stand and look out at the view. I'm here in my now, gazing over my future. I look back at Giovanni.

'Some things are so much better because of the people you share them with. I've stood here and looked at this view many times. But now I'm here with you I love it even more. It's not about where you are in life, but who you're with. And it's not about the recipe but who you share the experience with.' I smile. 'Like a good lasagne.'

In the background we can still hear the *nonna*s declaring loudly that they all have the best recipe for the tiramisu. And they're right: because they have each other and sharing food tastes so much better when you find someone to love. I want to share all my meals with the children, Stella and this man . . . the man I know I've come to love.

Somewhere in the wind that's bringing relief from the hot, hot summer, I hear Marco agree and give a hearty laugh, a laugh that loves life, and that is something I'll never forget.

Epilogue

'Happy birthday to you, happy birthday to you, happy birthday, dear Aimee, happy birthday to you!'

We cheer and clap.

'To Aimee!' says Alessandro, standing on a chair and raising a glass of water. 'And La Tavola!'

We cheer again.

There is still pizza on the long table, bowls of salad, and now a cake.

Stella arrives in the dining room, carrying a big box. 'Happy birthday! Sorry I'm late,' she says to Aimee.

'Is that for me?'

'It is!'

'Well, let's hope it's not another kitten.' I smile at Stella.

'No, not another kitten,' she says, and suddenly she seems a little sheepish.

There's a squawk.

'What's in the box?' asks Aimee, sliding off her chair in the beautiful party dress Caterina has made for her, with ribbons and netting from the clothes we found in

Casa Luna, all having a new life. Even Giuseppe is in a new suit that has been altered to fit him, as smart as paint. And the three nonnas are in their Sunday best, each wearing a rose he has brought for them, not singling one out from the others.

There's another squawk and Stella puts down the box as it starts to shake and move. She beams at Aimee. Suddenly a head pops out and squawks again.

'A chicken!' Aimee is delighted.

'Oh, Stella!' I say. 'I thought we said no more animals.'

'But it's a chicken! Well, two, actually . . . and a cockerel. A local farmer said they would make the perfect present. Think of all the eggs!'

'Excellent for pasta sauce, Tuscan carbonara,' says Nonna Rosa.

'The fresher the better,' agrees Nonna Teresa.

'I always use fresh eggs and a dash of cream,' says Nonna Lucia.

Nonna Rosa's hands fly to her cheeks. 'Cream? Never cream!'

'Yes, cream, a dash. My mother always used cream.'

'No, no! Pasta water and egg yolks.'

'And onion, a little shallot.'

'Never onion in a carbonara.'

'Our mother would be turning in her grave.'

'And always six egg yolks.'

Nonna Teresa shakes her head. 'Five. Six is too many.'

'No, no, six!'

'We'll have a competition. A Tuscan carbonara contest,' announces the mayor, clearly feeling buoyed up and brave.

'It's not even Tuscan!'

'We have to learn to grow and adapt, like we have as a village.'

'We're going to need more eggs,' says Giovanni to me, his arm snaking around my waist.

'Perhaps we could make it a party,' says Nonna Lucia.

'An engagement party,' says Nonna Teresa.

'But no one is getting engaged. Silly woman!' says Nonna Rosa.

'Actually . . .' says a voice from the corner of the room. We stop talking and turn. It's Alessandro's brother, Enrico. With his *nonna* on the mobility scooter. He looks around nervously. 'This place has been here when my brother and I, and Nonna, needed it. A helping hand on the way. And now we have more and more work coming in, thanks to Giovanni helping us set up. I have a job at the school, as the caretaker, as well as other jobs now that people are starting to discover our village through the cookery school and wanting to buy houses here. And we have some family news. Alessandro is going to college to study business in September.'

We erupt into cheers and rush forward to hug him. Giovanni is patting him on the back and I hug him hard. 'Just remember you can always come home when you need to. We're here!' I say.

'And, remember, cooking for people will always make you friends,' says Giovanni. 'I'll teach you *cacio e pepe* before you go.'

'But what about the engagement party?' I hear Nonna Teresa say, and we all go quiet and turn back to where Caterina is standing with her hands over her nose and mouth.

She is staring at Alessandro's brother, tears in her eyes, as he takes her hand from her mouth and says, 'Will you? Will you marry me?'

She nods and throws her arms around him.

'To hope and happiness!' says Pietro, and we raise our glasses as we echo the toast.

'Now, about the wedding menu . . .' I hear Nonna Rosa say.

I know that everything that is made will be made with love.

Acknowledgements

This book was inspired by my kitchen table and a number of people, working within their communities to feed others at their kitchen tables. As we know, sharing a meal with someone is about so much more than just the food itself. It's everything else that people bring to the table; company, storytelling, memories, friendship, shared problems, support and laughter. My kitchen table has brought all these things to me over the years. I love the marks and scars it has to remind me of our journey together. I was also inspired by the work of Danny McCubbin, founder of The Good Kitchen Sicily; do check out his Instagram page. Also Emiliano Amore, Emilianochef on Instagram, who I met on a food writing weekend and works helping so many different groups in society from the community kitchen in Brighton. Another inspiring project is The Long Table in Stroud, also on Instagram, and here in Wales, Cegin Y Pobl Cymru, dedicated to getting people cooking.

All of these people are inspiring others to get in the

kitchen, cook and share food with the ones we love, old friends and new ones . . . With our community, whether we are a family, a group with shared interests, or just trying to find a way from one day to the next, the food we share is the glue that holds us together, through the tough times and celebrations.

I really want to thank my editor Sally Williamson for her support and encouragement and loving this book as much as I do. The whole team at Transworld, many of whom are on new exciting journeys of their own and, as always, my agent David Headley.

And of course, my family; my wingman and husband for thirty-five years of togetherness. Our children, children–in–law and all of my younger gang who gather round my kitchen table in good times and in bad. You know who you are, and that there is always a place at the table for you . . .

This book is dedicated to the wonderful writer Belinda Jones. If you haven't read her books, do! She was a wonderful writer, whose books I loved. She was inspiring and supportive to me. She adored animals and wrote about them, but also followed her heart to work in a rescue centre in the States, looking after the ones that needed her the most. If you have a dream, a love, a passion, I hope you can seize the day and follow your heart too.

*Read on for some delicious
recipes and to discover
more of Jo's uplifting and
heart-warming books . . .*

Beef ragù lasagne

Lasagne is such a wonderful comfort food – the indulgence of the rich beef ragù combined with the creamy béchamel simply can't be topped!

Serves 6–8

Ingredients:

For the beef ragù
2 tbsp olive oil
1 large onion, finely chopped
2 carrots, finely chopped
2 celery sticks, finely chopped
2 garlic cloves, minced
500g beef mince
100ml red wine
2 x 400g tins of chopped tomatoes
2 tbsp tomato purée
1 tsp dried oregano
1 tsp dried basil
1 bay leaf
Salt and pepper to taste

For the béchamel sauce
50g butter
50g plain flour
600ml whole milk
A pinch of nutmeg
Salt and pepper to taste

For the lasagne
250g dried lasagne sheets
1 ball mozzarella cheese
50g Parmesan cheese (grated)

Method:

1. Heat the olive oil in a large pan over medium heat. Add the chopped onion, carrots, and celery. Cook for about 10 minutes until softened. Add the minced garlic and cook for another minute.
2. Increase the heat and add the beef mince. Cook until browned, breaking up any lumps with a wooden spoon.
3. Pour in the red wine and let it simmer for a few minutes until it has reduced slightly.
4. Add the chopped tomatoes, tomato purée, oregano, basil, and bay leaf. Season with salt and pepper.
5. Reduce the heat to low and let the ragù simmer gently for about 45 minutes to 1 hour, stirring occasionally. Remove the bay leaf before assembling the lasagne.
6. While the ragù is simmering, make the béchamel. In a separate saucepan, melt the butter over medium heat. Once melted, add the flour and stir continuously for about 2 minutes to form a roux.
7. Gradually whisk in the milk, a little at a time, ensuring there are no lumps. Continue to cook, stirring constantly, until the sauce thickens and coats the back of a spoon.
8. Season with nutmeg, salt, and pepper.
9. Preheat the oven to 180°C (160°C fan)/350°F/Gas mark 4.

10. Remove the bay leaf from the ragù. Then, in a large baking dish, spread a thin layer of the ragù on the bottom.
11. Cover with a layer of lasagne sheets, breaking them to fit if necessary, then spoon over a layer of béchamel.
12. Tear some of the mozzarella from the ball and place this on top of the béchamel.
13. Repeat the layers (ragù, lasagne sheets, béchamel, mozzarella) until all the ingredients are used up, finishing with a layer of béchamel sauce on top. Finally, sprinkle the grated Parmesan cheese over the top layer.
14. Cover the dish with foil and bake in the preheated oven for 25 minutes.
15. Remove the foil and bake for an additional 20–25 minutes, or until the top is golden and bubbling.
16. Let the lasagne rest for about 10 minutes, then serve!

Courgette Linguine

This quick and delicious pasta dish is perfect for a weeknight dinner. The creamy courgette sauce is balanced beautifully by the sharpness of the lemon, and it goes down a treat with a crisp white wine on a summer's evening!

Serves 4

Ingredients:

2 tbsp olive oil
2 cloves garlic, minced
3 medium courgettes, thinly sliced
400g linguine
150ml double cream
75g grated Parmesan cheese
A squeeze of lemon juice
Salt and black pepper, to taste
Fresh basil or parsley, chopped (optional, for garnish)

Method:

1. Heat the olive oil in a large pan over medium heat. Add the minced garlic and sauté for about 1 minute until fragrant, being careful not to burn it.
2. Add the sliced courgettes to the pan and cook for 5–7 minutes, stirring occasionally, until they are softened and have released some of their moisture.
3. While the courgettes are frying, bring a large pot of salted water to a boil, add the linguine and cook until *al dente*.
4. Once the courgettes have cooked down, reduce the heat and stir in the double cream, allowing it to warm through.

5. Add the Parmesan and stir into the cream until well combined, followed by the lemon juice. If the sauce is too thick, you can gradually add some of the reserved pasta water to loosen it up.
6. Add the cooked linguine to the sauce and toss carefully to make sure the pasta is evenly coated. Allow to cook for a minute or two longer so that the pasta can absorb some of the sauce.
7. Season with salt and pepper to taste, then dish up and sprinkle with chopped basil or parsley if desired. Serve immediately and enjoy!

Tiramisu

Nothing can beat the decadent layers of coffee-soaked Savoiardi biscuits and smooth mascarpone cream of this classic dessert. With an espresso on the side, I always think tiramisu is the perfect way to finish off any Italian meal!

Serves 6

Ingredients:

300ml strong brewed coffee, cooled to room temperature
3 tbsp Marsala wine or coffee liqueur (such as Kahlúa, optional)
4 large eggs, separated
100g granulated sugar
500g mascarpone cheese
200g Savoiardi (ladyfinger) biscuits
50g unsweetened cocoa powder
Dark chocolate shavings (optional)

Method:

1. Brew a strong pot of coffee and let it cool to room temperature. Mix in the coffee liqueur, if using, and set aside.
2. In a large mixing bowl, beat the egg yolks and sugar together until the mixture becomes pale and creamy.
3. Add the mascarpone cheese to the egg yolk mixture and beat until smooth and well combined.
4. In a separate clean bowl, whip the egg whites until they form stiff peaks. A hand-held electric whisk or stand mixer will make this process much quicker, but be careful not to overwhisk!

5. Gently fold the beaten egg whites into the mascarpone mixture, being careful not to deflate the egg whites. This will create a light and airy cream.
6. Quickly dip each Savoiardi biscuit into the cooled coffee mixture, making sure not to soak them for too long as they can become too soggy.
7. Arrange a layer of the dipped biscuits in the bottom of a rectangular dish (approximately 20cm x 30cm).
8. Spread half of the mascarpone cream mixture over the layer of biscuits, smoothing it out with a spatula.
9. Repeat with another layer of dipped biscuits and top with the remaining mascarpone cream.
10. Cover the dish with cling film and refrigerate for at least 4 hours, or preferably overnight, to allow the flavours to meld and the tiramisu to set.
11. Just before serving, dust the top generously with unsweetened cocoa powder and garnish with dark chocolate shavings if desired. Slice and serve chilled. *Buon appetito!*

Let the queen of feel-good Christmas fiction
whisk you off to the snowy countryside this festive
season with her brand-new novel . . .

CHRISTMAS AT HOLLYBUSH FARM

**Jemima Jones is driving home to her family's
magical hill-top farm for Christmas . . .**

And on arrival, she soon learns that her dad has been
keeping a secret – all is not as it seems, and Hollybush
Farm is struggling to make ends meet! Worried
about losing the childhood home she loves, Jemima decides
it's time to pull on her winter wellies and get stuck in.

Amid the chaos of chasing after escaping sheep and
organizing the Christmas tractor run, Jemima begins
documenting her slice of farming life on social media. As
she builds a supportive online following, she also forms an
offline connection in the shape of charming retired rugby
player Llew, her very own Santa's helper.

**With a sprinkle of festive cheer and a dash of
goodwill, might the community pull together to help
save the farm in time for Christmas?**

COMING SOON

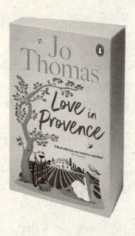

She found happiness in a new home,
but can she keep hold of it?

Del moved to the south of France three years ago and
hasn't looked back. She's found new friends, new purpose,
and new love with gorgeous Fabien.

But just as harvest on her little lavender farm is due to begin,
Del gets some shocking news. With no time to dwell as she
welcomes a new crew of lavender pickers, she unexpectedly
waves goodbye to Fabien for the summer.

Usually cooking – the thing she loves best – would help soothe
her troubles, but Del doesn't remember how . . . And then chef
Zacharie comes to town, dropping another bombshell!

Over one summer in Provence that's full of surprises, friends
old and new rally round. Can they complete the harvest and
pull the community back together?

**And if Fabien returns, will Del finally get her
happy-ever-after?**

The perfect place to raise a glass to love, hope, and new beginnings

When their grandfather dies, Fliss and her sisters are astonished to inherit a French château! Travelling to Normandy to visit the beautiful if faded house, they excitedly make plans over delicious crepes and local cider in the town nearby.

They soon discover the château needs major work and a huge tax bill is due . . . Unable to sell but strapped for cash, Fliss determines to spruce up the elegant old rooms and open a B&B.

But Jacques, the handsome town mayor, is opposed to her plan. When it becomes clear that the only way to save the magnificent castle is to work together, Jacques and Fliss discover that they have more in common than they think . . .

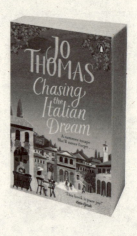

A summer escape she'll never forget

Lucia has worked hard as a lawyer in Wales, aiming for a big promotion she hopes will shortly come her way. Finally taking a well-earned break at her grandparents' house in southern Italy, the sunshine, lemon trees and her nonna's mouth-watering cooking make her instantly feel at home.

But she's shocked to learn that her grandfather is retiring from the beloved family pizzeria and will need to sell. Lucia can't bear the thought of the place changing hands – especially when she discovers her not-quite-ex-husband Giacomo wants to take it over!

Then bad news from home forces Lucia to re-evaluate what she wants from life. Is this her chance to carry on the family tradition and finally follow her dreams?

Take one woman longing for the perfect Christmas . . .

All Clara has ever wanted is Christmas surrounded
by loved ones, full of warmth and delicious food.
So when her new boyfriend asks her to move to
Switzerland, she can't help but say yes! After all, what
could be more perfect than Christmas in the Alps?

Add a dash of surprise

She quickly signs up for a tempting chocolate-making
class, but it turns out to be chocolate-making bootcamp!
And her boyfriend isn't all he seemed either . . .

And enjoy a magical festive treat!

Despite it all, Clara begins to make friends – including
the aloof yet intriguing Gabriel. With all of the
ingredients at her fingertips, will she finally be able
to whisk up her Christmas dream?

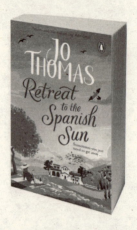

Sometimes you just need to get away . . .

Eliza has a full house! When her three children grew up and moved out, she downsized to a smaller property . . . but now they're all back. Every room in the house is taken and Eliza finds herself sharing her bed with her eldest daughter and her daughter's pug. Combined with the online course she's trying to finish, plus her job to fit in, there just isn't the peace and quiet that Eliza needs.

So when an ad pops up on her laptop saying 'house-sitters wanted', Eliza can't resist the chance to escape. She ends up moving to a rural finca in southern Spain, looking after the owner's Iberico pigs, learning about secret gastronomic societies . . . and finding a new zest for life and love along the way.